DEDICATION

*To Jen Safrey, whose dainty feet
provide big steps for me to follow,
to my mother and sisters, whose
magnificence humbles me, and to
Hazel Shannon (1921-2001), my
rock and my angel.*

SUDDENLY YOU

CRYSTAL HUBBARD

Genesis Press, Inc.

Indigo Love Stories

An imprint of Genesis Press, Inc.
Publishing Company

Genesis Press, Inc.
P.O. Box 101
Columbus, MS 39703

ISBN-13: 978-1-58571-302-8
ISBN-10: 1-58571-302-3
Manufactured in the United States of America

First Edition 2005
Second Edition 2008

Visit us at www.genesis-press.com or call at 1-888-Indigo-1

CHAPTER ONE

"Miss?"

Cady ignored the white-smocked nurse at the receptionist's station and marched down the wide corridor leading to the doctors' offices on the oncology ward of Raines-Hartley Hospital.

"Miss!" the nurse snapped loudly as she took after Cady. "You can't just bulldoze your way in like this!"

Cady read the nameplates on the doors lining each side of the corridor. Seong…Laugherty…Joyce…Bailey…

Bailey.

Cady's hand was firmly wrapped around Dr. Bailey's doorknob when the nurse madly lunged for the door, blocking Cady's way. "Do we have a problem here?" the nurse demanded. "You don't just breeze into my ward and bust your way into a doctor's office unannounced and without an appointment."

Cady glanced at the spitfire's nametag before she calmly said, "Get out of my way, Nurse Renyatta Runyon."

Renyatta Runyon was five and a half feet tall—six inches of which was in her heavily sprayed and intricately stacked hairdo. She had the figure and ferocity of a badger and protected the Raines-Hartley Oncology Department as though it were her lair. But like any creature in nature, Renyatta knew when to give way to a larger, more predatory animal. The fiery gleam in Cady's ginger eyes made Renyatta soften her hard stance on surprise visitors.

Renyatta's size-ten orthopedic wedgies took a pronounced step away from Cady and the door. "Do I need to call security?" she warned. " 'Cause I will."

"Do what you need to do, Nurse Runyon," Cady said, bending slightly to evenly meet Renyatta's feral stare. "Just as I'm doing what I need to do."

"Dr. Bailey won't like being disturbed," Renyatta said with a defiant lift of her chin.

Cady's determination to see Dr. Bailey showed in the set of her jaw. "Do I look like I care what Dr. Bailey will or won't like?"

A wide smile slowly bloomed on Renyatta's chubby, nut-brown face. Her gold upper incisor flashed as she took another step out of Cady's way.

"Thank you," Cady said.

Renyatta watched as Cady threw open the door and walked in, jumping when Cady slammed the door behind her. Renyatta, her polyester-wrapped thighs hissing noisily, crowded close to the door, listening. She furiously beckoned to the receptionist's station, to the nurses who had witnessed her encounter with Cady. Renyatta was well known for her generosity. She wanted to share this moment with her co-workers…the moment "the Iceberg" came face to face with a volcano.

When Dr. Keren Bailey failed to react to the slam of the door, Cady opened it just enough to smash it home once more. Keren remained hunched over the medical charts on his neat desktop, although he shifted his black eyes upward. His head followed his gaze as he stared at the woman approaching his desk.

Chic black boots covered the feet of the woman who quickly closed the carpeted distance between the door and the desk. Faded blue denim clung to her long legs and the curves of her hips. Her stretchy black top hugged the fullness of her breasts and offered a glimpse of her taut abdomen. In spite of himself, Keren's eyes lingered on that bare expanse of skin. Her lightweight leather jacket, perfect for a cool August afternoon, hung over her forearm as she stopped at his desk. The wrinkled and weathered butternut leather of the jacket contrasted sharply with the smooth, dewy appearance of her honey-brown complexion. Her full, cranberry lips did not smile and her light eyes held dark warning. Above her elegant eyebrows, which almost met in a grim scowl, was a wild tousle of shining wheat, copper, jet, sienna and auburn. She stood motionless, narrowing her jewel-like eyes at him. The slight quiver of her curls revealed the true depth of her carefully restrained anger.

Keren set down his pen. Without knowing why, he thought it better to stand to face his visitor. At his full height, he was nearly a foot taller than she was.

She didn't seem intimidated.

"I don't see patients without an appointment," Keren said.

His voice was much nicer in person than on the phone, Cady allowed. But it would take much more than a nice voice to alleviate the wrath that had been building up in her.

"I'm not a cancer patient," she said coolly. "Unfortunately, Claire Winters is."

"Mrs. Winters is under my care," Keren said, "but I'm not at liberty to discuss a patient's condition with—"

"You've already discussed it with me," Cady interrupted.

He was certain that he would have remembered her, had they ever met before, let alone discussed a patient.

"Zacadia Winters," Cady said, thrusting her hand forward as she slung her jacket over the back of a chair. "I'm Claire's granddaughter."

"Yes," Keren said, shaking her hand. "We spoke by phone yesterday."

"You spoke," Cady snapped. "I listened."

Keren put his hands in the pockets of his pleated slacks. "Was there something you didn't understand?"

"Yes." She planted her hands on his desk and leaned forward. "I don't understand how you could have been so damned callous."

"Your grandmother asked me to speak with you and I did," he said woodenly. "I'm sorry you didn't like what you heard."

Cady's anger reached another dimension as she recalled the brief conversation she'd had by phone less than twenty-four hours before this face-to-face encounter with Dr. Keren Bailey. Claire had been at Raines-Hartley for two days, presumably for the treatment of three pea-sized tumors at the base of her esophagus. Her doctors, the same team that had treated her breast cancer seven years earlier, had sent her there for complete bone and brain scans. Cady had called from Boston after the first battery of tests and x-rays. Dr. Bailey had come into the room while Claire was on the phone with her. Claire, slightly loopy from the medications and tired from all the procedures, had handed the phone to Dr. Bailey, so he could give the news to Cady.

"Hello, Doctor," Cady had said politely. "I'm Claire's granddaughter, calling from Boston. I was hoping you could tell me how she's doing."

"Your grandmother has an inoperable tumor, about the size of a walnut, located at the base of her brain. That's all I can tell you right now." And with that, Dr. Bailey had given the phone back to Claire.

Claire had gone oddly quiet through Cady's demands that Dr. Bailey be put back on the phone. "Cady, I think I need to speak to the doctor now," she had finally said, a tremble in her voice. And Claire had hung up.

Cady had sat a moment longer, staring at the phone, as dread and foreboding crept through her. At 71, Claire had beaten breast cancer, but only after losing the affected breast, her hair and about forty pounds. Seven years later, the cancer had metastasized to her stomach in the form of the three small tumors.

Through her own research, Cady knew that breast cancer liked to travel, and that it favored the lungs and bones. She had never counted on it moving to Claire's brain.

And never had she expected to learn of the new tumor the way she had. Her shock and sorrow at Dr. Bailey's words had combined with indignation at his bloodless delivery, and she'd spent the rest of the day and night talking to her mother and sisters by phone before taking the first available flight to St. Louis. She'd left Boston at six A.M. Eastern Time, and by 10:30 A.M. Central Time, she had been sparring with Nurse Renyatta Runyon.

That had been only the undercard for her main draw with Dr. Keren Bailey.

"She's an old woman and the pain medication confuses her," Cady told him. "That's why she had you talk to me. She deserved better than to hear the diagnosis not only secondhand, but in the way you dropped it on me."

Keren abruptly began gathering his charts. "I didn't have to speak to you at all, Miss Winters," he said flatly.

"But you did," she countered. "There's no good way to tell a person that she's dying. Claire shouldn't have heard it blurted out as if you were giving me a weather report. She's scared enough, and yesterday afternoon, you scared her even more."

"Claire is a strong woman. She's been through this before."

Cady wanted to grab him by his broad shoulders and shake him until he showed some sort of reaction—anger, defensiveness, guilt, something, *anything*—to her words. "She's never had a brain tumor!" Cady shouted. "Do you know how big a walnut is? That sort of thing doesn't spring up overnight. You've scanned her lungs and bones all along. Why didn't you scan her brain?"

"Are you a doctor, Miss Winters?" Keren's black gaze darkened.

"I'm a reporter," she said, "and a damn good researcher. Boston has some of the best oncologists in the world, and I've taken advantage of their expertise. I know far more about metastasized breast cancer than I ever wanted to know, *Doctor.*

"For weeks now, Claire's speech has been a little slurred, but I thought it was because of the drugs she was taking for her stomach tumors. She's been forgetful at times, and she's had pain in her left arm and leg. Aren't those symptoms consistent with the presence of a brain tumor?"

"Those complaints are symptomatic of any number of things," Keren said tonelessly.

"How long does she have?"

Cady stood before him as fearless as ever. But Keren read the plea that had come to her glistening eyes. "Perhaps you should sit down." He indicated the chair with a slight tilt of his head.

Cady crossed her arms over her chest and shifted her weight to her right leg. "Just spit it out. Like you did yesterday."

Her forced bravado didn't fool him. His trained eye noticed the rapid drumming of her pulse at the base of her throat. Her long lashes fluttered too quickly. Her pupils were dilated slightly, another sign that her adrenalin—and her anxiety—were elevated. She wanted the answer to her question just as much as she dreaded it. And if she were as good a researcher as she claimed to be, she probably already had an idea of what he would say. She hadn't asked about treatment. She had asked about time.

"Five months," he said.

Cady stopped breathing. She had hoped against hope that every opinion she had solicited in the past twenty-four hours had been wrong. Those opinions had shaped her decision to request a six-month personal leave from her newspaper job. She had packed four suitcases, put a hold on her mail and sent her landlord a check to cover the next half-year of rent. Even through her hurried yet thoughtful preparations, Cady had never entertained the possibility that her worst fear would be realized.

"Miss Winters…"

Cady took a slow, deep breath, but the air didn't seem to do what it was supposed to. She clutched the back of the chair and closed her eyes as her jacket slid to the seat.

Keren rounded his desk. "Miss Winters, sit down."

"I'm fine," she insisted, her voice little more than a croak.

The deep rise and fall of her chest and the subtle bobble of her chin showed him that she was anything but fine. Sure that she was about to faint, he put his left arm around her shoulders to support her. He was guiding her into the chair when she half-turned and clapped her left arm around his neck. She trembled against him, clenching and unclenching her fists. His right arm dangled at his side. With his left hand, he gave her two clumsy pats on her back.

"Five months," she whispered in anguish.

The warmth of her breath caressed his neck and he felt heat at every point where her body touched his. He cleared his throat. "There's a surgical procedure," he began. Until now, he'd never had a problem finding words in any situation. He struggled to push rational thoughts past the fresh-rain scent of her hair. "We can use the Leksell Gamma Knife to treat her with radiation," he said. "It allows us to precisely target the affected area and—"

"She won't agree to it," Cady said as she pulled away from him. She picked up her jacket. "You people took her breast seven years ago, and ever since then she's insisted that she never wants any more surgery. She told me so again when I called her last night. I have to see her now. She doesn't know that I'm here. Thank you for your time, Dr. Bailey."

"Raines-Hartley will make her comfortable," he said, offering the only solace he could.

"I'll make her comfortable," Cady said at the door. "She's going home."

"Claire's condition is only going to worsen," Keren said. "Even with surgery, radiation and chemo, the damaged tissue can't be restored. Because of the tumor, your grand-mother has other health problems that require constant medical care."

"You want her to die surrounded by strangers in this hospital?"

"She's going to die, Miss Winters. That fact is inescapable, and the sooner you face it, the easier it will be."

Cady's amber eyes turned liquid as she slowly shook her head. A moment earlier, the doctor had shown her a modicum of compassion, an apparent deviation in his personality in light of his last comment. "It may be easy for you to watch someone die, but it won't be easy for me, Dr. Bailey. I'm going to be here today, tomorrow and every day until…" Her words faded as she fought to maintain her cool before this man with the frozen heart. "Stay out of my way, Doctor," she finished coldly.

She threw open the door. Renyatta and the other nurses scattered as Cady left the office. Dr. Bailey stepped into the corridor. "This is my department, Miss Winters," he called after Cady, who was halfway to the elevators. He scowled at Renyatta and company. He hated being a spectacle for their amusement. "I don't take orders from the relatives of patients."

Cady blinked away the moisture in her eyes before turning around. Dragging her jacket alongside her, she returned to Keren, stopping two inches from him. "And don't talk to me, either," she said between clenched teeth. She went back to the elevators. Her boots clomped noisily against the polished floor. Keren watched her until the elevator swallowed her.

The stares of the nurses brought him out of his reverie. He scowled and started back to his office.

"I guess she told you," Renyatta muttered with an amused smile as Keren passed.

He whirled on the nurses, the tails of his white coat flying. "I will not ever see that woman again without an appointment!" With that, he went into his office and closed the door.

Renyatta shared looks of amazement with the other nurses. Ordinarily, she would have given Keren a dose of his own medicine for yelling at them, but they were too surprised to be insulted. This was the first time "the Iceberg" had ever shown his anger.

More than that, it was the first time he had ever shown any emotion at all.

Cady's bad feeling toward Dr. Bailey was put on hold the moment she saw Claire, who was asleep. Cady quietly moved to her grandmother's side. Claire didn't look terminal. In sleep, her face had a calm youthfulness that Cady hadn't seen in a long time. She knew, though, that the plumpness in Claire's cheeks came from the corticosteroids administered to help her breathing. Lovingly, Cady passed her hand over the soft white scruff that had grown in after Claire had lost her thick, silvery-black hair to chemotherapy. Radiation had darkened Claire's skin from a rich pecan with rose undertones to a flat, bittersweet chocolate brown. No matter the changes to her physical appearance, Claire was still the most beautiful person Cady had ever seen.

She kissed Claire's forehead and found the old woman's eyes upon her when she straightened.

"I told you not to come here," Claire said, her bright smile the evidence that she was glad Cady had disobeyed.

"And I told you that I am a grown-up woman and I can do what I want," Cady said. She took Claire's hand and brought it to her lips.

"I don't suppose Corman came with you?"

Cady gave Claire a reproving scowl. "*Courtland* couldn't get away from work."

"You mean he didn't want to get away from work," Claire said knowingly. "Did he make noise about you coming?"

Cady cast her eyes downward. "A little."

Courtland Prince, Cady's on-again, off-again boyfriend of two years, had tried to stop her from flying to St. Louis. Accusing her of using "any excuse" to put her family before him, Courtland had come to her apartment and picked a fight with her only hours before her flight.

"Are you making me choose between you and my grandmother?" Cady had bluntly asked him.

He'd had the decency to hesitate a moment before he said, "Yes."

"Is this an ultimatum?" Cady had asked

Courtland had crossed his arms over his chest. "Yes."

He had stood in her living room, the grey light of the pre-dawn sky cloaking him in ashen blues and shadows. He was an attorney and well accustomed to getting his way. He'd surprised her, all right, by coming out so early. She had first thought that he'd made a special trip, just to try to convince her to stay. But when she took in his sweatshirt and running shorts, she'd realized that he'd been up for his morning run anyway.

"If I go," she had said, "you won't be here for me when I come back?"

He had planted his feet more firmly, as if bracing himself for the delivery of a powerful closing argument. "Yes," he had said.

The petulant pout that she had once found so sexy was now utterly irritating. What she'd once seen as willpower was obstinacy; what she'd once thought was self-confidence, was selfishness. In that moment of decision she had finally seen him clearly for the first time.

"Make sure the door is locked when you leave," she had said. Then she had walked right out of her apartment and out of his life.

"I'm sure you and Corbett can make things right when you go back to Boston," Claire said, breaking into Cady's thoughts.

"He behaved like a club-swinging caveman," Cady said. "I don't need that. Especially now."

"I'm sorry to have been the cause of your breakup with Corwin."

"Courtland. And you weren't. When I first told you about him, you told me that he wasn't the man for me. It's taken me two years to see what you saw the first time you met him."

Claire sighed. "When you're my age, it's easier to see the man behind the handsome face. Cortez was sure nice to look at and he had a good job, but that's all there was to him. Looking good. You were part of that."

"How so?" Cady wondered aloud.

"You're beautiful, charming, smart as hell—dumb where *he* was concerned—and it made him look good to have a woman like you on his arm. You deserve better than Corpuscle."

"Corpuscle? You have definitely been in the hospital for too long."

"You've been without a good man for too long," Claire said. "What is it now…27 years?"

"I'm 31," Cady smirked. "Kyla is 27."

"You and your baby sisters need to find yourselves good men and settle down. Give me some more great-grandbabies to spoil."

Cady felt the pressure of tears behind her eyes, but she blinked them back. "Clara gave you three gorgeous great-grandchildren, one of whom is named for you."

Claire stubbornly raised her chin. "Danielle's *middle* name is Claire."

"Don't be greedy, old lady," Cady grinned. "Ciel named her son after you."

"Clarence is not the same as Claire."

"You're a rascal, you know that?"

"Our family tradition is that the Claires name their first daughters Zacadia, and the Zacadias name their first daughters Claire."

"I know, Grandma," Cady said. "That's why you gave the name Zachary to Daddy, isn't it?"

"Of course," Claire said. "Your mama's the one who insisted that they call their firstborn Clara instead of Claire. Abby thought we had too many Claires and Cadys in the family tree already."

Cady kissed Claire's forehead. "My Claire is one of a kind."

"So's my Cady." Claire gave Cady's hand a tender squeeze. "You know, you're my favorite grandbaby."

"Chiara told me that you said she was your favorite."

"She's my favorite youngest grandchild," Claire amended. "You're my favorite middle grandchild."

"And Clara's your favorite first, Ciel's your favorite second, and Kyla's your favorite fourth, right? You're my favorite grandmother, even as shifty as you are." Cady gently stroked Claire's hair. "Get some sleep, now. I have to check into my hotel."

"Hotel? Why aren't you staying at your mama's house with your sisters?"

"No room," Cady said. "And no quiet, with Ciel's kids there. And I like my privacy."

"Where are you staying?"

Cady smiled and went to the window. "Across the street." She opened the curtains and pointed to the high-rise luxury hotel sharing the view with Forest Park. "I reserved a suite on the south side of the fifteenth floor. If the hotel honored my request, your new view will include my room."

"You are so silly!" Claire squealed with joy. Then she softly added, "You constantly amaze me. I'm so glad you're here. And that Cornbread isn't."

Cady stepped away from the window. "As bad as Courtland is, he isn't as awful as Keren Bailey."

"Is Dr. Bailey still my doctor, or did you run him out of this hospital?"

Cady guiltily bit the right corner of her lower lip.

"When you called me last night, still hissin' and spittin' about Dr. Bailey, didn't I tell you to leave that man alone?"

"You told me not to call him," Cady said. "You didn't tell me not to speak to him in person." She refused to meet Claire's eyes. Claire had always been able to read her secrets in her eyes.

"He's nice-looking, isn't he?" Claire said knowingly.

Cady had seen little through her anger when she first encountered Keren, but her practiced reporter's eye had stolen a few details during the course of their meeting. In the aftermath of her anger, she now reflected on how serious and sad his black eyes had looked beneath the sheen of his shaved head. And how his mouth was a thing of sculpted beauty, even as it shaped his insensitive words. Hardest to ignore had been how good he smelled. If she inhaled deeply enough, she could detect the faint scent of him on her clothes. Sandalwood, she guessed, or some sort of mild musk. Whatever the scent was, she had already come to associate it with the beat of his heart behind the hard muscle of his chest.

"Dr. Keren Bailey is a monster." Cady stubbornly refused to agree with Claire. "He's rude and insensitive and that makes him just about one of the ugliest things I've ever seen on two legs."

"I hope you don't put lies like that in your stories," Claire chuckled. She used the button on the side panel of her bed to raise herself into a sitting position. The bed did all the work, but Claire still seemed exhausted afterward.

To hide her expression from Claire, Cady made a fuss of fluffing and arranging her pillows. She remembered a time not so far past when Claire walked two miles every day before breakfast and could stack 25-lb. bags of topsoil with little more than a grunt and a glow of perspiration.

It's not fair, Cady shouted in her head as she looked at Claire's thin wrists and listened to her labored breathing. Sitting on the edge of the bed, she gathered Claire into her arms. Claire tried to hold her tight, but her grip was weak. "I ain't gone yet," Claire said, letting a trace of her Mississippi dialect slip into her speech. She rested her head on Cady's chest. "Dr. Joyce says he's never seen anyone who wanted to live turn around and die of cancer. I beat it once and I'm beating it again. I've got a whole lot more living to do.

"I've seen all five of my grandbabies graduate from college and I've seen two of them get married. I've seen six of my great-grandbabies. I want to dance at your wedding, Zacadia. And at the rate you're going, I'll see 120 before that happens."

"I don't need a husband to be happy," Cady said, "and I'm not going to run out and get one just you make *you* happy."

"That's all I want for each of my babies," Claire said. "I want you all to be happy. I want you all to take care of each other and to be close. You're all scattered like dandelion floss in the wind, living so far apart. One day, all you're going to have is each other."

Cady's heart ached as she held the heart of her family. "Are you scared, Grandma?"

Claire's raisin-dark eyes twinkled as she laughed. "Scared of what?"

"Of dying," Cady exhaled softly.

Claire laughed even harder. "I'm not dying, baby. At least not yet."

"Has Abby been by today?"

"I really wish you'd stop calling her out of her name. Your mama deserves more respect than that."

"Does that mean no?" Cady asked.

"You know how your mama is," Claire sighed. "This is hard for her."

It's hard for all of us, Cady thought.

"She took yesterday off from school to be with me, but she didn't want to leave her kids with a substitute today. She'll be by after school. Did you tell her you were coming?"

"I didn't tell anybody. I didn't have time."

"How long are you staying?"

"As long as you need me."

"You didn't quit the paper, did you," Claire asked warily.

"I'm the only African-American news writer at the *Herald-Star*," Cady said. "I'm in the union and I'm a woman. I didn't quit. I'm using my accrued vacation and sick time. Let that paper even think about firing me for taking my contract-guaranteed personal leave, and I'll show 'em how cold a Winters woman can be."

"You're something else, Cady," Claire smiled. "But I don't want you putting your job at risk because of me."

"There are other jobs, Grandma." Cady laid her head beside Claire's on the pillow. "There's only one you. I love you."

"You love me enough to get me a pineapple triple-thick milkshake from Ted Drewes?" Though only the two of them were in the room, Claire whispered, tipping Cady off to the illicit nature of her request.

"Are you allowed to eat stuff like that?"

"I asked you a question first," Claire said.

Cady cast her grandmother a suspicious glance as she eased Claire's slight frame onto the bed, then stood up and grabbed her jacket. Claire grinned, and Cady saw a glimmer of the sharp-eyed woman who had devoted her life to her daughter-in-law and grandchildren.

"I'll be back in a half hour," Cady said. "Is there anything else I can bring you, Your Highness?"

"A couple of White Castles would be nice…"

"Why don't I just kill you myself, right now?" Cady said as she left the room, shaking her head. "Milkshake yes, Castles—no way."

Once she shut Claire's door behind her, Cady leaned heavily against the wall. Her exhaustion was complete, body, mind and soul. With four words, *She's going to die*, Keren Bailey had destroyed Cady's lifelong source of comfort and security. Each minute she spent with Claire brought her another minute closer to the time she would have to know a life without her. That was something Cady couldn't even imagine. The mere suggestion left her achy and weak. Her back against the wall, she slid to the floor. Hugging her knees, she hid her face in the wreath of her arms. Her tears came in a silent rush and this time, they wouldn't be stopped. She cried soundlessly, her shoulders quaking.

Damn it! her heart cried as she gritted her teeth. *I write stories covering murderers and rapists and child molesters and wife batterers who live long lives without ever catching even a cold. Why does this have to happen to my grandmother? It's not right! It's not fair!*

"Are you okay?"

Cady swiped her eyes across her forearm before lifting her face to the person standing before her. A pudgy brown hand heavy with chunky gold rings lit on her shoulder as Cady hesitantly smiled at Renyatta, who was bending over her. "I'm fine," Cady said, wiping her reddened eyes as she stood. "I'm just tired. It's been a long couple of days."

"Okay," Renyatta said, her understanding in the warmth of her tone. "If you need anything, you just let one of us know."

Cady nodded. "I'm sorry about the way I spoke to you earlier. I shouldn't have taken my feelings out on you."

"Don't think twice on it," Renyatta said. "Emotions tend to run high on this ward. Besides," Renyatta said with a wink, "Claire warned us about you."

"I don't know if I should be flattered or offended." Cady smiled sadly.

"And I don't know if I should be impressed or afraid, if everything Claire said about you is true," Renyatta said. "Your mama and your sisters seem to be a little on the mild side."

"Don't let them fool you," Cady said. "We're all made from the same stuff."

"Good stuff," Renyatta said confidently, "if I judge by Claire. She's a real sweet lady. They don't make 'em like Claire Winters anymore. I'm gonna miss her when—"

"She'll outlive you and me put together," Cady cut in. "We're going to get through this, same as we got through the other times."

Renyatta smiled, but it didn't quite reach her eyes. "Claire said you were the stubborn one."

"No Winters woman has ever turned away from a fight," Cady said. "Grandma's not about to start now."

"Mrs. Runyon, may I speak with you in private?" Keren asked as he passed the nurses' station. He kept walking while Renyatta hastily wrapped what was left of her chicken salad sandwich. She furiously chewed the last bite she had already taken as she scurried into Dr. Bailey's office. The doctor only called her into his office to discuss his most serious cases, and then only when the situation was at its most dire…not that things were ever truly good on the terminal ward.

Renyatta knocked before entering, even though the doctor expected her. Each of the oncologists on the ward had their own peccadilloes. Dr. Bailey's involved his peculiar attachment to his privacy.

"What can I do for you, Dr. Bailey?" Renyatta asked. She stood before his desk, notepad and pen in hand.

Keren brought a chart from his filing cabinet to his desk. He offered Renyatta a seat before he sat down himself. Renyatta slowly lowered herself into it, her suspicion roaring to full strength. Dr. Bailey never offered her a seat unless the news was very, very bad, and even then he always wore a blank, emotionless face.

This time, Dr. Bailey looked…nervous.

Renyatta bit back a grin. Dr. Bailey refused to meet her gaze and repeatedly rearranged the already tidy surface of his desk. Renyatta relaxed and with curiosity awaited the doctor's next move.

Keren placed his silver Cross pen in the breast pocket of his white lab coat, once he realized he had clicked the end of it several times in quick succession. Renyatta was an excellent nurse and a superior gossip—which was why he'd called her into his office. She had information that he wanted. And he wanted it fiercely enough to risk the chance that she would rebroadcast their conversation all over Raines-Hartley.

"Miss Winters," Keren began, his gaze firmly fixed on the unopened chart before him. "How is she?"

A bit disappointed that this meeting was to be business as usual, Renyatta sat back in the chair. "She seems to be handling things well. She ate well this morning and she's asked a few questions about the surgical procedure. Her pain's not too bad, or so she says, but I think she's holding off on the medication. It makes her drowsy and incoherent, and she wants to be alert for her granddaughter."

Keren clenched his jaw. "I've seen *Mrs.* Winters," he carefully clarified. "I'm well aware of her condition. I was referring to *Miss* Winters. Zacadia Winters."

Renyatta's ears perked up and she smiled. Keren closed his eyes in a long blink.

"Oh…" Renyatta began, her expression and posture revealing her delight. "You want to know about Cady."

"Yes," he almost snapped. "I saw her earlier, in the corridor. I believe…" He hesitated, baffled by his interest in the she-beast from Boston. "I believe she was crying. You were speaking to her."

"She's alright now," Renyatta said tenderly. "It's always hard to get news like that. That girl's got a spark. A real fire. She's sure that Claire will pull through this. I half believe it myself."

"Don't be foolish," Keren said.

"Faith is never foolish," Renyatta said gravely. "Especially when it's all you have to pin your hopes on."

Keren kept quiet. There was no point in arguing with Renyatta. The woman held to her beliefs tighter than a starving pit bull held onto a pork chop.

"You know, Dr. Bailey," she went on, "Claire looks like she's been touched by an angel. All of her girls visit regularly, but she was missing something until Cady showed up. That Cady is something else. Claire wanted a pineapple milkshake, and do you know Cady went out and brought milkshakes back for Claire, me and all the nurses?"

"Claire shouldn't be consuming empty calories," Keren said flatly.

"This is the perfect time for Claire to eat and drink and do whatever she wants," Renyatta said. "I think the only thing she truly wants is to have that wild granddaughter of hers near. That girl is like a battery, charging Claire up every time they're together."

Keren sat back and spun his chair toward the window. "Thank you, Mrs. Runyon."

He didn't hear Renyatta excuse herself or the door softly close behind her. He gazed through the window, not seeing the cloudless blue sky or the rich green view of Forest Park from fifteen stories up. His mind's eye was focused on Cady and the way she had looked crouching in the corridor, silently sobbing. He had been leaving a patient's room when he'd spotted her there outside Claire's door. He hadn't expected to see her, and even less had he expected to catch her in a moment of complete vulnerability.

When they first met, she had shown him her strength and the heat of her anger. By flying to her grandmother's side, she had revealed the depth of her capacity to love. He reasoned that it only followed that her sadness would run just as deep.

Keren reckoned that he had never met anyone with such life.

"And such passion for it," he muttered.

He forced his thoughts to the chart on his desk. *Where in the hell is my mind?* he inwardly chastised himself as he opened the folder. Ten terminal patients needed his attention far more than the very alive and very healthy Zacadia Winters.

But even as he tried to evict Cady from his mind, he wondered aloud, "What kind of name is Zacadia?"

CHAPTER TWO

Keren pushed past the common area, scarcely blinking at the tiki torches flanking the archway. He was already ten minutes late for a briefing of incoming oncology residents. Suddenly he stopped cold in his tracks, then doubled back to the common area and stood in the wide archway, staring. He couldn't believe what he was seeing.

Clifford Williams, accompanied by his oxygen tank and heart monitor, sat in a wheelchair that had been decorated with palm fronds and long, thick green grass. Clifford's rheumy eyes twinkled above the oxygen tube snaking under his nose. Beneath it, he wore a broad smile. A Polynesian headdress made of bright feathers and flowers sat on his bald head, and he wore a red Hawaiian-print shirt over his green hospital gown. The ancient brown slippers he always wore sported glowing yellow tiger lilies. Clifford's arthritic hands lightly clapped in time to a recording of "Tiny Bubbles," which played softly from a boom box beneath a table. Clifford was 83 years old, but right now his wrinkled brown face looked twenty years younger.

Clifford's wife Gloria, a pink lei dangling from her neck, held a coconut-shaped mug to his lips. Plastic spears holding chunks of pineapple, strawberries and maraschino cherries jutted from the neck of the mug, along with a pair of flexible-neck straws through which Clifford sipped a pale yellow concoction.

A number of patients were in the large room. Among them was Adele Harrison in a pale blue lei that matched her eyes. Rod Millbrook sat cross-legged atop an orange plastic sofa cushion transplanted to the floor. Rosina Ippolito sat in an armchair, a bouquet of red tiger lilies resting in her lap. An orderly manned a table with a blender and small tubs of cubed fresh fruit, multicolored plastic spears and coconut mugs. Two nurses and Dr. Raymond Seong stood beneath strands of paper lanterns near the wall of one-way glass, talking among themselves, coconut mugs in hand. And there, by a giant fake palm tree, stood Cady. A crown of fuchsia hibiscus and pink iris adorned her curls and a white lei graced her neck. A grass skirt hung low on her hips, revealing the satiny expanse of her lightly muscled abdomen, the dimples just above her tailbone and tantalizing peeks of her long, sleek legs. A top made of thin leather cord and a pair of appropriately placed coconut shells completed her outfit.

Keren took an involuntary step into the common area when a speeding wheelchair sideswiped him. Claire, wearing a lemon-yellow lei, was the passenger. Renyatta, sporting a coconut-shell bra over her pink smock, was the reckless driver. After she parked Claire next to Clifford, she scooted off to the beverage table.

Cady went to Claire's side. "All cleaned up?" she asked softly.

Claire sighed and smiled sadly. "I sure hate to make a mess like that. Renyatta never complains, but—"

Cady clutched her grandmother's hand. "Renyatta's honored to clean up after you."

"Even so, I hate being like a baby."

"We'll talk to your doctors about your medication," Cady assured her. "I'm sure something can be done to help things out down there."

Claire patted Cady's hand, which still clasped hers. "Dr. Bailey's right over there. No time like the present." Claire gave her a gentle push toward the archway.

Keren moved farther into the room, his eyebrows drawn in a severe line, his jaw muscles tightly clenched and his dark eyes pinned on Cady. They met in the middle of the room. "Six weeks ago, you told me to stay out of your way," he ranted before she could even open her mouth. "In fact, you told me not to speak to you either, a desire I've been only too happy to satisfy. But I am still the supervising physician on this ward and I will not have you turning it into a traveling circus!"

"It's on now," Renyatta muttered ominously as she inched closer to the pair facing off in the center of the room.

The doctor's forceful declaration vaporized any inclination toward civility Cady might have had. Her light eyes burned darkly into his as she planted a hand on one hip. Keren had to force his gaze to remain on hers, rather than the curves and plains of smooth brown skin exposed by her skimpy top.

"This isn't a circus," Cady said with forced calm. "It's a luau. This is Hawaii." And then, because she just couldn't help herself, she removed her lei and slipped it over Keren's head as she said, "I can tell it's been a while since you were leid."

"No. She. Didn't," Renyatta said, her eyes wide.

Keren snatched off the lei, snapping the cheap plastic. "I want you in my office," he demanded, pointing at Cady. "Now!"

Cady planted both hands on her hips. "The air pollution is just bad enough today to give us a perfect, tropical sunset." She glanced at the western sky. The sun was just beginning its showy exit in shades of purple, magenta and cobalt. "I'll report to you as soon as I can. Aloha, Doctor." Cady turned and started back to Claire and Clifford.

Keren grabbed Cady's wrist, stopping her. She turned, her wrist still caught in his strong hand. His grip wasn't uncomfortable. It wasn't so tight that she didn't notice the way his thumb whispered over the highly sensitive skin of her inner wrist.

"If you aren't in my office in the next ten minutes, I'll have you banned from this floor, Miss Winters," he said gruffly before turning her loose and storming toward the archway. "I want this room cleared immediately," he announced as he disappeared into the corridor.

The common room fell silent but for Don Ho's mellow crooning.

"If I'd known Hurricane Bailey was in the forecast, I'd have stayed in St. Louis," Rosina said dryly. Her comment earned a few laughs and broke the tension, but Renyatta and the nurses began gathering the flowers and plastic idols.

Claire beckoned Cady over. "You riled him up good this time," she said. "You probably should have asked him before you took over the common room."

"It's called a common area because it belongs to everyone, not just one ill-tempered, big-headed, pain-in-the-butt doctor," Cady said. She grasped the handles of Claire's wheelchair and turned her to face the windows.

"You undermine his authority when you backtalk him in front of his people," Claire said.

"He's the one who came in here and started bullying *me*," Cady said. "He's not *my* boss."

Claire looked up at Cady. "He was wrong, too. And you're right. He can't fire you. But he *can* ban you from this floor. Go on and talk to him."

Cady brought Clifford to Claire, and helped Rosina to the sofa that faced the windowed wall. The nurses and doctors stood near the patients, gazing at the beauty of the September sunset. Cady quietly backed out of the room and headed for Dr. Bailey's office.

Against the backdrop of the island-like sunset, Keren paced behind his desk. He swiped a hand over his head. Frustration, annoyance and anger took turns governing what he would say to Cady once she showed up. If she bothered to.

Cady Winters was the most aggravating person he had ever met. She got under his skin like no one else ever had. Thoughts of skin conjured up the image of Cady in her hula dancer's costume. She should have looked silly. She should have looked ridiculous.

But she looked stunning.

All day, every day, he was witness to the ravages of one of the world's most feared diseases. Hair and weight loss, ulcerating sores, skin lesions—he had seen them all. Cady's obvious good health was like shock therapy, reminding him that life was still out there, too, and that it glowed with color and heat, and smelled like sunlight and roses. And it was all right there within his grasp, if he only knew how to take it.

He stared at the door, wishing Cady would enter in her coconut shells and grass skirt. His wish came true when the door opened and she stepped into his office.

"Do you knock?" he asked, if only to hide his relief that she had finally arrived.

"Is that why you demanded that I come here? So you can school me on the proper way to enter an office?"

He stuck his hands in his pockets. "Look, Miss Winters. I—"

"Cady."

"What?"

She bit the inside of her lip to keep from giggling. Her interruption had caught him off guard, and his expression of surprise tickled her. "You can call me Cady."

He stared at her for a second, the amount of time it took for him to get used to calling her anything other than Miss Winters. "Cady," he began. Already he liked the way the name felt as it left his lips. "I tolerated the masseuses and the manicurists you've had come in for your grandmother, but I can't allow you to drag the other patients into these…events…of yours."

Cady strolled to the wall bearing Keren's diplomas, accreditations, certifications and affiliations. She casually studied each one.

"Are you listening to me?" he demanded.

Hands on her hips, Cady leaned over his leather sofa and peered especially close at his medical school diploma. "I didn't know that there was a Harvard University in Hackensack, New Jersey."

Keren rushed to the wall and examined his med school diploma. Cady slipped over to his bookcases, choking back a laugh. "This says Cambridge, Massachusetts," he grumbled, glaring at her back. It was such a pretty back, he decided to let her get away with her little joke. "Have a seat, please, Cady," he said.

She ran her fingers along the blue leather spines of a row of books. "The last time you wanted me to sit down, it was to tell me that my grandmother is dying. I'll stand."

"Fine."

Cady eyed him, put on guard by his lack of fight and the odd quality that had crept into his voice. In that one word, he had managed to sound less like a robot and more like a man.

As he watched her move through his office, Keren had never felt more like a man. Like a match to kindling, her presence ignited his senses. The scent of the flowers in her hair, the silky swish of her grass skirt, the sight of her perfect skin…it was too much.

"Doctor?" she asked, noticing his peculiar expression and the way he stood motionless, staring at her. "Is there something wrong?"

He squinted his eyes shut, forcing himself to take care of the matter at hand. "Yes. There is definitely something wrong. Your activities on this ward have to stop." He took a deep breath and hoped that he'd expelled his preoccupation with Cady's lovely curls and penetrating eyes. "I let you get away with the aromatherapist you hired. I looked the other way when you smuggled Mrs. Ippolito's Chihuahua onto the ward. I have to draw the line now. Your antics have got to stop. These patients are here because they are dying. No amount of pulled pork, mai tais and sunsets will change that."

"They aren't dead yet, Doctor," Cady argued. "They can still enjoy a massage or flowers or a little party. I've read that 'friendly' hospitals lessen anxiety, which can promote healing. Aromatherapy, entertainment, a scenic view, in-room massages and special meals would go a long way toward improving the well being of most hospital patients, particularly the ones on this floor."

Keren returned to his desk and sat on the edge of it, near a stack of patient folders. "Do you know anything about Clifford Williams?" Before she could answer, he took up Clifford's folder and slapped it against his desktop. "I can't discuss specifics with you because of confidentiality, but I can tell you one thing. Your luau didn't help Clifford's condition one bit. The best thing you can do is avoid getting too attached to them, to any of them."

Cady's lips slightly parted as she stared at Keren in utter disbelief. The small movement brought his gaze to the full, berry-colored bow of her mouth. When she spoke, it took him a moment to focus on her words rather than the sultry prettiness of her mouth as she shaped them.

"I know that Clifford turned 83 today and that he's always wanted to go to Hawaii," Cady said forcefully. "I also know that he probably won't see too many more sunsets like the one we saw tonight. I know that his wife loves him, and that when he's gone, she will finally find peace, knowing that he's no longer in pain. I also know that the patients on this ward would much rather see me than you coming to their rooms."

"Is that right?" he said defensively.

"Yes," Cady charged. "That's right. These patients like me, and I like them." She moved closer to him.

"You bring them ice cream and stuffed animals and Don Ho," he said. "Of course they like you. I'm a doctor, Cady, an oncologist. I'm not running a summer camp here. I don't need my patients to like me."

Cady stood so close to him that the fronds of her grass skirt caressed his knee. "Have you ever wondered why they don't like you?"

"Whether or not they like me is immaterial. Why should I care one way or the other?" he asked, drinking in the scent of her flowers.

"Because it's important," she said.

"Then enlighten me."

She moved even closer to him, almost stepping her bare foot on his Cole Haan wingtip. She placed her left hand on his desk and leaned on it. "Your patients don't like you because in you, they see what they're going to be."

"And what's that?" He traced her collarbone with his gaze.

"Dead."

The word shocked all sense back into him. He stood and took a step back.

"You've captivated everyone in this ward, Cady," he said. "Everyone loves you. Will they still love you when you pack up and leave? Are you going to take the aromatherapy, the leis, the masseuse and the lobster dinners with you? Where will these terminal patients be when you go back to Boston five minutes after Claire is in the ground?"

He had barely finished uttering his last word when Cady's right hand smacked him across his left cheek. She stood before him, her chest and shoulders heaving. Tears welled in her eyes as she waited for him to respond to her outburst. Keren knew that he had fought unfairly, that he had deliberately used Claire to wound her. He had hurt her far more than she had hurt him. He placed his hand over hers. Cady looked at their hands and tears rushed down her cheeks. She pulled her hand from his to wipe her eyes.

"Cady, I'm...I apologize," Keren said formally.

"Don't," she said, dismissively waving a hand. She willed her tears to stop. "You were just being you." She started for the door.

"Cady, please—"

"Miss Winters," she said without turning around. "I would prefer it if you would call me Miss Winters."

Raines-Hartley wasn't a 'friendly' hospital like the ones Cady had read about, but it wasn't unfriendly, either. Visiting hours were quite liberal, which allowed Cady to stay the night in Claire's room. Hours after their clash in his office, Keren found her nestled around Claire during his late-night rounds.

He stood in the semi-darkness of Claire's room, watching Cady sleep. It was such a contrast to see someone who lived life so fully, so energetically, at complete rest. Her beauty was ethereal and delicate in sleep, but every bit as striking as when she was awake. He wanted to touch her skin and to feel the softness of one of her wild rotini curls. He wanted to taste the berry of her lips. Before he knew it, he found himself standing over Cady's side of the bed. As if it had a mind of its own, his right hand was poised to touch her face.

But when Keren's eyes met Claire's, his hand froze.

Keren reached past Cady and began fussing with Claire's IV line. A sleepy smile came to Claire's face as she brought a finger to her lips, signaling for Keren to be quiet while Cady slept.

Keren wouldn't dream of waking her. The last thing he wanted was another confrontation.

"I think Dr. Bailey is a virgin."

Cady's orange juice left her mouth in a violent spray. She couldn't decide which shocked her more: Claire's opinion or the fact that she actually had spoken it aloud. "What…*what?*"

"Try as I might, I can't picture him puttin' on the bedroom eyes and romancing some lady," Claire said. She pushed her bed table aside, having picked at rather than eaten her breakfast, and was using the remote control embedded in the bed panel to find Bob Barker and "The Price Is Right."

"Is this you or your brain tumor talking?" Cady asked. She wiped her mouth with her napkin, and then took her breakfast tray to the counter at the sink. Sitting on Claire's bed, she pulled the bed table back in place and took up Claire's fork. "You have to eat, Grandma, to keep your strength up."

"I'm really not too hungry," Claire said. "There he is," she cooed lovingly as she settled back into her pillows. "My Bob Barker."

"Bob Barker would want you to eat your French toast," Cady wagered. "Open."

Mesmerized by the living room set the first lucky contestants were bidding on, Claire opened her mouth. Cady fed her a bite of French toast.

"He's not a virgin," Cady said under her breath.

"One dollar!" Claire yelled to one of the contestants.

Until a commercial break, Cady knew that she was left on her own to consider Claire's speculation on Keren. Like hell he's a virgin, she decided. The success of her work depended largely on how well she read other people. Cady knew when folks were lying, when they were hiding something, when they were scared, satisfied or just plain bad.

She had also learned to divine the intimacies of nature revealed by a person's body language. Keren knew how to dress his well-shaped physique, and he moved with a confidence that bordered on arrogance. For such a tall man, he was graceful, and elegant in a wholly masculine way.

In the brief moment of their first meeting, when they had almost shared an embrace, he had responded to her in a way that she should have found offensive, under the circumstances. She hadn't. It had been too easy, too comfortable, to find solace in the wall of warmth of his solid body. His lack of warmth in all other areas had kept her at bay ever since.

Dr. Keren Bailey was no virgin. At least not physically. Cady had no doubt that the doctor had been with women before. The piercing black eyes and sensuous mouth set in flawless dark caramel skin were enough to attract women, not to mention his perfect nose, his high cheekbones and the devil's cleft in his chin. Keren was sinfully handsome. He had surely known women in a carnal sense, but Cady doubted that he had ever shared more than his physical being with them.

Why should I even care? Cady wondered to herself. Her answer came in the memory of his hand on hers, after she'd had the ill-conceived audacity to slap him. Though that contact had been so fleeting and so innocent, its effect remained with her, just as the memory of his thumb across her wrist still gave her goose bumps.

"He's gonna fall…he's gonna fall…" Claire muttered as the little mountain climber in his lederhosen neared the peak of the price mountain.

Cady popped a forkful of scrambled eggs into Claire's mouth. A commercial came on and broke the spell the game show had on Claire.

"Grandma," Cady said, "why did you say that about Dr. Bailey?"

Claire shrugged a thin shoulder. "It just seems to me that Dr. Bailey didn't know what to do when he was watching you sleep."

"Watching me…He was in here last night?" Cady said.

"Sure was," Claire said, her eyes still on the television as the commercial ended. "Looked to me like he was gonna lean right over and…Now you know that's too much to bid! That's an Escort, not an Escalade!"

Cady continued to feed Claire between exclamations but gave up trying to question her about Keren. Unless she were in Contestants Row, Claire would be oblivious to her until after her show.

CHAPTER THREE

"I wish I'd thought to come over here before," Renyatta said as she slowly scanned the mountainous greeting card display at the back of the Forest Park Plaza's gift shop. "They have a much nicer selection of cards than Raines does."

"The masseuse and the aromatherapist I sent to the hospital came from the hotel," Cady said. "I've tapped a lot of the resources here for Claire. It makes sense. You'd think the hospital could work something out with the hotel, considering that they're neighbors and that the two provide similar services."

"High-priced amenities and slow service," Renyatta chuckled. "You got that right. But I know what you mean. That 15-minute chair massage that Swedish man gave me left me as loose and happy as a worm in a puddle. It was just what I needed after Clifford's chart review."

Cady picked up a tri-fold card and glanced at the words written on it. She got past the first sentence before she put it back in its slot. "What's a chart review?"

"You don't want to know about chart meetings." Renyatta hurried past Cady, to a different section of cards.

Cady followed. "Yes, I do. Tell me."

Renyatta sighed heavily, considering her answer before speaking. "After a patient passes, the doctors and the nurses who handled his case carefully go over the chart and the patient's history, to make sure that every medication and treatment was in order. We review the chart to make sure no mistakes were made that might have caused the patient's death."

"That's the last you see of a patient?" Cady asked quietly. "Their medicines, complaints and the caregiver's notes?"

"I go to the services, sometimes. I can't go to all of them. There's only so many funerals a person can take."

"You have a hard job, Renyatta. I know I couldn't do it."

"There's worse." Renyatta finally settled on a large card with embossed gold flowers and bright rays beaming heavenward. A long passage from the Bible was written in it. "There's always the pediatric oncology ward."

Cady showed Renyatta the card she had selected. It was taller and not quite as wide as a regular-sized card. The front featured an abstract fuchsia, gold and lavender watercolor. "Do you think Mrs. Williams will like this one?"

"She'll love the artwork," Renyatta said. "It'll remind her of the time she spent in 'Hawaii' two weeks ago." She opened the card and found it blank inside. "There's no condolence."

"I like to use my own words," Cady said.

"I've been on the terminal ward for so long, I don't have any more of my own words left for days like this. Hallmark says it just as well as I do."

The two women took their cards to the cashier and paid for them. Renyatta tucked the waxy paper bag containing her card into the heavy handbag slung over her shoulder as they exited the gift shop. "They sure fixed this place up nice," Renyatta said, gazing up at the chandeliers glittering from the high ceilings. "I can't believe this is the same place that almost got condemned ten years back. The papers said these floors are made of yellow-gold tile that came all the way from Italy. If I hadn't spent my whole lunch break in the gift shop, I'd have made you show me your room. It sure must be costing you a small fortune."

"This is St. Louis," Cady said. "I can get a whole suite here for a week for what it would cost to have a single in Boston for two days."

"Everybody tells me that Boston is so expensive and that the traffic is just the worst in—"

"Renyatta?" Cady said as they traveled the length of the wide corridor leading to the revolving doors in the front lobby.

"Yes?"

"Was it quick?"

"Clifford?"

Cady nodded.

"I imagine so," Renyatta said. "He arrested in his sleep at three A.M. Dr. Bailey was there, but he didn't handle the code."

Cady stopped. Her eyes seemed to glow with the reflected golden hue from their surroundings. "Keren was with him?" That knowledge both warmed and surprised her.

"Clifford was one of his patients," Renyatta said, taking a few more steps toward the main door. "He probably didn't have anything better to do. He's a living ghost, haunting the ward at all hours."

"Doesn't he have family?" Cady took a few quick steps to catch up to Renyatta. "A girlfriend? If anyone knows, it's you."

Flattered, Renyatta smiled and answered both questions the same way. "Not that I know of. And not that I know of." She linked her arm through Cady's and pulled her into the moving chamber of the revolving door. "Why do you ask?" she said as they stepped into the chilly fall day.

"Reporter's curiosity," Cady said.

"Uh huh," Renyatta said, giving her a sideways glance.

The two wasted no time crossing the street and scurrying into the hospital lobby. They were in the elevator and slowly rising to the fifteenth floor before Renyatta said, "That birthday luau you gave Clifford meant a lot to him and his wife. I think it bought him these last two weeks. You won't ever guess what he wanted to be buried in."

"Those old brown slippers he always wears?" Cady guessed.

Renyatta's eyes misted. "That loud-ass Hawaiian shirt you gave him for his birthday."

Cady caught a tearful laugh in her hand.

"He's gonna scare the heck out of St. Peter when he shows up at the gate looking like Toucan Sam!" Renyatta and Cady shared a laugh in the otherwise deserted elevator. Their laughter was a pleasant release, a respite from the grief stinging their hearts. "Okay," Renyatta said. "Now I know I'm gonna be okay. If I can find something to laugh about on a day like today, then I know I'll get through it."

"You don't ever get used to it, do you?" Cady asked, her laughter tapering into sadness once more.

"Nope. When I get used to it, then I'll know that it's time for me to retire." The elevator opened at Floor 15. "Now come on. Let's get these cards off to Mrs. Williams."

After writing something in her card for Mrs. Williams, Cady found Claire in the common room, tucked into her wheelchair with her IV bags dangling from the pole attached to the back of the chair. She sat at the windowed wall, staring at the cloudless sky.

"Grandma?" Cady said, kneeling beside her. "Are you okay?"

"Folks keep asking me that," Claire mumbled. She mustered a smile for Cady. "The service is Thursday afternoon. You want to take me?"

"Take you where? To Mr. Williams'…? Thursday is the day after tomorrow. His service is that soon?"

"It's been planned for a long time, honey," Claire said. "Clifford and his people knew it was coming. Gloria has been saying goodbye for a long time. She wants to finish it. You can understand that."

Cady dropped her gaze and noticed Clifford's ratty brown slippers on Claire's tiny brown feet. Her heart flipped as she fought back tears. "Dr. Bailey doesn't even want you to eat ice cream. Do you think he'll really let you leave the hospital? Did he say you could go?"

"I can leave anytime I want to, Cady. I'm a patient, not a prisoner."

"Grandma, the service is all the way out in Florissant. It's a long drive. Anything can happen. You're still connected to the IV, you're on medication—"

Claire cupped Cady's face. "I want to say goodbye to my friend," she said gently. "I'll ask Abby to take me. Clifford is being interred at Forest Glade. Abby and I can go to Clifford's service and put some flowers on Zachary's grave while we're there."

On Thursday afternoon, Cady paid a visit to the *St. Louis News-Chronicle*. The *Chronicle*'s newsroom was just as loud, dusty and cluttered as the one she worked in at the *Herald-Star* in Boston, but she was surprised at the extensive research tools available in the *Chronicle*'s library. On a personal assignment, Cady made use of InfoSysTracker, a tool by which any reporter can learn just about anything about any person or corporation.

Cady sat at a computer in the rear of the *Chronicle*'s library, logged on to IST and typed two words into the Search region: Keren Bailey.

Thousands upon thousands of "Baileys, K." popped up, so Cady narrowed her search to Keren Baileys in St. Louis.

Only one name popped up.

In less than ten seconds, Cady knew Keren's full name—Keren Royce Bailey—a partial of his social security number and the state in which it had been issued—Missouri—his current home address, his past three home addresses, and any aliases he might have used—none.

IST was a stalker's best friend and in principle, Cady hated that it was so easy for people to learn so much about her and everyone else. But Cady knew that she'd never get the information from Keren himself, so she felt just a little less guilty learning about him this way.

She still had plenty of guilt about what she was doing, though, because she screamed out loud when a large, doughy head wearing wire-rimmed glasses appeared over the back of her computer monitor.

"Sorry," the head said as it stood. The body attached to it was just as doughy. "You're visiting from the *Star* in Boston, is that right?"

"News travels fast," Cady said. She had signed in at the security desk down in the front lobby not more than fifteen minutes before the head's interruption.

"So what are you working on?"

Cady turned the monitor off as her pesky inquisitor rounded to her side of it. She gave his slouchy, wrinkled khakis and boat shoes a quick glance. "It's top secret. A scoop, actually."

"Wow," the head said, his pale blue eyes flashing. "I knew it! Nothing ever happens in St. Louis, and when it does, they bring in a heavy-hitter from Boston."

"Is there something you wanted?" Cady asked. "I don't mean to be rude, but I have some research to do."

The head removed his glasses and began cleaning them with the untucked tail of his striped Oxford. "Oh…no," he said casually. "I was just, you know…" He laughed. It sounded like a rusty hinge battered by a strong wind. "I was passing through." He indicated the library with a nervous sweep of his arm. "I thought, 'Hey, I'll go say hi to the ringer.' You know."

Cady crossed her arms over her chest and leaned back in her chair. "You're lying, Todd."

He froze, his smile melting. He swallowed hard. "H-How did you know that my name is Todd?"

All guys like you are named Todd or Doug, Cady thought. "Wild guess," she said. "You're not a reporter, either, are you?"

"Uh…no," Todd said. He stole an anxious glance over his shoulder.

"I think you're an intern, Todd. You're still in school. St. Louis University, I'll bet. You work in sports. And all those editors I passed on my way in here put you on this little reconnaissance mission. Stop me when I miss something, Todd."

"Okay," he said meekly.

Cady leaned forward, planting her hands on her knees. "I'm very busy, Todd. I don't have time to entertain you or anyone else. If there's something you want to know, come right out and ask me. Don't pussyfoot around. Now. What is it?"

"Y-Your name," he said. "They want to know your name." He chuckled nervously. "Security wouldn't give it to me. Some investigative reporter I'd turn out to be, huh?"

A blush crept into Cady's face. With her name, they could learn about her just as she was attempting to learn about Keren. "My name is Kyla Winters," she said. "K-Y-L-A. If I look familiar, it's probably because I've done a little television and movie work."

"I knew it!" Todd exploded. "I kept telling the guys that I'd seen you before and they just laughed at me!" He grabbed her hand and vigorously wagged it up and down.

"It's so cool to meet you. Oh man, I have to go tell the guys." Delighted, Todd ran off, looking back to wave at her.

Cady limply waved her hand at him and turned her monitor back on. "Newsmen," she muttered under her breath. "They're the same everywhere you go."

Armed with a full name and a partial SSN, Cady broadened her search to include any newspaper or magazine article that featured the name Keren Bailey. She learned that he had attended Washington University for his undergraduate studies, majoring in biology and graduating with high honors. He had attended Harvard Medical School and graduated in three years, summa cum laude. He had spent his internship and residency at Raines-Hartley, and was the youngest department head in R-H history. He had written numerous articles that had been published in medical journals all over the world.

Cady took her search farther back in time and learned that Keren had spent his high school years at the prestigious Warwick Country Day School on a full scholarship that included boarding, and that he had been the first African-American named valedictorian. Cady was searching the final address on her original list when Todd returned with another intern, a young Asian man with hair the color of orange Kool-Aid. Determined to escape before the boys could engage her in conversation, Cady was about to log off when Keren's name appeared once more. This time, it was in an obituary.

Cady had sat through the inane chitchat of the star-struck young men for as long as it took her to print out the obit. Back at her suite, she read it at her leisure:

Samuel Keren Bailey, 32, of St. Louis, Mo., died at New Baptist Hospital after a prolonged battle with lung cancer. He worked at Gerritson Chemicals, Inc., for over ten years and was one of the plaintiffs in a landmark lawsuit that saw GCI forced to pay $115 million to ten of its former employees in wrongful death and negligence awards.

He is survived by his nine-year-old son, Keren.

He was preceded in death by his wife, former Gerritson employee Elizabeth Kay Bailey, who previously succumbed to liver and ovarian cancer…

Cady read the obit over and over, and realized that if she had started her research at the end, she would have had the key to Dr. Bailey's beginning. The obit was so short, yet revealed so much about what had made Keren the man he'd become.

"Nine years old," Cady whimpered. So young to lose his father…to have already lost his mother. As much as the obit revealed, there was so much more Cady wanted to know. Keren had been listed as the only survivor. If that had been the case, who had taken him in after his father's death? Who had cared for him as his father was dying? What had become of him in the years between his parents' deaths and his arrival at Warwick?

Cady didn't dare speculate, and she promised herself not to go back to InfoSysTraker. She wanted her next answers from Keren himself, although she had no idea how she would go about getting them.

She sat in the living room, curled up on the sofa and facing the window. She could see that Claire's room was still empty. Renyatta had gone to Clifford's service with Claire and Abby, so Cady had a certain peace of mind. But she wouldn't feel totally comfortable until Claire was safe and in view.

Claire had always enjoyed funerals, if that was the right word. She had never seen them as mournful occasions. While the circumstances surrounding a death might have upset her, she viewed a funeral as a time to celebrate and remember a life that had been woven in some way with hers. Cady appreciated the sentiment, but couldn't bring herself to that level of understanding and generosity.

Maybe I'm just selfish, she thought. I want my angels close to me, not up in heaven.

Claire's room was so dim and lifeless. Cady got up and closed the curtains, unable to stand the sight of her grandmother's absence.

Cady stood before the wall of vending machines lining one end of the cafeteria. There was so much to choose from that it all looked the same. Claire had sent her for a bag of Ozark barbeque potato chips. Cady couldn't remember the last time she'd seen the brand on the shelves. This was only the most recent of Claire's peculiar cravings. There was no substitute for the Ozark brand. The bright red and orange flavoring heavily coating the thin, crispy chips made them truly one of a kind. The closest thing Cady could find was Doritos, and they weren't the same thing at all.

Maybe I can find a bag online, Cady thought. She'd done a story on online auction sites and had discovered that people collected a dizzying variety of innocuous things, from character jelly jars to special issue cans of Spaghettios. *Or maybe I can get the recipe from the company and hire someone to duplicate it.*

She dragged herself to one of the vacant tables in the empty cafeteria. Although the cafeteria had been closed for hours, patients and medical personnel continued to stream in and out intermittently to dine at the vending machines. In her two months in St. Louis, Cady had come to know much of the late-night staff, and many of them greeted her as she sat alone. None, Cady noticed, asked her how Claire was doing.

Cady put her elbows on the table and used her hands to hood her eyes. Claire had fared well at Clifford's service, but it had been a long day. First the church service, then the interment, then visiting her son's grave, and then a stop at the Williams home. Claire had been asleep by the time Renyatta and Abby had returned her to the hospital, where they were met in the lobby by a very tense and anxious Cady. The three of them had put Claire to bed. Abby had kissed her mother-in-law and left for the night while Cady brushed Claire's hair. Claire had roused briefly, just enough to give Cady a reassuring smile and to send her on a quest for Ozark potato chips.

"Ozark chips," Cady muttered. "She never liked Ozark chips. I was the one who liked them." Cady's shoulders shook in a melancholy laugh. "That old rascal."

"You're Cady," came a voice at her left. "You're one of Claire Winters' granddaughters."

Cady lifted her face and rested her hands on her forearms on the table. An attractive doctor stood close to her, his hands in the slit pockets of his white coat. His short dreadlocks and the bright smile radiating from the warmth of his burnt caramel complexion were a distinct contrast to the stone face of the doctor accompanying him—Keren.

Who wants to know? was Cady's first thought. Instead she said, "How do you know Claire Winters?"

"Well," began the new doctor, "I've treated her. My name is Zweli Randall." He offered his hand.

"*Doctor* Zweli Randall?" Cady presumed aloud.

Zweli took a seat. Keren stepped over to the vending machines, but remained within earshot. "Doctor is so impersonal," Zweli said. "But yes, I'm a doctor. I'm a cardiologist."

"That's nice," Cady said shortly. "But I didn't ask you about you. What sort of treatment have you given my grandmother? What exactly is wrong with her heart? Has something new cropped up?"

Zweli chuckled and his hazel eyes glittered. "I heard you were a handful."

Cady arrowed a look at Keren. He kept pressing a button that caused a tower of boxed sandwiches to revolve before him.

"Your grandmother's heart tends to beat a little too fast at times," Zweli said, returning Cady's attention to him.

"That's her tachycardia, right?" Cady said.

Zweli nodded. "All things considered, she's got a very good heart. I mean that in every possible way."

"Thank you," Cady said, softening a bit. "How did you know that I was her granddaughter?"

Zweli held her gaze as he leaned forward and gave her a sly smile. "Word travels fast around here. Every single man in this building has heard about Claire Winters' beautiful granddaughters. They say that each one is prettier than the next." He put an elbow on the table and leaned in toward Cady. "Apparently, the best came last. Has anyone ever told you how beautiful you are?"

"Yes, actually," Cady said. "There was this man who came up on me once with that same exact tired line. He actually thought that he could get in my good graces by commenting on my physical appearance. I don't think he ever considered that I had a brain, too, and would see him for the superficial fool he was."

Zweli excitedly clenched his fists as he stood. "You are something else, Cady. I love a woman with beauty, spirit and brains." Just as Cady would have stabbed him with a sharper piece of her mind, his beeper went off. He looked at it, then said, "This is urgent. I have to take it." He waved at Keren as he started off. At the entrance he called back to Cady, "I'll make it my business to catch you later, gorgeous."

Cady uttered a profanity that turned Keren's head.

"Sorry," she said. "And...sorry."

"For what?" He dropped coins into one of the machines, pressed a few buttons, and then bent over to retrieve his purchases.

"For swearing," she said. "And for popping you the other day."

He brought a shiny Red Delicious apple and a boxed tuna sandwich to Cady's table. "That was two weeks ago. And I accept your apology."

He hovered near the table for another moment or two, unsure if he should stay or go. Cady decided the matter for him when she used one of her graceful legs to kick a chair out for him. He took it, setting his meager meal before him. Cady watched him as he set the apple on its side on top of a napkin, and then used a plastic knife to cut the apple in half. He offered the top half to Cady before taking a big bite of his own half.

"I've never seen anyone eat an apple like that," she said. She looked at her half, and then displayed it for him. "Look. There's a star." Her tired eyes were playing tricks on her, because for a second, she thought Keren almost smiled.

"I dated a man who ate glazed long johns with a knife and fork, but I think he was just *trying* to be odd. Low self-esteem disguising itself as eccentricity."

"You've dated a lot of men?" he asked.

She stared at his profile, watching the muscles of his jaw work as he ate the juicy apple. "Dated yes," she said. "Slept with, no."

He faced her. "I didn't ask you that."

"You didn't have to."

Keren finished his apple and then removed the film covering the triangular halves of his tuna sandwich. Cady quietly nibbled around the star in the center of the apple. The silence between them was far too comfortable, even when he passed her half of his sandwich.

You're getting too thin, he wanted to tell her, but kept his tongue for fear of disrupting the perfect peace between them. She had a superb figure, curves and flesh in all the right places, tight and lean in all the other places. But since she'd arrived to be with Claire, she had gotten thinner. With the colder weather, luxuriant and loose sweaters and turtlenecks had replaced her form-fitting sleeveless tops. Her leaner face betrayed the weight loss hidden by her clothing. Where Zweli Randall had seen only Cady's beauty, Keren now saw shades of the anxiety and fear she fought to keep concealed.

"Is your shift over?" Cady asked quietly as she half-heartedly ate her sandwich.

"I don't really have a shift, per se. I set my own hours."

"That would explain why you're always here."

"I go home," he said.

Thanks to her computer search, Cady knew where that home was. Keren lived less than three blocks from the hospital, in one of the best neighborhoods in the West End.

"You should go home, too," he said. "You need sleep, Cady."

"Today was a long day for Claire," she said wearily. "My mother told me that Grandma insisted on doing everything today. When they brought her back to the hospital, I couldn't tell if she was just tired, or if the reality of Clifford's passing finally hit her. Adele took it pretty hard. I stopped in her room before I came down here, and all she wanted to talk about was the horses she used to ride down South on her father's farm when she was a girl."

"It happens every time," he said. He set his sandwich aside. "This is the most closely-knit group of patients I've had in a long time." Thanks to you, he bit back. "When one of them goes, malaise tends to set in among the rest. Adele and Clifford were admitted at the same time. They knew each other longest. Everyone liked Clifford."

Even you? Cady almost asked. "My mother said that Grandma didn't eat at Gloria's house. Grandma says that food just doesn't taste right to her anymore. I think she was overtired." Keren met her gaze but Cady looked away. She couldn't bear to see the truth in his dark eyes. "She was asleep when I came down here. Would you…"

Anything, his eyes seemed to say.

"Would you look in on her before you leave tonight?" she asked. "She was so tired and…I worry about her."

"You need to get some sleep, too," he told her. "Those beds really aren't made for two."

The word "bed" was enough to make her whole body give in to exhaustion. She couldn't wait to fall into her king-size bed and stretch her limbs within the soft embrace of clean, flannel sheets. She longed to bunch the pillows up under her shoulders, reserving just one to tuck under her head and to hug close as she settled in for a full night's sleep. She liked snuggling up with Claire. Even now, it gave her the sense of safety and peace that it had when she was a little girl afraid of hobgoblins behind her closet door. And since her job required so much traveling, Cady had grown accustomed to snuggling up alone, with nothing but her hotel pillows for comfort. But now, as much as she wanted to climb into a warm bed, Cady also felt the need for a warm man. She wanted someone strong and rested, someone capable of wrapping her in a pair of powerful arms and taking her burden of worry for just a little while, just long enough for her to regain her full strength. Her eyes drifted shut and she saw herself in Keren's arms. This time not in his office, but filling the empty expanse of her big hotel bed.

"Is there anything else I can do for you, Cady?" he asked, drawing her from her daydream.

Yes, she answered in her head. You can tuck me in tonight, and stay with me until I fall asleep. But what she said was, "No. Thank you. Just check on Claire for me."

Claire's monitors beeped and hummed and clicked and whispered as Keren moved around her, adjusting her pillows and blankets and checking her pulse and respiration. Claire was as good as she could possibly be, given her condition. Cady could get a good night's sleep without worry, if she'd let herself.

Keren looked at Claire's sleeping form and couldn't blind himself as Cady did. Claire wasn't responding to treatment. She was thinner, weaker. She was having moments of complete mental confusion. His experienced eye told him that her fierce will to live, and the daily boost she got from Cady, were more instrumental in keeping her alive than anything else was.

He turned off Claire's bedside lamp, leaving the night-lights on. He had started to close her curtains when across the street he caught sight of Cady. She sat at a small desk in the living room of her suite. She faced the window, though her attention was on whatever she was working on at the desk. She had changed from the red chenille mock turtle-neck and black velvet pants she had been wearing earlier, and now wore a plain white tank-style nightgown.

Cady looked up from her work, oblivious to her audience of one, and stood up. She turned off the desk lamp, plunging the living room into darkness. Light from a back room of the suite was just strong enough to make her gown sheer, giving him a shadowy outline of her breasts, torso and parted thighs before she retreated deeper into the suite.

Keren stopped breathing and stared at the space where she had been, still seeing her beautiful form against the night. His blood churned as he clenched his fist around Claire's sheer curtain. His brain had been able to keep Cady Winters at a distance, but his body roared to life as this latest sight of her reminded it of how she had felt against him. He hated to think of how quickly and how strongly his flesh had responded to her upon their first meeting, all because she had spontaneously sought a moment of comfort in the face of her sorrow.

Each time he saw her, in passing or up close and personal, her effect on him had grown stronger rather than weaker. His body refused to cooperate with his mind, and as he stared at her empty window, picturing her in her shadowy glory, his heart tried to get in on the action. His whole self was at war over his feelings for Cady Winters.

Keren left the curtains open as he tore himself from the window. He checked Claire's vitals one more time, then rushed to his office. He grabbed the duffel bag from behind his desk and took the stairs three at a time down to the hospital gym. He had changed and was in the middle of his weightlifting circuit before he declared his body the victor in his battle over Cady Winters. Dropping the barbells where he stood, Keren raced to the showers, blasted the cold water and jumped in fully clothed.

CHAPTER FOUR

Cady threw open the door to her suite, expecting to see Renyatta behind Claire's wheelchair. The eager smile on her face slowly vanished as she stared at Keren, who stood there uncomfortably in his lab coat.

"What's wrong?" Cady demanded, instantly at full panic. "Where's my grandmother?"

Keren wanted to put her at ease, to tell her that everything was fine. But Cady's appearance stole his power of speech. She hadn't dressed for the dinner date with her grandmother. In fact, she had mostly undressed. She wore a white ribbed man's-style tank top and a pair of jersey shorts. Judging from the effect the cold blast of air from the hallway had on her breasts when she opened the door, what he saw was all she wore. And once again, Dr. Keren Bailey was at the mercy of something he couldn't control—his body's response to Cady Winters.

Cady grabbed him by the lapels of his white coat. "Is something wrong with Claire? Tell me!"

Keren gently covered her trembling hands with his and lowered them. "She's fine. She's tired, that's all. She asked me to come over and tell you that she couldn't come for dinner tonight. She thought that if she called to cancel, you would guilt her into coming out anyway. If she thinks she needs to rest, she should rest."

Cady breathed deeply, collecting her thoughts. "Don't scare me like that," she finally said. "I thought that…" She closed her eyes and pushed the rest of her statement from her mind. "She's been tired more and more over the past few weeks." Cady pulled her hands from Keren's and went to the kitchen area. "If she moved around more, she'd have more energy. She's always been active. She took care of Ciel's kids up until she was diagnosed with the brain tumor."

Keren reluctantly followed her into the suite. The aromas of Cady's cooking had him salivating almost as much as her appearance had.

"Where's Renyatta?" Cady asked. "She still could have come. She's been dying to see this place for the past three months."

"Claire said that she felt more comfortable having Renyatta there with her," Keren said. He eyed the busy kitchen. The countertops were lined with various dishes filled with food, and still more food steamed and sputtered in pots and pans on the stove.

Cady followed his gaze. "I got a little carried away," she explained. "I made all my grandmother's favorites. I thought it would help her start eating more."

Keren rubbed his hand over his mouth to make sure that he wasn't drooling. Cady was beautiful, she had a good sense of humor and, from the looks of things, she could cook, too. His heart seemed to beat twice as hard, twice as fast. He had to get out of there.

"Good evening, Cady," he said, and started for the door.

She outran him, beating him to the door and blocking his escape. "Where the hell are you going? I spent the day in that kitchen, and somebody is going to eat that meal in there."

"Cady, I didn't come here for dinner."

"Neither did Claire and Renyatta, and like I told you, someone has to eat this stuff," she said. "Besides, you look hungry to me." She took a step forward, forcing him to walk backward. She moved past him and put her hands on his shoulders, taking his white coat. She removed it slowly, taking guilty pleasure in the way the muscles of his shoulders felt against her fingers.

Keren straightened his tie while Cady hung up his coat. Her bare feet moved soundlessly on the plush white carpet as she led him to the counter that divided the kitchen and living room. "Have a seat." She indicated one of the stools at the counter, then went into the kitchen to put the final touches on the meal.

"Do you drink wine?" she asked him.

"Uh…occasionally."

She opened the refrigerator and retrieved a bottle of white wine. "I picked this one special for Grandma. It's a California muscat. It's the perfect wine for people who don't think they like wine."

"Claire doesn't drink?" He accepted the bottle and the corkscrew Cady dug up for him.

"She used to drink a capful of brandy in a cup of RC Cola every night before she went to bed," she said as she rolled fresh basil and parsley leaves into a tight tube. "She'd let my sisters and me take sips of it."

Keren opened the wine while Cady cut the tube of herbs into ultra-thin slices. "Do you have glasses?" he asked.

"They're here somewhere," she said. She searched through cabinets until she found them. "This is why I love staying in a suite. It has practically everything you need for normal living. Pots and pans, a full-size refrigerator, a dishwasher, dishes, cutlery. The only thing I needed for tonight was serving bowls. My mother let me borrow a few of hers."

"It looks like you were expecting an army." He poured the wine, filling her glass half full and his own a mere third of the way.

"I was, sort of." She took the bottle and filled both glasses to within a half inch from the lip. She handed a glass to Keren, gently clinked them together, and took a sip of the sweet, refreshing wine. "Claire wanted me to make enough to take back to the hospital. She thinks it's hospital food that's keeping sick people sick."

"That's a distinct possibility," he said. He tasted the wine. "You're right. This is nice."

She looked up, her eyes smiling. "You almost made a joke. You go, Doc."

He felt a blush creeping from under his collar. "Who are you feeding at the hospital?"

"Claire, Renyatta, Adele and Rosina. Rosina's never had fried okra before so I promised her a plate." Cady began ticking off the rest of her list on her fingers. "Two of the nurses on fifteen and that one housekeeping lady whose name I always forget. She's got that one long hair that grows out of her right eyebrow. Dr. Randall—"

"Zweli?" Keren interrupted. "You cooked for *him*?"

Cady bit back a smile. If this was jealousy from the good doctor, she liked it. "He's been very attentive to Claire lately. He was there while I was making plans with Claire and Renyatta and he dropped so many hints that Claire took pity on him and promised him a plate."

Keren swirled his wine and then watched the "legs" form on the inside of the glass. "I got the impression that you didn't care for Dr. Randall."

Cady indifferently shrugged a shoulder. "I don't." She tasted her tomato sauce before dropping her chopped herbs into it. "It's just food. What do I care?"

"Can I help you?"

She smiled. Keren almost oozed off of the stool. No woman, no mortal person on earth, had the right to be so damn beautiful. He wondered what God was thinking by giving Cady such a gorgeous smile. It was a weapon man was powerless to resist.

"Sure," she said. "You can start carrying."

She hefted a huge dish of Cornish hens and tried to pass it to him over the counter. He was so captivated by the movement of her untethered breasts that he almost let the little roasted birds slide to the carpet. "Maybe we should just fill our plates here in the kitchen," he suggested. "Since it's just the two of us."

"I like the sound of that," she said, meaning the "just the two of us" part.

He joined her in the kitchen, where she gave him a white dinner plate. He didn't know where to start. She had prepared a feast, and there was food everywhere. "What do you recommend?"

"Everything," she said. She helped him out by spearing a Cornish hen and placing it in the center of his plate. He served himself collard greens slow-cooked with smoked turkey, macaroni and cheese, butter beans, cornbread that was as sweet and moist as cake, oyster dressing, cucumber and beet salad, fried corn, smothered cabbage and oven-braised sirloin tips. His plate was so heavy, he had to carry it with both hands to the glass-topped table in the dining room area.

Cady brought their wine glasses, then returned to the kitchen for her own plate. On it, she had a Cornish hen and a dab of macaroni and cheese. She had a separate bowl for her collard greens.

Keren draped a linen napkin across his lap before he began eating. Cady grinned as she watched him tackle the Cornish hen with a knife and fork. "That ain't no long john," she said.

"I beg your pardon?" Keren said.

Cady picked up her hen and bit right into the breast. She chewed the moist, succulent meat, then sucked the tip of her index finger. "I used Claire's recipes. These birds are 'finger lickin' good.' "

Keren wondered if she would notice if he stepped into the bathroom and gave himself yet another in what had become a long string of cold showers. The food would surely satisfy his appetite but the sight of her golden-brown skin and elegant limbs only piqued a baser appetite. He focused his energies on the food before him, and following her example, devoured the bird caveman-style in a matter of minutes. Cady watched him eat. He sampled everything first, then ate his sides in order. He started with the collard greens and finished with the cornbread. He had three slices of the cornbread in all, and when Cady was convinced that he couldn't hold any more, he had another serving of butter beans.

As he ate, she had watched him. He was fastidious and well mannered, but he ate with a hearty appreciation for the food. When she got a glass of water for herself and brought one, unasked, to him, it seemed the most natural thing in the world to do. To wait on him. To serve and to please him.

I need my head examined, she thought dryly.

"Cady," he said as he pushed away from the table, "that was the best dinner I've ever had."

"I'm glad." She took their plates and set them in the sink. "You're staying for dessert."

"I can't."

"Yes, you can. You are." She turned off the kitchen light. She grabbed the wine bottle and their glasses and moved into the living room. "I made sweet potato pie and a coconut cake. You're too bloated to leave anyway. I'll be amazed if you can drag yourself over to the sofa."

Cady sat on the deep, wide sofa, elegantly tucking her legs beneath her and crossing them at the ankle. Keren joined her, sitting at the opposite end. "The remote is on the coffee table there, if you want to watch television."

"I'm fine." He was content watching her pretty legs.

"If you weren't here with me, what would you be doing right now?" she asked.

"Probably checking out the vending machine specials," he said.

"Nice," she smiled. "That was funny. There's hope for you after all."

"What would you be doing?" he asked. "If I weren't here?"

"I'm working on a story. I got the idea shortly after I got here. I'm not sure if I'll pitch it to the *Herald-Star* or if I'll treat it as a freelance piece and submit it elsewhere."

"What's it about?"

"I never talk about my works in progress," she said. "It's like letting someone watch you shower."

His gaze became more intense and his jaw tightened as he pictured that very image. It was too easy to envision the sheen of her skin as water coursed over her body, as her slender hands traced the lines of her torso and legs.

"That was a joke," she said, hoping to ease the sudden tension in his face.

"I'd like to read your work sometime," he said, clearing his throat. "Your job seems very exciting." He turned toward her, resting his left arm on the back of the sofa.

"It is, at times. It can be very boring, too. And frightening. News takes lots of shapes."

"Did you always want to be a reporter?"

She stretched her legs toward him and stared at her feet. "I think so. My father was a reporter."

"Was?"

"He died when I was seven," she said, raising her gaze to meet his. "Chiara was just a baby and Kyla was only three. They never knew him. I don't remember much about him. Claire kept him alive for us."

He loosened his tie and undid his top button. He was caught off guard by the tenderness that had crept into her voice. Her bluster and bravado were gone, leaving her exposed and vulnerable.

"My father wrote for the *St. Louis News-Chronicle*, the *Chicago Tribune* and the *Washington Post*. He covered Watergate and was nominated for a Pulitzer for his work. He was killed covering a story in Israel. It was a suicide bombing at an outdoor café."

His natural response was to say I'm sorry. He knew how inadequate I'm sorry was, so he kept his silence and listened.

"Abby...my mother...fell apart when he died. Daddy's life insurance only went so far, and Abby eventually took a second job to support us. She taught all day, she worked nights at a grocery store, and she tutored on weekends. We hardly ever saw her; Clara, my oldest sister, was basically raising us. She was only twelve and she had four children.

"That's when Claire stepped in. She moved in with us. She raised us, for the most part. It was hard. We never had enough money. I was always in Clara and Ciel's hand-me-downs. That's an adolescent complaint, really. My sisters and I turned out great and I know it. For a long time, I hated my father for getting himself killed. But once I became a reporter, I understood what drove him. I'm at peace with him, most of the time. In my memory, my father is a handsome and smart man who loved me. But Claire is what's real to me. She's the one who taught me how to change the oil in a car and how to make oyster dressing. She's the one who always told me that I could do anything I put my mind to. She's why I'm the person I am today."

"She's quite a lady," he said.

"Tell me about your family," she said carefully.

"I don't have any." He abruptly stood. "I can't stay for dessert, Cady. I have rounds."

She kneeled on the sofa and took his hand, stopping his retreat. She had taken a chance and it was blowing up in her face. Her first instinct was to shove him back down on the sofa, pin him there and batter him with questions until he caved to her will. Going completely against her nature, she softly said, "Don't go. Please. You don't have to talk about it. You don't have to talk at all."

His lax hand involuntarily tightened around hers. He sat back down heavily, jostling her a bit so that she fell forward. She caught herself by gripping his thigh and his shoulder. He covered the hand on his thigh with his own. The room was too warm or maybe the wine was affecting him. Whatever it was, his thoughts were jumbled. His heart filled with all the things he suddenly felt compelled to tell her, but he couldn't spill them with her looking at him so tenderly and touching him and sitting so close. All he could do was touch his head to hers and pray that she wouldn't draw away.

She turned him, just enough to properly wrap her arms around him, and hugged him, pressing her cheek to his temple and flattening her breasts against his upper chest. His arms went around her middle and they both nearly groaned in pleasure. Her soft warmth and compassion fed a hunger far removed from food, just as his strength and support gave her what she had needed for so long. Like two sides of a coin, they had come together, and were pleased to find that they fit.

He pulled from the embrace just enough to see her face. Her breathing was rapid, matching his, as her amber gaze studied his lips. She closed her eyes, sure that she would burst into flame if he didn't kiss her. He cupped her face with one hand, and she tilted her head into his palm. Her thighs quivered in anticipation when his lips touched the base of her throat. His hands warmed her skin through the thin fabric of her shirt. As they moved along her back, he discovered that she was indeed braless. His kisses became bolder as they traced her throat and moved up to her chin with maddening stealth.

Her skin was sweeter and softer than he had imagined. Her minute movements against him sent fire raging through his lower belly. He lifted her just enough to place her astride his hips. He wanted to kiss her, to taste every part of her, to sample her flavors and textures as heartily as he had partaken of her delicious cooking. Any indecision he might have had was erased when she slightly repositioned herself on his lap. She placed her left foot flat on the sofa and curled her right leg around him. She had barely moved, yet her small action brought the center of her heat directly over his. This was a whole new world of want. Their breaths came hard and fast as he threaded his fingers through her curls and tipped her head back. He moved to kiss her, then suddenly caught a movement in the tail of his eye.

It wasn't just the two of them after all.

The living room curtains were wide open, and every light in the room was ablaze. The astronauts on the International Space Station could probably see into Cady's suite, so Keren had no doubt that Claire and Renyatta had a stellar view.

Cady saw them just after Keren did, and the two parted like guilty teenagers. Cady went to the window, straightening her clothing as she did so. Keren had to look away. The sight of her backside was enough to make him change his mind about grabbing her and giving Claire and Renyatta a show they would never forget.

He buttoned his shirt and realigned his tie while Cady made wild hand signals at Claire and Renyatta. Claire's bed faced the window, and Renyatta had pulled a chair up beside the bed. "She has the nerve to be eating popcorn," Cady reported with a laugh.

Keren didn't respond. Cady turned from the window in time to see him making a beeline for the door.

"You're not embarrassed by this, are you?" Cady asked, trailing behind him.

"I'm not interested in becoming fodder for the hospital's overactive grapevine." He took his white coat from the closet and put it on, but not before Cady caught sight of the evidence of how much their interlude had affected him. "I'm sorry. I never should have let things go so far."

"That's supposed to be my line," Cady said.

"I have late rounds," he said. "Thank you for dinner. And everything else. Good night, Cady." He flung the door open and dashed through it.

She stood in the corridor and watched him go. He never looked back.

━━━━━

Keren stripped off his white coat and nearly tore off his tie as he rushed through the lobby and burst onto the street. The October chill was in the night air, but steam seemed to rise from his collar and his waistband as he stood in the cold. He stepped farther away from the building, so he could look up at the fifteenth floor. Her suite was in the center, and her lights glowed into the dark night.

I could go back up there, he told himself. I could go right back up there and finish what we started. "But what would the finish be?" he mumbled. Just tonight? Just while Claire is here?

The more he thought about it, the more he didn't want to finish anything. On the contrary, he wanted it to be a beginning. He wanted Cady. He wanted her so much that it caused him physical distress. But he didn't want her for a casual fling. He wanted her forever.

She was passionate, caring, generous, smart, beautiful, she could cook…there would never be a dull moment. His mind, body and soul were harmoniously in sync, agreeing that they wanted Cady Winters.

Just as he turned to go back to her, the lights in the center suite on the fifteenth floor died, leaving only cold stone in the moonless night.

━━━━━

Fresh from a long, hot shower, Cady sprawled on her back on her bed. She had left the dishes for the housekeeping staff—along with a big tip—and she had shoved all the leftovers into the refrigerator. She had tried to watch television, but nothing held her interest.

She couldn't stop thinking about Keren.

Even her shower couldn't remove his scent. She hugged her pillow to her face. He had never made it into her bedroom, but she could still smell the sexy musk of him. She rolled onto her stomach and tried to get comfortable, but the bed was too big. And too empty. Her mind replayed the moments she had spent with him, then projected more intoxicating images of what they could have done right there on her giant bed.

"What is wrong with me?" she moaned, exhausted by the relentless memory of Keren's lips on her skin and his hands on her body. She had been attracted to men before, but this was ridiculous. She wanted him the way she wanted air to breathe. Just being in his arms had made her respond as she had never responded to any other man. He gave her goose bumps in all the right places just by turning his lovely, unreadable eyes on her. From the moment she met him, he had by turn annoyed, frustrated, offended, insulted and just plain bothered her. Yet she couldn't get through a day without smiling at the way he stood with his hands in his pockets when conducting his rounds, or the way his nose wrinkled when he caught the nurses telling a risqué joke. Lately, she had started feeling antsy and cranky until she saw him in the course of a day.

"I'm like a damn seventh-grader with a crush," she said out loud. And God help any seventh-grader who wants what I want from Keren Bailey, she added to herself.

The man's body was incredible. She had seen him only in his typical uniform: starched button-down, tie, pleated slacks, wingtips and white coat. But her casual touches here and there had told her what their after-dinner romp had proved: that he had a fine build underneath it all. He was certainly handsome, and she had suffered little darts of jealously when she once overheard a gaggle of female interns talking about which doctors were the sexiest at Raines-Hartley. Dr. Bailey had tied with Dr. Randall, but Cady only felt territorial about Keren.

He was the proverbial still water that ran deep, and Cady longed to do a cannonball right into the middle of it. While most people had a complete lack of mystery for her, Keren was nothing except mystery. He had revealed nothing about himself, which only captivated her even more and made her more willing to share parts of herself with him. She had revealed more to him about her father than she had to any friend or lover she had ever had.

"Maybe that's the problem," she thought. "I'm too much for him. I'm too emotional and impulsive."

A darker thought invaded her head as she sat up in the bed. Or maybe he's just like every other man, she thought. Maybe he just wants sex. Maybe he doesn't want *me* at all.

She curled up and buried her face in her pillow. This is what I get, she thought. I came here for Claire. I didn't come here to get laid. And I definitely didn't come here to fall in love with a man incapable of returning it.

CHAPTER FIVE

"Maybe I should have been one of the Munchkins," Renyatta said. "I look like a giant ball of cotton candy."

Cady crawled on her hands and knees around the circumference of Renyatta's frothy, bell-shaped skirt. Plucking the straight pins from between her lips, she pinned up the hem of the layers of pink tulle forming the skirt of Renyatta's Halloween costume. She was Glinda the Good Witch, complete with a tall miter-style crown and magic wand.

Renyatta had the height of a size six but the girth of a size 20. It would have been easier to just hack the skirt in two rather than pin up the foot or so that Renyatta kept tripping over.

"I brought the stapler, in case you run out of pins," Renyatta said. "Hurry up, Cady, the trick-or-treating starts in a few minutes."

"I'm almost finished." Cady planted two more pins. "There. You're done. I'm warning you, Renyatta, do not go near the lobby doors. You'll short circuit the metal detectors. I used a whole box of pins on that skirt."

Renyatta looked at herself in the full-length mirror tacked to the door of the nurses' locker room. "I look like cotton candy all right," she said. "Sweet and bad for you!" She wrapped her thick arms around Cady. "You never cease to amaze me, girl. Claire told me she taught you how to sew, but I didn't know that you could *sew*."

"It's been a long time since I sat down at a machine," Cady said. "I don't usually have much time to sew."

She'd had plenty of time in the past couple of weeks. Throwing herself into the ward's Halloween party preparations had given her the perfect way to avoid Keren. With Claire spending so much time sleeping or medicated, Cady had needed something to occupy her restless moments.

In keeping with Renyatta's theme, Cady had decided to dress as the Scarecrow. She set her patched black hat on her head and adjusted the raffia braid that looked like straw sticking from her dark green sleeves. After blackening the tip of her nose with mascara, she pulled out a few curls at the opening of her burlap hood to give herself a suitably shabby look.

"You look so cute," Renyatta said. "Everybody kept asking me what you were going to dress up as. I told them that I was gonna be the Wicked Witch of the West, and you were gonna be one of my Flying Monkeys."

"You're so bad," Cady said. She opened the door for Renyatta, who needed both hands to mash her skirt enough to fit it through the doorway. They emerged to applause from the other nurses, each of whom was in costume.

"Ready ladies?" Renyatta asked. "We have twenty minutes to cover the ward."

Armed with buckets of goodies, the nurses began their circuit of reverse trick-or-treating. They stopped in each room, delivering treats to those allowed to have them. Cady and Renyatta lingered in Adele's room to help her into her Dorothy costume.

Adele had recently received the good news that her stomach tumor was responding well to radiation therapy, that it had shrunk by forty-six percent. She was almost well enough to continue her treatment on an outpatient basis. While her physical health was improving, her mental and emotional well-being were suffering, and had been since Clifford's passing.

"I'm so glad you agreed to be Dorothy," Cady said. "The little ones on the pediatric ward are going to go nuts when they see us."

Adele sat on the edge of her bed in her blue and white gingham dress while Cady buckled glittery red shoes onto her feet. "Every year when I was a little girl, I would dress as an equestrian," Adele said. She gazed dreamily into the darkening sunset as she spoke. "My father was a trainer. I used to spend every summer and every weekend working with him and the horses. Oh, I loved to ride. This is the only time in my life that I haven't had a horse. I sold Camelot, my last horse, right after I got sick."

"Well, you're getting better now," Cady said. She held Adele's hands, helping her onto her feet. "You can get Camelot back and start riding again."

"No," Adele said, her voice fading. "I love my horses the way I love my family and friends. It would be too hard to say goodbye again. I can't do anything about the people, but I can stop the heartbreak of having to leave my horses."

"That's no way to think and you know it, Ms. Harrison," Renyatta said. She picked up Adele's chart and made a note to have a psychologist visit her.

"Your tumor is in your belly but you talk like it's in your head," Cady told Adele. "Why the hell can't you ride anymore?"

"I can't explain it, Cady," Adele said. Her pale eyes began to fill. Adele was 51, but she looked older. Though her disease seemed to be letting go of her, her inability to let go of it was wearing her down. For a month now, Cady had watched Adele withdraw further and further into herself. All at once, Cady was sick of it. A determined gleam in her eyes, she turned in her clunky oil boots and clomped toward the door.

"Cady, where are you going?" Renyatta asked. "I know that look. Whatever you're about to do, don't. Please. Dr. Bailey's been as prickly as a grizzly bear for the past couple of weeks and I don't want you getting into any trouble. I don't want you getting *me* into any trouble."

Cady swung the door open wide. She looked over her shoulder as she walked away and said, "The less you know, the better."

A crowd of patients and staff, most of whom had followed Cady to the fifteenth floor common room, gathered just outside the archway as Glinda the Good Witch, the Cowardly Lion and Dorothy entered. Glinda and the Cowardly Lion stood in wide-eyed shock as Adele, her eyes brimming with tears, approached Cady and her guest, her hand outstretched.

"His name is Rufus," Cady said as Adele carefully placed her hand on the silky black mane of the horse Cady held by its reins.

"You have got to be kidding me," the Cowardly Lion, aka Dr. Zweli Randall said. "Cady, I thought you'd pulled off the impossible when you talked me into putting on this cat suit, but this…this is…this…"

Renyatta doubled over, laughing so hard that her pink crown and her gold tooth cover popped off. Adele stroked the horse, which seemed to enjoy the affection. "You're a good boy, aren't you?" Adele cooed. "I can tell that you're a good fella."

Zweli approached Cady, circling away from the horse. "Cady, you have to get that animal out of here. This is a hospital," he explained slowly, as though she were mentally deficient in some way. "This is a building for people."

"This is a building for healing people," Cady said. "This is medicine, for Adele."

Zweli glanced at Adele, who smiled happily as she laid her head on Rufus's shoulder. Rufus, the big softie, gently nibbled at Adele's hair.

"Okay, well, let's continue this treatment outside," Zweli said. He began to sweat in the furry costume. "Did you bring him up on the elevator?"

Cady's eyes merrily sparkled above her blackened nose. "No, we took the stairs. We needed the exercise."

"Very funny, Scarecrow," Zweli said. He trotted to the archway and pushed his way through the crowd. He checked the corridor, then went back to Cady. "The coast is clear. Let's move it."

"Him," Cady said.

Still laughing, Renyatta now had tears running down her face. She used a layer of her skirt to wipe her eyes.

"Him, then," Zweli said. "Let's go before you-know-who shows up."

"You can say his name," Cady said. "He's not Satan, you know."

"You'll wish he were if he catches your friend here. Satan would go easier on you."

Cady patted Rufus's neck. "Dr. Randall, for a Cowardly Lion you're very brave. The costume suits you."

Zweli grinned and puffed with pride. "You already owe me one for getting me into this costume. After we get Mr. Ed back in the wild, I expect to collect."

"Fair enough," Cady said. She moved to Adele's side. "Will you help me get Rufus outside? He wasn't really cooperating with me when I brought him up here. He knows I'm not a horse person."

Adele threw her arms around Cady and gave her a tight hug. "Thank you, sweetie," she said. "Thank you so much."

"Ladies, save the love fest for later," Zweli urged. "Let's go. Too many people are gathering up here."

Adele drew from Cady and wrapped Rufus's reins around her hand. With a click of her tongue, she started the enormous horse forward. There were so many people in the corridor that it took longer than it should have to reach the elevator, and Adele and Rufus missed the first empty car. When the doors of the second car opened, they were face and nose to its occupants, Dr. Keren Bailey and a St. Louis Mounted Police officer.

Keren absorbed the scene before him: Adele dressed as Dorothy, a horse dressed as a horse, Cady dressed as the

Scarecrow, Zweli dressed as the Cowardly Lion, Renyatta laughing so hard that she made only pips and wheezing sounds, and beside him a St. Louis Mountie in jodhpurs, riding boots and a smart white helmet. Keren stared at Cady. This was their first face-to-face since their ill-timed encounter in her hotel suite. He had tried to catch her alone, to explain himself, but she was never alone. He hadn't dared to visit her at her suite, not with its two-way view of Raines-Hartley.

He'd known that he'd see her again.

But he'd never counted on it being at the scene of her arrest.

The officer stepped out of the elevator and said, "There you are," as he approached Cady.

Thinking fast, Keren rushed to circumvent the policeman. "Officer, I can explain," he began. "And I take full responsibility for the, uh, abduction of your horse. I'll accompany you to the station house right now to accept whatever charges you have to press. I assure you, Officer, your animal wasn't harmed in any way."

Cady's eyes widened as she listened to Keren. She would never let him take the heat for her actions, but the fact that he was trying to protect her made her heart flutter.

"Doctor," the officer said, "it's fine. I was supposed to pick him up here. I thought it would be outside, however." He approached Adele, removed his helmet and bowed. "Officer Adam Walker at your service, ma'am. I was told that you like to ride."

"I did," Adele said. She stroked Rufus's velvety coat. "I do."

Officer Walker offered his right elbow. "Then let's go."

"You're not arresting me, are you?"

Officer Walker looked at Cady, his eyebrows raised. "You didn't tell her?"

"You were able to clear it?" Cady said.

"Yes. It's fine," he said.

"What's going on here?" Keren demanded.

"Officer Walker is taking Ms. Harrison riding in the park tonight," Cady explained.

As one, the onlookers oohed and aahed. Zweli chuckled in relief. "Nobody's going to jail tonight!"

"I'll need my coat," Adele said. Her dark curls bounced as she giggled like a schoolgirl. "I came here in July. I don't believe I have a fall coat here."

"You can borrow mine," Cady said. She hurried through the crowd to get it. Keren hastily thanked the officer for his understanding and rushed after Cady. Her leather jacket must have been close by, because she was giving it to Adele before Keren could get past Rufus. "Have fun, Dorothy," Cady said as she helped Adele into the jacket. "Don't jump over any rainbows."

The crowd applauded as Adele, Rufus and Officer Walker stepped into the elevator. Thank you, Adele mouthed to Cady. She blew her a tearful kiss as the doors closed. The excitement over, the crowd quickly dispersed. Zweli lifted Cady's hand and placed a tender kiss on the back of it. "You're something else, Miss Winters." He glanced past her. "And God be with you."

Cady turned, following Zweli's line of sight. Keren was the only other person standing in the corridor. And he didn't look happy.

Cady sat without being asked. Keren paced on his side of the desk, fighting to contain his irritation. "Do you have anything to say for yourself?" he asked.

Cady slumped in the chair. "Adele was starting to give up. It's like she's scared to be getting better because she's terrified of getting sick again. She likes riding. There are always mounted policemen in the West End at night, and the park is right across the street. It all just came together on the spur of the moment."

"You mean you decided that you'd go out and steal yourself a horse," he said angrily. "I was in the basement, in pathology, and I heard there was a horse on fifteen before the elevator even made it up here. The second I heard 'a horse on fifteen' I knew you were behind it."

Cady tugged off her hat and hood and shook out her curls. "I didn't steal him. I saw Officer Walker and explained the situation, and—"

Keren slammed his palms on his desktop, startling Cady with the force of his emotion. "Was he drunk? What could you have possibly said to him, to get him to turn that animal over to you?"

"Why?"

"Call me curious," issued from between his gritted teeth. "He probably broke a dozen or more laws by letting you take that horse."

"Rufus. The horse's name is Rufus, and he's an officer, too."

Keren tugged at the knees of his pants and sat down in his leather chair. He clasped his hands on top of his desk blotter. "What did you tell him?"

"I told him that it was his job to save lives, and that I needed him to save Adele from herself. He was on a break. It's not encouraged, but he's allowed to take civilians for rides, if a situation calls for it. He's not on duty for another hour.

"I think he liked Adele, once he saw her. They're about the same age, and he's single."

Keren spent a silent moment looking at her. Cady held his eyes. They revealed nothing, which unnerved her more than his silence. "I want you to see one of our grief counselors," he finally said.

Totally unprepared for his request, Cady gasped. "You want me to see a counselor? Why?"

"What you did for Adele was kind but it was completely ill-advised. This is a hospital, Cady. Bringing a horse to the cancer ward was a completely irrational act. And it was the last straw. Either meet with the grief counselor, or you will not be permitted to visit anymore."

"You're actually going to ban me from this floor?"

If she kept staring at him with her heart in her eyes, he would leap across the desk and gather her into his arms. He would allow her to bring the Anheuser-Busch Clydesdales up to the ward if she asked. He looked away from her, before he backed down from his demand.

"I'm going to ban you from this hospital, Cady. You crossed the line tonight."

Her grip on her felt hat became murderously tight. "You would keep me from Claire all because of a horse?"

"It's not just the horse and it's not just Claire. It's everything. You have tried so hard and spent so much time, money and energy trying to make everyone happy. Why?"

"Because they need it!" she shouted.

"This is your way of avoiding the truth about Claire. She isn't getting better. Your good deeds won't buy her more time. See the counselor. She'll help you work through your feelings in more constructive ways."

"Hypocrite."

The word slithered from her lips like the foulest curse. He swallowed hard. "Excuse me?"

"You're a damn hypocrite, Keren Bailey." Her voice wavered under the weight of her fury. "You need that counselor more than I do. How dare you talk to me about constructive ways to manage my feelings. I feel too much, and that makes me bad? You don't feel enough!"

"You don't have the slightest idea about what I feel," he said coolly.

"How would you behave, Keren, knowing that someone you love more than you love your own self is dying?" she challenged. "Would you do everything you could to make her and the people around her happy, or would you just shut down and refuse to feel anything? What would *you* do, Keren?"

Her pointed questions nicked parts of himself that he meant to keep hidden from plain sight. He recalled something she'd once said, about being a good researcher. He saw her knowing in her wounded eyes. "See the counselor, Cady. You're banned from the hospital from this moment until you do."

Keren caught up with Renyatta in the cafeteria. She was in the cashier's line when he stepped up to her and paid for her chicken pot pie and scrambled eggs.

"What's the matter with you today?" Renyatta asked suspiciously. "I know something's going on when you treat me to lunch. If you're feeling guilty about what you did to Cady last night, maybe you should be buying lunch for her instead of me."

"I'd like to speak with you, Nurse Runyon," Keren said. He escorted her to a table for two behind a column in the farthest corner of the cafeteria.

Renyatta set her tray on the table and waited for Keren to begin.

"Your performance up until a month or so ago was exemplary, Nurse Runyon, but ever since—"

"You never told me that before," Renyatta said.

"Told you what?"

"That you appreciated my work. We've worked together for four years and you never told me how good I am."

"Well…now you know. But your work has suffered since Claire's granddaughter—"

"Clara?"

"No."

"Ciel?"

"No." He frowned. "Listen—"

"Chiara?" Renyatta asked.

"You know who I mean," Keren grumbled.

Renyatta touched the scarlet nail of her left index finger to her lip and crinkled her brow in thought. "Kyla?"

"Cady, damn it!" Keren erupted. Other diners turned at his outburst. "I mean Cady and you know it," he said quietly.

"Oh," Renyatta said innocently. "What about her?"

Keren's exasperation threatened to burst through his professional demeanor. "You have allowed that woman to turn you into her willing accomplice in every single one of her silly escapades. We run a cancer ward for the terminally ill. It was never a picnic and it's not meant to be a traveling circus. By the time these patients reach us, they need constant care and attention, not balloons, mai tais and a petting zoo. These patients—"

"Are dying," Renyatta said somberly. "Dr. Bailey, you were still in high school when I began working with terminal patients, so maybe you should listen to me for a minute. I have watched people die from this disease for 20 years. I have never seen terminal patients respond to medicine, surgery or psychiatric counseling the way they respond to Cady Winters.

"She treats those people with respect and dignity, not pity and sorrow. That girl has enough life and love in her for ten people, and she shares it. Cady is medicine to my patients. She's using herself up, not just for Claire but for all of us. She tends to the dying. I respect you, Keren, as a doctor. You have a remarkable talent for diagnosis and prescription of treatment. Not too many people leave our ward to go on and live happy lives, but I've seen it done more often since you took over. But as a man, Doctor, you have a lot to learn."

"I didn't come here to talk about Cady or me," he said. "Your job is at stake."

"Fine," Renyatta said. "But before you say one more word, consider this: I'm not going back to the way things were around here. I'm not going back to the way I was. Cady has the right idea. These patients are people, first and last. I won't treat them like they're just a collection of symptoms waiting to fade away. And if you ban Cady from this hospital, I'll betcha half the staff will walk out with her."

"Including you?"

Renyatta took a tiny bottle of Crystal hot sauce from her giant handbag. She unscrewed the white cap and began shaking the spicy sauce onto her scrambled eggs. "I'll beat her out the door." She took a hearty bite of the fiery eggs. "Now what was it you wanted to tell me about my job performance?"

Keren, fresh from his talk with Renyatta, was on his way back to his office when he spotted Cady in Claire's room. Good sense told him to keep on walking, but the taskmaster in him made him backtrack into the room.

"Good to see you today, Dr. Bailey," Claire greeted. Her words were a bit slurred. Her left eye had begun to droop and wouldn't shut completely. The tumor was beginning to assert its pride of ownership.

"It's good to see you, too, Mrs. Winters," he said, taking her chart from the foot of her bed. "How are you feeling today?"

"Good as I can, I guess," Claire said. "Did you get tricks or treats last night?"

"Neither." He glanced at Cady. She sat in an armchair beside Claire's bed. She'd been reading the Psalms to Claire, and she used her fingers to hold her place in the book. She didn't look at Keren. "I'll be back tonight, Mrs. Winters. You rest today."

Keren left and was halfway down the corridor when Cady ran into the corridor and called after him. "I spoke with Carmen Ortega this morning," she said. "I'm not here illegally."

He walked back to her. "I'm glad. I wasn't trying to hurt you, Cady."

"It was okay." She pulled the cuffs of her fuzzy blue sweater down over her hands. The movement stretched the boat neck of the garment, giving him a glimpse of her collarbone. "It helped to talk about it with someone who isn't family. I didn't realize I'd been holding so much inside."

He moved closer to her, bowing his head to speak into her ear. "You can talk to me."

She raised her face, inhaling the warm, sensuous scent of him. Reluctantly, she stepped away from him before his scent drove away what she wanted to say to him. "No, Keren. I can't talk to you."

"You can," he said. He would have taken her in his arms if there hadn't been so much traffic. Visitors and patients were traveling the corridor. Dr. Randall and Renyatta were at the nurses' station, discussing a patient.

"You don't talk back," she said, taking a step back toward Claire's sunlit room. "You don't…give back."

Her tiny steps returned her to Claire's door, but all she wanted to do was run into Keren's embrace and tell him every fear and every ache that currently weighed on her heart. As angry as she had been at him the night before, she now saw that he had cared enough to force her into the meeting with a grief counselor. The meeting had helped settle her and had forced her to acknowledge that there were things that she just couldn't fix.

The counselor had been referring to Claire's health, but the lesson also applied to her situation with Keren. Her two-hour session had been about learning how to let go. Easier said than done.

"I miss her already." Cady gazed upon Claire's sleeping form, her eyes sparkling with tears.

"Cady…" Keren started. Not knowing what else to say, his voice trailed off.

"I forgot to thank you for trying to cover for me with Officer Walker," Cady said. "Why did you do that?"

"I didn't want to see you thrown in jail."

"Is that the only reason?"

Her hopeful expression almost disarmed him. "What other reason could there be?"

Her shoulders sank. "None. None at all." She wanted to kick herself for even hoping that his caring went any deeper.

"Dr. Bailey, I need to speak to you about a man with a heart problem," Dr. Randall said from the nurses' station.

"My office," Keren said. "I'll be right there." He turned back to Cady. "You made Adele very happy yesterday. She's a different person today."

"Aren't we all."

"I have to meet with Dr. Randall now, but I have some time this afternoon if you want to talk," Keren offered.

"No," Cady said adamantly. "But thank you. Talking to the counselor helped me see that I've lost sight of why I came to St. Louis. I came for Claire. I can't waste any more time on distractions."

"Okay," he said dully. "Good luck to you, Cady."

She watched him turn and walk down the corridor. Disappointment and sadness churned through her. His easy acceptance of her decision proved what she had suspected—that what had happened between them in her suite hadn't meant a thing to him.

"Which patient are you here to talk about?" Keren asked Zweli, who lounged on the sofa.

"You."

"I don't have time for games, Zweli." Keren said. He went to the appointment book on the corner of his desk and checked his afternoon schedule.

Zweli, his fingers laced behind his head, settled more comfortably on the sofa. "No one has secrets in a hospital, K. Patients talk, nurses talk, even doctors talk. Right now, they're all talking about you."

Keren flashed a dark look at Zweli. "Me? Why?"

"Man, are you really this out of touch? We're all talking about you and Cady Winters."

"There is no me and Cady Winters."

"Take my advice, Keren. Consider that it comes from a man who would give his right eye to be where you are. Cady is the kind of woman that comes around once in a lifetime, and then only if you're lucky. She's intelligent, vibrant, gorgeous—"

"I don't need to be schooled," Keren said. He was well aware of her gifts. He dreamt of them. "I know what she is."

"Then you should also know that if you leave even the slightest opening, every available man in this hospital will do his damnedest to win her."

Keren sat on the edge of his desk and crossed his arms over his chest. "Does that include you?"

Zweli sat up and uncrossed his legs. Resting his elbows on his thighs, he leaned forward. "All's fair in love and war and medicine."

"She doesn't belong to me," Keren said. "She'll be going back to Boston. We don't have anything even close to a relationship. We had dinner together one time."

Zweli rolled his eyes. "For a smart man, you are mad stupid, K. That dinner was a setup. Why do you think Claire insisted that you go over there personally to cancel for her?"

"It was just dinner."

Zweli didn't fail to notice the way Keren's eyes dropped guiltily. "Yeah, because you ran out on her."

Keren was annoyed by the accuracy of Zweli's gossip.

"She's going to need someone to be there for her soon," Zweli said. "You know that."

"She's got plenty of family to fall back on."

"She'll need someone other than family," Zweli explained. "Claire is the keystone of that family. Cady's mom and sisters will have their own grief to deal with. They won't be able to handle Cady's too. And you've seen how Cady is. She's a slave to her emotions. She feels everything fully. Grief can be lethal to someone like her."

"I've already put her in touch with a grief counselor," Keren said.

Zweli launched himself to his feet. "I'm not talking about therapy, you stubborn fool! I'm talking about friendship and affection and—do I actually have to spell it out for you?"

"Please do."

"Love, Keren. I'm talking about love. Did you see the way she looked at you last night when you tried to fox that cop to save her ass? Did you listen to what she said to you just now, out in the hall?"

"Of course I listened," Keren said impatiently.

"You heard her with your ears but did you listen with your heart?" Zweli pounded his palm against Keren's chest. "She loves you. But you're too much of a goat to see it."

"You're overromanticizing my situation with Cady," Keren said softly.

"And you're underromanticizing it. I don't exactly know what the two of you were talking about just now, but she needed you. She needs someone. I'm a doctor, K. I'm silly and flirtatious and goofy, but I'm good at easing the pain of others. I'm going to find Cady and offer her the support you seem incapable of giving her." Zweli went to the door. Before he exited the office, he turned and caught Keren's eye one last time. "It was Cady's idea to dress up to hand out candy to the kids in pediatrics last night, and she made the costumes. I wasn't crazy about wearing that lion suit, but Cady has a way of convincing people to do things they otherwise wouldn't. She got me to be the Cowardly Lion. Me, the man who was set on being Luke Cage."

"Who's Luke Cage?"

"You're ignorant, K. Luke Cage, Hero for Hire? Marvel Comics. Black superhero, alias Power Man. He had superhuman strength and skin of steel. You never heard of him?"

"I was never into comic books," Keren said.

"Apparently you have a lot to learn about a lot of things. You know, I begged Cady to let me be the Tin Man. She said that the fifteenth floor already had one. Now I know what...or rather, who...she meant."

CHAPTER SIX

Dr. Randall's words stayed with Keren, and he began to try harder to be what Cady needed. But so did every other man between the ages of 20 and 50 at Raines-Hartley. Now that Cady was spending her time exclusively with Claire, all sorts of people began finding their way into Claire's room. Keren had to restrict non-family visitors to two per day. Flowers came almost every day, men competed to pay for her tea in the cafeteria, and she had countless offers to go out to restaurants, movies, sporting events, long drives—anything "just to get away from all that sickness."

Cady resented all of it. She distributed the flowers to the patients and staff. "Claire's room was starting to look like a funeral parlor," she told Renyatta as she handed the nurses a vase of three-dozen long-stemmed yellow roses. When her admirers paid for her tea, she made sure to purchase another cup, and gave the gift cup to Adele. She politely declined every date invitation.

On Thanksgiving, Cady caved and accepted Zweli's invitation to go on a walk around the hospital. She had no idea that he would walk her right up to the stars. He took her to the 16th floor, then up the access stairs that led to the roof of the hospital. Cady breathed deep of the air, enjoying the chill.

"Me and my bright ideas," Zweli said with a shiver. "Aren't you freezing?" He flipped up the collar of his white coat and pulled the coat closer about him. "I'll be a gentleman and give you my coat, if you want it."

"I like it when it's like this," Cady said. "It's just cold enough to put roses in your cheeks and the air smells ripe for snow. I got used to winters in New England. This is nothing compared to how cold it can get in Boston."

She led them to the northern side of the building. She rested her elbows on the cold stone edging and leaned on them. "It's nice up here. Quiet. Peaceful."

"You've been cooped up in your grandmother's room for a week straight," Zweli said. "Renyatta says that now you only leave to get clean clothes from your hotel." He nodded toward the Plaza, which filled their view. "You can't be getting much sleep on that rollaway in Claire's room, and I know you aren't eating the hospital food. My sources tell me that the cafeteria boys are giving you free meals but that you leave the trays virtually untouched."

"So Renyatta appointed you to check up on me," Cady said. She looked at the wide window of her suite and caught glimpses of two of her sisters, who were setting the glass-topped dining table they had moved into the living room.

"Renyatta's worried about you. So am I. When was the last time you slept through the night, Cady? I'll bet you haven't had a good meal since that feast you cooked for Ker—for the cancer ward. I know that's the last good meal I had. Those hens and that cornbread were off the hook."

"Claire taught us to cook," Cady said. Still looking across at her hotel, she added, "My sisters are almost ready to serve Thanksgiving dinner in my rooms."

"Then why are you here, on the roof, in the cold with me when you could be over there, in a nice toasty hotel suite with your fine sisters and all that good food?"

"Claire might wake up again. I don't want her to be alone."

Zweli set a hand on her shoulder. "How was she the last time she woke up?"

Cady watched her sisters bring food out to the table. Abby was somewhere in the suite, but she wouldn't appear until Clara was ready to cut the bird. "Her mind…" Cady couldn't go on. She couldn't tell Zweli that Claire didn't recognize her, that she had no idea where she was or what was happening to her. Claire's moments of lucidity were becoming farther and farther between.

"Which one is that?" Zweli asked softly, turning Cady's attention back to her sisters.

"Clara," Cady said. "She came in last night from California."

"She's cute."

"You can't really see her from this angle," Cady grinned.

"Oh, I can see enough," Zweli leered.

"Can you see her wedding ring?"

"Children?"

"Three."

Zweli snapped his fingers in mock regret. Two more sisters caught his eye. "Who are they?"

"Ciel and Kyla. You've met Ciel."

"She's the one with the long, glossy black hair that gleams blue in the sunlight," Zweli said.

"Ciel's got our great-grandmother's hair. Claire's mother was part Osage Indian. We all got her cheekbones and none of her height. She was six feet tall." Cady gave Zweli a sideways glance. "You've been thinking about Ciel?"

"It's hard not to. You Winters women leave an impression. Is Ciel dating anyone?"

"No."

Zweli happily rubbed his hands together.

"She doesn't date," Cady said.

"Why not?"

Cady yawned and rubbed her eyes. "She doesn't like leaving her children with a babysitter."

"How many kids does she have?"

"Three," Cady said. "All under the age of seven."

"That's a handful. I like kids, though. I could take them all out."

"I suppose you could, but I don't think her husband would like it."

"Damn, Cady. Are there any available Winters girls?"

"Kyla." Cady pointed to the woman placing a serving spoon in a big bowl of candied yams. "She's the one laughing by the candied yams. The one with the big teeth and enough hair for two women."

"That smile is dynamite," Zweli said. "How old is she?"

"If I'm 31, that makes her 27 this year. She's an actress. She was a Budweiser swimsuit girl before she moved to Los Angeles. She played Alien Victim #3 in some space flick last year. Her head was bitten off but her body stayed alive and was controlled by the aliens. She majored in theater arts in college, but she minored in languages. She's fluent in Spanish, French and Russian. And flirting."

"I like that," Zweli said lecherously. "Who else is available?"

"Chiara, but she's not down there. She works for a computer company and she's stuck overseas on a two-year contract. She's the baby. Well, she's 25, so she's not really a baby, but she's not here so I guess Kyla's the only one on the market."

"And you, Cady. Or aren't you available?"

"What I am is tired," she said.

"Okay. If you don't want to talk about Keren, you don't have to."

"There's nothing there to talk about."

"He misses you."

"Is that why he hasn't said more than ten words to me in three weeks?"

"He's not much on talk," Zweli said.

A dry chuckle escaped Cady.

"Judge him by his actions," Zweli said. "You're one for words. They're your stock and trade. It's harder for Keren."

Cady faced Zweli, her hands on the hips of her wool slacks. "How hard is it to look at someone and say, "I think I've fallen in love with you. I never meant to embarrass or hurt you. Can we start over, because I feel lost and empty without you?' "

He reached out to touch her hair, but forced his hand to her shoulder instead. "If those things are so easy to say, why haven't you said them to Keren?"

"It's too late."

"Are you sure?" Zweli asked gently.

"Yes," Cady answered, though it sounded like no.

"There are plenty of people here for Claire. You should go over there and have dinner with your sisters. I'd much rather be over there with them than here at Raines."

"Then go over. They won't mind."

"Are you serious?"

"Kyla in particular would love to have you."

Zweli's eyes narrowed at the dual meaning of Cady's statement. "Do you mean what I think you mean?"

Cady's cell phone rang, saving her from having to elaborate. "Hello?…What?" She turned toward her suite and saw her sisters crowded at the window. Clara had her arms around Kyla. Ciel, one hand tensed in her hair, spoke animatedly into a cell phone gripped in her other hand. There was no mistaking the panic on their faces. "I'm going now!" Cady ran for the door with Zweli close on her heels. "Something's happening in Grandma's room!"

"Charge!" Keren barked as Cady and Zweli raced into the room. Zweli held Cady back, stopping her from interfering with the code team working on Claire. Keren led the team.

Renyatta squirted gel on the defibrillator paddles Keren wielded. He quickly rubbed them together as he said, "Clear!" He placed the paddles on Claire's exposed chest, on top and on the side of her heart, and shocked her. Her tiny body went rigid, then flopped against the mattress.

"Help her!" Cady begged Zweli.

He held Cady tight. "Keren's got it under control," he said. "What do you got?" he called to the code team.

"Seventy-nine-year-old woman with grade-4 brain stem tumor arrested," one of the code nurses said. "Floor nurses responded to the alarm and performed CPR until the code team arrived approximately two minutes later. She's been shocked twice with no response."

"Charge!...Clear!" Keren directed.

Cady jumped as though the electric charge had gone through her.

"I've got a pulse," a nurse said.

"We've got a rhythm," said another voice. "And blood pressure's rising."

"She's back," Renyatta said.

"Good work, K.," Zweli said. He released Cady and stepped forward to examine Claire.

When Keren moved out of the way so the nurses could clean and dress Claire and pack up the crash cart, he noticed Cady standing in the doorway. She had the doorframe in a white-knuckled grip.

"That line on her heart monitor," Cady started in a thin, reedy voice, "that flatline...that meant..."

"We got her back," Keren said.

Cady never heard him. In that moment, her knees buckled and she hit the floor.

Cady woke up on her back with two concerned faces staring down at her. "Don't get up, Cady," Renyatta said.

Cady felt Renyatta's fingers on her wrist, taking her pulse. Ciel, her fine black eyebrows angled in worry, stroked Cady's hair.

"Girl, you hit the floor like a bag of cement," Ciel said. "You smacked your head pretty hard."

"Where am I?" The words were thick and fuzzy in Cady's mouth. She felt heavy and weak, like she'd been asleep for a month.

"I can't believe you just said that." Kyla's voice came from nearby, but Cady couldn't see her.

"Hush, Ky," Clara said. Her face appeared beside Ciel's. "You're in Dr. Bailey's office. On his sofa. You passed out in Grandma's room."

"No, I didn't." Cady awkwardly sat up. Her right temple and cheekbone throbbed painfully.

"We saw you from the window," Kyla said. "One minute you're standing there, the next…SMACK! Ass in the air."

Keren and Zweli entered the office. Cady's sisters and Renyatta scattered to give them access to Cady. Keren sat beside her and placed her hand around a paper cup of water. "Drink this."

Cady took a cautious sip.

"All of it," Keren said.

Cady gulped the water down.

"Follow my finger." He moved his index finger from left to right before her face. "Use your eyes, not your whole head."

Kyla giggled, and Clara pinched her arm.

"That hurt!" Kyla whined.

"No, it didn't," Clara said. "Shut up."

"Knock it off you two," Ciel warned.

Cady followed Keren's finger with her eyes. When his finger stopped, she kept her eyes on his. "Is she okay?"

"She's still alive, Cady," Keren said. "She's got a strong heart. The tumor is interfering with the signals her heart needs to get from her brain." He placed his hands on her neck, just under her jaw. The unexpected contact made her shiver. He tilted her head from side to side and front to back. "I'm making sure that nothing was sprained or broken when you fainted."

"It'll take more than a bump on the head to break that skull," Kyla said.

"I didn't faint," Cady said. "I've never fainted in my life."

"Well, you did faint once," Clara said. "Remember that time when you were ten and I chased you around the block with that dead locust?"

"I don't remember that." Cady savored the feel of Keren's hand as it trailed over her shoulder.

"Do you remember the time you fainted at school, right in the middle of that play about those cats?" Clara said.

"You mean *Cats*?" Cady grimaced. "No. Can I go now?"

"Not so fast," Keren said. "Are you feeling nauseous or light-headed?"

"Light-headed, no. Nauseous yes, but it has nothing to do with *slipping* and hitting my head." She glared at her tattletale sisters.

"I think you'll be fine," Keren said. He stood and offered a hand to Cady. She took it and began to stand, but her wobbly legs wouldn't support her weight. "Okay," she said. "Now I feel light-headed."

Keren pinched the back of her hand. Cady yipped in pain. "What the hell is wrong with you?" Cady snapped, rubbing the painful spot on her hand.

"I told you it hurts when you get pinched," Kyla said to Clara.

"Your skin tented," Keren told Cady. "You're mildly dehydrated. I believe that's one of the reasons why you fainted. You haven't been taking care of yourself. You're not leaving this office until you drink sixteen ounces of water and eat a full meal."

"I'm not your patient, Dr. Bailey," Cady said, wishing she had more will and more energy to fight him.

"You will be, if you force me to admit you."

Cady pursed her lips. Keren wanted to kiss them. "First you tried to ban me from this place. Now you're trying to ban me from leaving?"

"He didn't exactly say you couldn't leave," Kyla said.

Zweli pinched her. Kyla rubbed the painful spot as though the pinch were a gift.

"I'll bring you a plate from the hotel," Clara said.

"Bring me one, too," Kyla said. "Now that the scare is over, I'm hungry."

"Me, too," Zweli said.

"It would be easier to just take Cady to the food," Ciel said. "That way, we could all eat. Thanks to Dr. Bailey, we have something very important to give thanks for."

"I'm not leaving Grandma again," Cady said.

"Mama will stay with Grandma," Clara said. "You need a break, Cady."

Cady stared at the door. She didn't feel like arguing, but she wasn't going anywhere.

Her sisters recognized that look of stubborn determination. Kyla grabbed Zweli's arm. "Would you help us bring some plates over here for Cady and Mama?"

"My pleasure," Zweli smiled.

"Let's just bring everything over," Clara said. "We made enough to feed the whole hospital. Dr. Bailey, would you mind if we took over your common room?"

"Not at all," he said, his eyes locked on Cady, who refused to look at him.

"I want to see Claire," Cady said.

"You can see her later," Keren said, "when I'm satisfied that you aren't going to collapse again."

"I told you, I didn't collapse or faint or pass out. I slipped," she insisted. "Someone…someone pushed me."

"Cady, you passed out," Zweli said. "Keren and I gave you a cursory examination right there on the spot. Your pupils were reactive but you were out cold. You were like a limp noodle when Keren carried you in here."

A blush raged in Cady's cheeks. "Whatever. I'm fine now. And I'm going to see Claire." She started to rise but Keren planted a hand on her shoulder and shoved her back down.

Cady looked at him as though he had grown a third arm. "Do you know that I *will* hurt you?" she said.

"No, but I'll tell you what I do know," Keren said. "I know that you are going to remain right there on that sofa until your sisters bring a hot meal back here for you."

"Oh, yeah?" Cady's head throbbed, this time with anger. "Who's gonna make me?"

"I am." He dropped to one knee before her. "I've watched you put yourself at risk for too long now. I won't let you hurt yourself anymore. I care about you too much."

"Finally!" Zweli said as he put his hand over his heart. "It's about time, man!"

Zweli and Cady's sisters left to transfer Thanksgiving dinner from the hotel to the hospital. Cady sat on the sofa, still stunned by Keren's offhand admission.

She wanted to read more into it. It was nice that he cared about her, but she already knew that. He was a doctor. He cared about most people.

Keren went to the mini-fridge tucked on his bookshelf and took out a bottle of spring water to refill Cady's cup. There was so much he wanted to say to her. He wanted to tell her how pretty she had looked in the plaid skirt she had worn one day, and how lovely she was when she sat in the window to write or read. He also wanted to tell her how concerned he was by her drastic weight loss, and how scared he had been the day he heard her sobbing in Claire's bathroom.

He wanted to tell her how much he missed her, and how he dreamed of her even when he was wide awake.

"I want you to drink the whole bottle," was all he could say to her.

"I want you to tell me why you've been avoiding me," she blurted.

"You wanted no distractions."

"Well, I've been distracted," she said testily. "There are times when I look at Claire and I feel sick because I want to stop what's happening to her and can't. I want to undo what this awful illness has done to her. Sometimes, all I want to do is hide my head and cry. Those are the times that I think about that night you had dinner with me. I think about what it felt like to be in your arms and what it could be like now, if you hadn't run away."

He surprised her when he sat beside her and said, "I think about it, too. I think about what might have happened, if I'd been willing to take a chance. But I suppose it's too late now."

"Why do you say that?"

"You'll be heading back to Boston one of these days."

"Yes," Cady said softly. "I guess so."

"I guess it wasn't meant to be," he said.

"I never thought of you as a distraction," she confessed.

"I never wanted just a fling."

"So what happens now?"

"I guess…we can just be friends now."

"I'd like that," she said. She meant it, but her heart broke as she mourned the loss of something she'd never had.

"This is the most civil conversation we've ever had," she chuckled sadly.

"I'm trying to talk back," he said. "It isn't easy for me."

"I know." She blinked back unshed tears. "I appreciate it. I really want to hug you now, but it wouldn't be the kind of hug one friend gives another friend."

"I don't think I'd take it the way a friend would."

"Then I guess that's that. Friend," Cady said.

"That's that."

A cold ache settled into Keren's belly. He had done the right thing. He knew it. She was leaving. That fact alone was enough to prevent anything serious from developing between them. But how could doing the right thing feel so utterly wrong?

"What happened while I was out with the sisters?" Zweli asked Keren first thing the next morning as the two worked out in the hospital gym.

"We agreed to just be friends," Keren said. He exhaled sharply as he began his set of twelve bench presses, starting with 150 pounds.

"What the...?" Zweli uttered. "Why? What went wrong?"

Keren finished the set and replaced the bar before answering. "Bad timing. She's going back to Boston. I didn't want a casual hook-up." He used a small white towel to wipe his sweaty face.

"You're in love with the woman, and you show her by telling her that you just want to be friends?"

"Her grandmother is dying," Keren said. "A friend is what she needs right now. You're the one who told me that, remember?"

"Yes, but the stakes have changed. You love her. She loves you."

"She's leaving, Zweli."

Keren started for the next weight station. Zweli stayed close on his heels. "But what if she weren't? What if she were staying here?"

"It's not even worth thinking about," Keren said. He adjusted the straps of his weightlifting gloves, tightening them before he began his biceps routine.

"But what if she stayed in St. Louis?"

Keren contemplated the implications of Zweli's "what ifs" as he worked his right bicep with the 40-lb. barbell. If Cady stayed in St. Louis, he would do his best to become the kind of man she wanted. Someone she could talk to and someone who would give as much as he would get from a magnificent lady like Zacadia Winters. He had thought that keeping away from her would make his feelings for her diminish. Not so. His feelings had only grown stronger, so strong in fact, that he had almost flown into a full panic when she fainted in Claire's room. Now he knew why doctors should never treat their loved ones. It was hard to think like a doctor about proper treatments and procedures when the man in you was worried senseless.

If Cady stayed in St. Louis, he wondered if he could stay mad at her. And he was mad at her, for making him love her. He'd never had a chance not to. From the moment she first set foot in his office, she had turned his world upside down and inside out, and given it a good shake. No one around him was the same. Clifford Williams had died a happy man, and had been buried in a shirt Cady had given him. Adele Harrison was being released in time to spend Christmas at home with her family. He had caught Renyatta talking to a patient's liver, telling the tumor to get out. And then there was Claire…that she had lasted as long as she had was nothing less than the miracle of Cady's undying love.

If Cady's love could keep Claire alive, Keren could only wonder what it could do for him. Zweli had said that Cady loved him, but Zweli was a sickening romantic. Zweli fell in love with women based solely on how they looked walking across a room and as often as most people passed through doorways.

Keren dropped the barbell and stretched his burning bicep. Cady didn't love him. He was sure of it. How could she, when all of her love was spent holding on to Claire?

"If you're going to stay here every night, you should let Mama stay in your suite," Ciel said. "That way, she'll be close when Grandma passes."

Cady sat in one of the big, vinyl-covered armchairs in the common room. It was Saturday, so the room was more crowded than usual as patients visited with relatives. Their conversations were a soft hum in the background as Cady had lunch with her sister, who sat facing her on the opposite side of a low, wide, circular table. She unpacked an insulated picnic basket set at her feet. Ciel was only two years older than Cady, but she had always seemed so much wiser, so much more mature, than the rest of her sisters.

"You say that so easily," Cady said.

Ciel tucked a lock of her dark hair behind her right ear as she set covered plastic containers on the table. "It's not going to be a surprise, Cady. Grandma knew, even before they took the scans. She started planning her service back when the cancer in her breast was first discovered."

Cady harrumphed. "Grandma's been talking about it since forever. Remember those shoes she bought for Clara's college graduation? She said they made her legs look so nice, she wanted to be buried in them."

"She was kidding back then," Ciel said. She popped the lid on a bowl of cranberry-orange relish. "Actually, she probably wasn't."

Cady let her sister lay out a sampling of Thanksgiving leftovers: the relish, turkey slices, green beans with new potatoes, scalloped potatoes, rolls and Cady's favorite, cornbread dressing.

"How are you feeling today?" Ciel asked. Her work done, she crossed one elegant knee over the other. If Cady was the impish roughneck of the family, Ciel was its regal matriarch-in-waiting. Cady admired her sister's constant calm and classy style.

"I still feel a little funny," Cady admitted. "Like my head is connected to my body with a piece of balloon string."

"Renyatta said that she thought you'd fractured your skull when you…slipped." Ciel's wide, expressive eyes twinkled.

"I fainted," Cady sighed. "You can say it."

"It's nothing to be ashamed of, Cady. You've been running yourself into the ground since you came home. You've really been here for Grandma."

Cady propped her feet against the edge of the table and ran her hands over her denim-clad legs. "That's me," she said. "I come in at the eleventh hour and burn hot and fast. Ciel, you're the one who's done the hard part. You're the only one of us who still lives in town. Ever since Grandma first got sick, you were the one who took her to all of her doctor's appointments and treatments. You took her shopping and to church when she couldn't drive anymore. You took care of her until she had to come here.

"The rest of us stayed where we were, content to let you and Abby face the day-to-day trials of Claire's illness."

"You're here now, Cady. You got here at the perfect time." Ciel put food on a plate and served her sister. "I've always envied your relationship with Grandma. I think that you really are her favorite."

"She treated us all the same," Cady said.

"Yes, but you were the one who did all the things she wanted to do. She lived vicariously through you. She was so excited that time you went to the White House and interviewed the president."

Cady lowered her feet to the floor and took up her plate. "We fought like rabid squirrels until I moved away from home. No one could bug the hell out of me like Claire."

"It's because you loved her so much." Ciel nibbled a knotted roll. "And you understood each other so well. You never seemed to have to explain things to each other. Like the time you decided to dye your hair pink. Mama almost had a stroke. Grandma didn't say a thing, just acted like nothing was out of the ordinary."

"She didn't have to say anything. She knew I'd regret that dye job. I did, three minutes after it was done. I looked like I had an Afro made of cotton candy. My hair hasn't been the same since."

The sisters sat in silence, each sorting through her memories. Cady broke the silence with, "I left her alone only for a few minutes. She almost got away from me."

"Where did you go?" Ciel asked. "We thought you'd changed your mind and were coming to the Plaza."

"I was on the roof."

Ciel's left eyebrow hiked a bit higher. "Alone?"

"With Zweli."

"Really," Ciel said thoughtfully.

"I wanted some air. Zweli was window-shopping for a girlfriend."

"What do you mean?"

"We could see into my suite. Zweli liked everything he saw."

"I think he's happy with Kyla," Ciel said.

"That's like liking like," Cady said. "They're two of a kind and the biggest flirts I've ever seen. God help them if one actually falls for the other."

"Kyla has her doctor, at least for the time being. How are things between you and yours?"

"Hmmm?" Cady pretended not to hear the question.

"Grandma told me that you and Dr. Bailey had dinner last month." Ciel smiled. "Renyatta told me the rest."

"Keren and I—"

"Keren? You're on a first name basis already? He's been treating Grandma for three years and I still call him 'Doctor.' Not even Dr. Bailey. Just 'Doctor.' "

"We're just friends."

"He didn't look like just a friend Thursday night," Ciel said. "He almost caught you before you fell. He wouldn't let anyone else touch you."

"A relationship just wouldn't work out between us," Cady said. "I've only known him for four months. And I'll be going back to Boston. I don't think either of us wants a long-distance thing."

"Why do you have to go back to Boston?"

"Is that a trick question? My job is there. My apartment is there."

"There are jobs and apartments in St. Louis," Ciel pointed out. "Your family is here, too. So is Keren Bailey."

"I would never move fifteen-hundred miles for a man unless we were crazy in love," Cady said with a sigh.

"Well," Ciel began, "I don't think either of you is crazy…"

"Grandma likes him," Cady said.

"Dr. Bailey?"

Cady nodded.

Ciel perked with interest. "What did she say about him?"

"Nothing. That's how I knew she liked him. She never talked about his breath or his hair or his shoes, and she never accused him of looking at her funny. That's why she didn't like Courtland. She said he looked at her funny."

"Cady, has Grandma responded to you since Thursday?" Ciel asked.

Cady set down her plate, her appetite fleeing. "I think so." To be more truthful, she added, "I hope so. She hasn't opened her eyes since the cardiac code. She'll be back, after a good long rest."

Ciel's expression softened. "Cady…"

"What?" she said too sharply and too quickly.

"Why are you snapping at me?" Ciel asked.

Ciel's constant calm and even-temper had always been her best defense against Cady's explosive responses to anything that hurt her feelings.

"Because I know what you're going to say to me about Claire," Cady said defensively.

"I don't have to tell you anything about Claire that you don't already know," Ciel said in her mellow, lyrical voice. "I was going to tell you to eat before your lunch gets cold." Her eyes shifted to the right. "And before the scavengers pick up the scent."

Cady turned to see Zweli and Renyatta trotting toward them. Cady and Ciel were on their feet in an instant, ready to sprint for Claire's room. "What?" she called to them. "What is it? Another cardiac code?"

Renyatta spoke to Ciel while Zweli caught Cady by her shoulders. His smile put Cady at ease, even though his words sent her racing for Claire's room.

"Your grandmother is awake and asking for you," Zweli said.

CHAPTER SEVEN

"You've been wearing that same expression for the past two weeks," Keren said as he wrote his notes in Claire's chart following his exam.

"What expression?" Cady's wide, happy eyes sparkled like the crystal Christmas ornaments strung over Claire's bed.

Keren almost smiled. "That 'I told you so' face," he explained.

"There's nothing I can do about my face, Doctor," Cady said.

Keren watched her for a moment as she tucked a blanket snug about Claire's frail frame. Two weeks ago, he never would have thought that he would be standing at the foot of Claire's bed, watching her interact with the granddaughter who stood firmly between her and nature. Cady had insisted that all Claire needed was rest, and then she would be ready to battle once more. Claire's little body had taken all a body could, yet somehow, some way, her system had found the strength to fight on. Keren gazed at Cady and knew that he was looking at the source of Claire's strength.

With Claire holding on, Cady had taken a turn for the better. She was eating regularly and sleeping better, although she still insisted on staying in Claire's room on the rollaway bed. Keren had provided her with an air mattress to go on top of it, giving her a little more comfort.

Food and rest had further enhanced Cady's singular beauty. She was so pretty in a black turtleneck, gold hoop earrings and a slim black skirt, Keren couldn't stop staring at her, even after he'd reached the point of embarrassment.

"Are you going to the party next week, Doctor?" Claire asked, stealing Keren's gaze from Cady. The words weakly wheezed from her as she lay on her back. She rarely sat up anymore, and she was fed intravenously. In her moments of lucidity, she was the Claire Winters everyone on fifteen had come to know and love, but those moments were rare.

"How did you know about the hospital party?" he asked her.

"Oh, I have my ways," she said, a feeble laugh escaping her. "Dr. Randall came by and asked my Zacadia if she wanted to go. That's the only reason I asked. Be nice if you were going, too."

"Dr. Bailey and I are just friends, you crafty thing," Cady reprimanded.

"I don't have time to fool around with 'just friends,' " Claire smiled. Her eyes drowsed shut.

"And 'just friends' don't fool around, Grandma."

"I want to see your dress." Claire's words faded as she drifted to sleep. Cady looked at each of Claire's monitors, assuring herself that her grandmother really was just sleeping.

"So you're going to the Christmas party," Keren said softly, so as not to disturb Claire.

"It's in the Corazon Ballroom at the Plaza," Cady said, "right there in my hotel. I'll probably pop in."

"You need an invitation." He took his time replacing Claire's chart. His moments in Claire's room always seemed too short, even when Cady wasn't there. He had come to care for Claire almost as much as Cady did, if for no other reason than because Cady loved her so.

"No, I don't," Cady said. "When I was in high school, I used to dress up and go to the parties of strangers at the Corazon all the time. I went to wedding receptions, bar and bat mitzvahs, fraternity formals. If you act like you belong, no one suspects a thing."

"You've become a fixture around here, but you aren't a Raines-Hartley employee," he said. "Why are you going to an office party for an office you don't officially work at?"

Cady chewed the inner corner of her lower lip. That meant she was contemplating a lie, or that the truth was painful to say. "Claire is making me go," she said. "She thinks I need to get out. Have some fun. 'Leave her in peace,' is the way she put it."

Keren took two steps toward her. Cady turned to face him. She never tired of watching him move. Whether he was hurrying to a patient's room, strolling with a nurse as he explained something to her, or pacing before the vending machines, deciding what to have for dinner, he moved with the powerful grace of a jungle cat, or a dancer. So many times she had cursed the moment she'd agreed to be just his friend. Her thoughts toward him hadn't been the least bit friendly as the weeks passed. They had been downright animalistic.

"She's right," Keren said. "A night out would do you a world of good."

"I'm only going because she told me to. She's being very stubborn about it. Kyla's going with Zweli. You should go, too."

"Why?" His black gaze met and held her cinnamon eyes, almost daring her to tell him the reason she wanted him to attend the party.

She blushed, which was an answer in itself, and began to chew her lip. "Because Zweli says that in all the time you've worked here, you've never been to a Raines-Hartley holiday party."

"He would know," Keren said. "Zweli is always the first one there and the last one to leave. From what I've heard."

"You should come just to see Kyla's dress," Cady said.

"Zweli tells me that it's rather low cut."

Cady snorted. "It's J.Lo cut, not just low cut. It's a disgrace. But in a good way."

"Do you have a dress for the party?"

"Why?"

"Because if you had a dress, then I'd actually believe that you were serious about leaving Claire for one night."

Keren fidgeted.

He sat on a stylized settee of leather and chrome. He looked at his watch twice in the space of five minutes. For Dr. Keren Bailey, that was fidgeting.

"Relax, man," Zweli said. Standing on a small dais before the center panel of a giant, three-way mirror, he turned and twisted, studying the cut of the tuxedo he'd had custom made for the hospital holiday party.

"When you said you had an errand to run before lunch, you didn't say anything about it being a fashion show," Keren said. He glanced at his watch again.

"I am too pretty," Zweli said, smoothing his hands over the satin lapels. He turned to Keren. "Ain't I pretty?"

Keren was looking at his watch.

Zweli stepped off the dais as he motioned for the tailor. "Am I keeping you from an appointment, K.?"

"Yes," was Keren's immediate response. Then he told the truth. "No."

Zweli slipped off the tux jacket and handed it to the white-haired tailor.

"You chose exactly the right cut, Dr. Randall," the tailor said happily in a heavy Italian accent. "This suit…it puts the other one to shame."

"Thank you, Octavio, but the suit is only as good as the man who makes it," Zweli said, unfastening his shirt. "You do excellent work. I'm trying to talk my friend here into letting you suit him up."

Octavio turned his pale eyes on Keren and thoughtfully gripped his chin as he scrutinized Keren, who fought the urge to run straight back to the hospital.

"Basic black," Octavio decided. "Striking. Powerful. Seductive." Octavio tossed up his hands. "Oh! The tuxedo I could make for you! You would stop hearts."

Zweli leaned toward Keren. "If you wore it to the party, I'd be there to jumpstart them all."

"Even the great Octavio can't make a tux in three days," Keren said.

"*Si,*" Octavio agreed, shaking his head regretfully. "It would be less expensive for you to fly the Concorde to Milan and buy off the rack." Octavio took Zweli's tux and left the fitting room.

"This will be my fifth tux," Zweli said. "I have a Calvin Klein, a Richard Tyler, an Armani and two Octavios now." He pulled his slacks on over his maroon silk boxers.

"Do you moonlight as a lounge singer?" Keren asked. "Why do you need so many tuxes?"

So surprised by Keren's rare flash of humor, Zweli misbuttoned his grey shirt. "You get funnier everyday, man," he said. "I don't know what's gotten into you lately, but—" Zweli chuckled lightly to himself.

"Yes?" Keren prompted when Zweli didn't finish his thought.

"I know what's gotten into you," Zweli grinned. "Or rather, I know what you want to get into. Or should I say who?"

"There is nothing between me and Cady Winters." Keren stood to leave, with or without Zweli.

Zweli grabbed his white coat. "There's nothing between you and Cady like there's nothing between me and Kyla."

"You're not...you didn't..." Keren started.

"Seduce her?" Zweli finished seriously. "No."

"Really," Keren said. "Five tuxedos and one failed conquest."

Zweli led Keren to Octavio's desk, where he settled his bill for the tux. "I wouldn't call it a failure, at least not on my part. I turned her down."

"You turned *her* down," Keren said skeptically. Zweli's success with women was the stuff of legend around Raines-Hartley.

"Unbelievable, I know," Zweli said. He pocketed his receipt and thanked Octavio. "I still don't believe I didn't make the most of that very interesting occasion."

Keren led the way to the door and opened it. A rush of December air hit him in the face. It smelled like snow. They were halfway down Market Street and getting into Zweli's Alfa Romeo before Zweli worked out a response to Keren's disbelief. "She didn't really want me," he said, easing the shiny, blood-red roadster into the downtown lunch hour traffic. "She was scared. Claire's code on Thanksgiving genuinely scared her. Kyla puts on that carefree, party-girl persona to camouflage her true feelings."

"I've never heard you talk about a women's feelings before," Keren said. "Could we skip lunch today? I need to get back to fifteen."

"You're not fooling me, K.," Zweli said. "You're itching to get back because this is the time Cady goes to get her lunch."

Keren rested his right elbow on the door and kept his face toward the window. "I'm looking out for her health. I make sure she eats."

"Three squares, two snacks and a dessert or two, from what I hear," Zweli said. "When do you plan to take her out right, for some real food instead of that cafeteria swill?"

"I don't want to start something I can't finish," Keren said.

The Alfa Romeo darted in and out of traffic, making the other cars on the road look like they were standing still. As he pulled into the Raines-Hartley parking garage, Zweli said, "Cady's talked about staying in St. Louis."

Keren snapped to attention.

"Kyla said that Cady mentioned something to Ciel about coming back home, for good," Zweli said. "The Winters girls are circling the wagons, to prepare for when Claire is gone."

Zweli pulled into the parking spot marked by his name. He continued to talk, and Keren caught odds and ends about Kyla. But Keren gave his mind over to the thing Zweli had said which interested him most—that Cady had mentioned staying.

The mere possibility tantalized and tormented him as he and Zweli entered the hospital and began the maze of corridors that led to the cafeteria. His breath snagged in his chest as a flood of scenarios played out in his mind. Cady would eventually leave Raines-Hartley, but how wonderful it would be if she went only as far away as the *St. Louis News-Chronicle*. If she stayed, he could ask her on a proper date, to dinner at Tony's or Balaban's. Better yet, he could cook for her. He could take her to a movie or for boat rides in Forest Park or to Six Flags for a death-defying spin on a rollercoaster. Things he never would have done otherwise leaped into his head as he imagined activities he wanted to share with Cady.

Granted, he could do any of those things, except for Six Flags, now. But what would be the point? Even if Cady were willing to leave Claire, spending time alone with her would only get him addicted to her presence in his life.

Unlike Zweli, Keren knew that he couldn't be satisfied with a short-term relationship. Not with Cady.

"Keren!" Zweli almost hollered.

His name startled Keren out of his reverie. He realized they were in the cafeteria, at the buffet line. "Yes? What?"

"Have you heard a word I've said since we left the car?"

"I was thinking," Keren said. "Sorry. What did you say?"

"I said Cady isn't here. We missed her."

"Don't keep watching the door, honey," Renyatta said. "It makes you look pitiful."

"I'm not watching the door," Cady said. She leisurely crossed Claire's room to sit in the chair on the window side of the bed. She hadn't exactly lied. She wasn't watching the door. She was specifically watching for Keren. Most days, she ran into him in the cafeteria, usually at lunchtime. Brief as it was, she'd come to treasure the time they spent together at midday. She knew that he was meeting her to make sure that she ate, but he seemed to genuinely enjoy their conversations.

She had learned more about him with each lunch, though he never revealed anything too personal or intimate. And he never spoke of family. Cady found his reticence daunting, but she valued his skill as a listener. His curiosity and interest in the Winters family was endless.

Cady had told him tale after tale, hoping that he would reciprocate, but he never did. That bothered her, but not enough for her to miss a single meeting with him.

She couldn't help wondering why he'd missed this one.

"He's probably with a patient," Renyatta said, easily translating the look on Cady's face.

"Who's caught up with a patient?" Cady asked, feigning ignorance.

"Don't you try to snow me, woman." Renyatta adjusted the flow rates on Claire's IV bags. "You and your 'friend' Dr. Bailey are drivin' us all crazy up here with your pussy-footin' around. Between you and me, the best thing you could do for Dr. Bailey would be to grab him by his tie, drag him into that office of his, and get him so hot it melts that icicle he's got lodged up his—"

"Renyatta!" Cady cried, shocked by her frank description.

"That man needs some like no man since Adam," Renyatta declared. "You're his rib." She patted Claire's leg before moving away from her. The gesture was spontaneous and affectionate. While Claire was unaware of it, it deeply touched Cady.

"How do you know that about Keren?" Cady asked.

"Because all men need it," Renyatta said. "I've been a nurse for a long time, Cady, and I've seen the meanest, crankiest, most irritable men on God's earth turn into sweet, cuddly teddy bears after a long private visit from a wife or girlfriend.

"Dr. Bailey keeps his private life private, but he doesn't fool me. That's a man who sorely needs a little less starch in his britches. We nurses had a pool going as to when you and the doctor would be bumpin' booties, but you two are hopeless. The both of you went and fell in love and messed up everything. Nobody had that in the pool."

"I'm not in love with Keren Bailey," Cady insisted, though it had no strength behind it.

"Yes, you are. You just don't know it because your love for Claire overshadows it. You know," Renyatta began in a conspiratorial tone, "your Grandma told me that she hoped to see you with a good man. I think she's gonna get her wish."

"She likes Keren," Cady said. "But all the rest is just wishful thinking."

Renyatta dismissively waved a chubby hand. "You're gonna sit there and tell me that you don't love that man?"

"I—"

"You talk in your sleep, Cady. You talk *loud*."

"I've always talked in my sleep," Cady said. "I shared a room with Ciel and Kyla when we were little. They complained about my sleeptalking all the time. They said it was just nonsense syllables."

"It is," Renyatta said. "But I understood the word 'Keren' and the long sigh and giggle that came with it."

Cady pulled her knees up to her chest and hugged them, resting the heels of her athletic shoes on the edge of her seat. "I dream about him," she admitted. She rested her cheek on her right upper arm and gazed out the window. The sky was heavy with powdery grey clouds the color of her sweats. "Day and night, awake or asleep, I dream about him."

Renyatta grabbed the straight-backed chair from the sink area and dragged it over to Cady. "You're not the only one," she said as she sat down. "I think Dr. Bailey has been the stuff of dreams for a lot of women who pass through Raines-Hartley. When he first came here, he was the talk of the building. Women would come all the way up here from radiology in the basement, just to borrow paper clips and to catch a look at Dr. Bailey. They thought he was shy and mysterious. Before long, they realized the man was just not turned on right.

"That's the difference between Dr. Bailey and a man like Dr. Randall. For Zweli, this hospital is like a box of candy. He can have what he wants, when he wants. He shows 'em a good time, but not one of them has ever touched his heart."

"I'll bet he's let them touch everything else," Cady said. "Zweli is a player's player."

"Zweli throws his passion into clothes, cars and seduction," Renyatta said. "But nothing ever goes deeper. Keren is the opposite. He keeps his passions hidden."

"The ultimate odd couple," Cady said. "One lays it all out there, the other keeps everything locked up tight."

"And both are sinfully fine," Renyatta said.

Cady laughed. She caught herself and glanced over to make sure that she hadn't disturbed Claire. Her grandmother continued to sleep, and Cady watched the slow rise and fall of her chest. Moments like this, when she stood sentry over Claire, made her dream of Keren even more.

Her mother and sisters came by regularly enough, and Renyatta had become a good friend, but Keren bolstered her spirit more than anyone else. Their talks in the privacy of Claire's room had been far more enlightening than their conversations in the public forum of the cafeteria. In Claire's room, he made good on his promise to become someone she could talk to.

He had told her about the papers he had published and breakthroughs in cancer treatments. He actually made it all sound interesting, so much so that she had suggested that he consider teaching…in Boston, for instance. He had been receptive to the possibility and had seriously discussed it with her.

He never tried to tell her that her vigil with Claire was pointless. Keren respected her need to be with Claire. He never tried to compete with it, or steal her from it. He shared it, which made Cady want him all the more.

Earlier, she had waited for him in the cafeteria for so long that she hadn't had time to eat before she had to go back to Claire's room. That was another thing: Keren made sure that she ate and drank and slept regularly. He wasn't overbearing about it, which made her truly appreciate his concern.

She wished for him then, even as Renyatta said goodbye to her and stood to leave.

Cady's wish came true when Keren entered the room as Renyatta exited.

"This is so…unexpected," Cady said, smiling as she accepted the grease-splotched white sack Keren offered. She set the bag on her knees and opened it. Keren's hand hung in the air until he could break the paralysis caused by the unexpected sight of Cady's smile. It had been a long time since he'd seen her smile in full bloom. He hadn't realized how much he missed it.

"Thank you," Cady said. She pulled two steaming French fries from the bag and lightly blew on them. In her sweatshirt and sweatpants and with no makeup, she looked like a fresh-scrubbed coed, yet the pucker of her mouth as she blew on her fries gave Keren goose bumps.

"You skipped lunch?" he asked. He gave Claire and her equipment a quick once-over, and scanned the notes Renyatta had made in Claire's chart.

"I didn't mean to," Cady said, chomping a few more fries. "I didn't see you down there."

"Zweli dragged me on one of his errands and it ran long." Keren went to the window. He leaned against the wall and looked out at the sky.

"His final tuxedo fitting?" Cady guessed.

Keren nodded.

"Kyla says that Zweli has four tuxes already," she told him. "One for awards dinners, one for weddings, one for the cruises he goes on every year, and one he keeps in his office for 'formal emergencies.' Now he has a new one for the R-H party. He's Prom Date Ken."

Cady munched a few more fries, then licked the salt from her fingertips. The bottom half of the bag was practically clear with grease. She set it on the floor on top of a faded *Chronicle* so it wouldn't leave a slippery spot on the linoleum, and then joined Keren at the window. "Do you have a tux?"

He looked at her, but she kept her face toward the window. "No," he said. "Why?"

She turned to face him, and braced her left hand on the windowsill. "Because I have a dress."

The neck of her baggy sweatshirt was wide enough to give him a nice view of her collarbone and the angle of her shoulder and neck. He shook his head, amazed that she could look provocative even in a pair of gym sweats.

Hell, she looked downright sexy. The formless garments hid her figure, but that made her all the more appealing. He knew what the sweats hid, and it was too easy to picture her wrapped in something silky or satiny with a pair of high heels.

"So you're going to the party," he said, his voice thick.

"That's the plan. I keep telling myself that it's only across the street and that I can get back over here in less than three minutes, if I need to."

"You won't have fun if you're just going to worry about Claire the whole time."

"I've been worried about Claire since I came back to St. Louis."

"I know." He took a step closer to her. "You need to let go of some of it. Zweli can tell you what stress does to your health, particularly your heart."

"My heart's been through a lot lately," she said softly.

Before he could comment, if he were going to, she suddenly jumped. "Look!" she said. "It's snowing."

There were no warning flakes. The snow started all at once, falling softly and heavily, like a flurry of silent lullabies. Keren didn't look at it. He had seen snow before. What he had never seen before was the reflection of freshly falling snow in Cady's eyes. The image was beautiful, so much so that it made him uncomfortable. The longer he gazed at her eyes, the less friendly he began to feel.

"I have to go," he said abruptly. He backed away from her before he gave in to the urge to take her in his arms and kiss her. "Excuse me, Cady."

She opened her mouth to call him back, but decided against it. For all the progress they had made toward building a friendship, he was still as unpredictable as a St. Louis summer. She never knew when a tornado would come along and blow them apart.

CHAPTER EIGHT

"If the cancer doesn't get me, those hairspray fumes will," Claire said. Her soft, thready voice penetrated the noise issuing from the bathroom. The lavatory was larger than those in most of the rooms at Raines-Hartley, but it was a tight fit for the four Winters girls.

"Sorry, Grandma," the granddaughters said in unison.

Cady sat on the edge of the bathtub while Ciel used a brush and a blow dryer to put the finishing touches on Cady's upswept hairdo. Kyla sat in the shower seat at the sink, so Clara could do her makeup in the best light.

"Hurry up in there," Claire said. "It's past my bedtime."

"What did she say?" Kyla asked. "I can barely understand her half the time."

"She said hurry up, it's her bedtime," Cady said. Claire slurred her words all the time now, and only Cady seemed to speak her language. She felt thankful that Claire was making sense.

"She just woke up," Kyla muttered.

Clara's hand froze in the middle of applying Kyla's eyeliner. "Do you want a poke in the eye? Then shut up."

"You're just mad that me and Cady are going to the ball and you and Ciel have to stay with Grandma," Kyla said.

"We don't *have* to stay with Grandma," Ciel said. "We want to. It took the two of us to replace Cady tonight." Ciel gave Cady's hair a final check. "You look good," she said, admiring her own work. "Maybe I should do hair for a living."

"That's a sharp idea," Cady said dryly. "Leave Brown, Fuller, King & Winters four months after they finally made you a full partner."

"I could do hair right there in the office," Ciel joked. "I could relax a client's new growth and take their depositions at the same time."

Cady went to the mirror. "Ciel, I don't even look like myself," she gasped. She lightly touched her hair and ran her fingers through it. She hadn't worn it straight in years. It was easier to wash it while she was taking a shower and let it do what it wanted from there. Ciel had straightened her hair with the brush and blow dryer, and had kept the style simple and sleek. It perfectly complemented Cady's dress and makeup.

Cady studied her face. Clara rarely wore makeup, but she knew how to use it. Smoky grey and shimmering purple, softened by warm gold and honey, made Cady's eyes sultry and striking. Whispers of brick and café au lait blush highlighted her cheekbones and brought out the rose undertones in her skin. Her lips, naturally perfect in shape and color, had only a light swipe of clear gloss. Cady's face was a masterpiece.

"If Ciel does hair in her law firm, you can do faces in your lab, Clara," Cady said. "You made me beautiful."

Clara smiled at her sister's heartfelt compliment. "You started out beautiful," she said. She finished up with Kyla, who crowded Cady out of the mirror so she could look at her own face.

"Can you imagine me doing makeup in the virology lab?" Clara laughed. "I can see it now: I put the blush brush in the wrong pot and I end up swiping the Ebola virus all over someone's face. No thanks." Clara hugged Cady from behind. "You have a good time tonight. Ciel and I will take care of things here."

"What about me?" Kyla said, turning from her reflection.

"What about you?" Clara said flatly. She began collecting her cosmetics and loading them into her makeup case.

"You're all, 'Have fun!' to Cady and 'So long, see you, 'bye,' to me," Kyla complained. She set her fists on her hips. Cady and her sisters were all too familiar with Kyla's petulant pose.

"Cady deserves some relief," Clara angrily whispered. "She needs a break from worrying and being in this hospital. You, on the other hand, act like you came home for Zweli Randall."

"So what if I spend time with Zweli?" Kyla demanded. "Sitting there constantly breathing down Grandma's neck isn't going to change anything. What does she need me for anyway? She's got Cady."

"Knock it off in there," came Claire's weak voice. "I won't have you girls fighting."

"Okay, Grandma," they said as one.

Cady looked at her sisters and easily read their thoughts in their eyes. They all were thinking the same thing she was, how Claire's voice, even the shadow of it, could cut their petty squabbles off at the root.

"Grandma's been waiting to see you all dressed up," Ciel said. She gently pushed Kyla into the bedroom.

"Lord, have mercy!" Renyatta squawked. "Is that dress missing a piece?"

Ciel held Cady back. "I don't want you to come rushing back here at nine o'clock," she said. She wrapped the cord of her blow dryer around its handle as she said, "You have your cell phone and your pager. I'll call you if Grandma needs you, for anything."

"Do you promise?" Cady asked somberly.

"Cross my heart," Ciel said, and she did so.

"Me, too," said Clara. "You turn on the charm and steal some hearts tonight."

"I don't want any hearts," Cady said as she started for the door.

"Not even one?" Ciel asked pointedly.

Cady blushed. It warmed every inch of her exposed skin, making her even prettier.

"She won't have to steal that one," Clara grinned, following her sister's meaning. "He'll hand it over to her as soon as he lays eyes on her."

"Stop it," Cady said as she left the bathroom with her sisters on her heels. "He's not even going to be there tonight. He's not the party type."

"Heaven help us!" Renyatta howled when she saw Cady. Her dark eyes darted from Cady to Kyla. "It's so nice to see sisters sharing clothes. Cady got the front of the dress and Kyla got the back."

"You don't like it?" Kyla asked. She strutted across the room in her four-inch heels and did a runway turn at the window. Kyla's black micro mini-dress was an understated wool jersey. The neckline, which plunged down to Kyla's midriff, made a howling statement all its own.

"Girl, if I had what you got, I'd be wearing that same dress, but in red," Renyatta said. "Aren't you worried about your bosom fallin' out?"

"Toupee tape," Kyla said. "It keeps the fabric over everything that needs to be covered."

"Aren't you worried about catching a chest cold?" Renyatta asked.

"I think she's relying on heated stares to keep her warm tonight," Clara said as she picked up the phone and dialed a four-digit extension.

Kyla scowled at her.

"And you, Miss Cady," Renyatta said, "you look like a goddess."

"Thank you, Renyatta," Cady said. "I wish I felt like one. You don't look half bad yourself. Show us that outfit."

Renyatta elegantly moved about, raising her arms to spread the folds of her silk tunic. The red, gold, blue and green floral pattern was lovely on Renyatta. Her hair had been styled high on her head and accessorized with live roses that matched the colors of her pantsuit.

"You look great, Renyatta," Ciel said.

"I look great, you look great, we all look great. Let's go," Kyla said. "Zweli is waiting in the lobby to walk us over."

Cady went to Claire and leaned close to her. "Grandma, I'm leaving now. I'll be back early, okay?"

"No, you don't," she said. "I don't want you running back here tonight. You go to that party and you have a good time. You have a good time for me, too. I'm tired, and I need my rest. I've earned it. I don't want to be lying here, worried that you're gonna come running back here no sooner than you leave."

"It's just a party, Grandma. I've been to plenty of parties."

"There's something in the wind tonight, Zacadia," Claire said. "Can't you feel it? Maybe it's some Christmas magic come early. I don't want you to miss it, baby."

"Grandma—"

"Cady, I don't have the strength to argue with you. So I'm telling you. Go on out tonight and take the biggest bite of life you can. Do that for me, okay?"

Cady nodded. She closed her eyes until she was sure she wouldn't cry and ruin her makeup. She kissed Claire's hand, and then her lips. "I love you, Grandma."

"You know I love you, too," Claire said matter-of-factly.

Cady giggled in spite of herself. "I know. You rest, so I can tell you all about the party when I come back very, very late tonight."

"That's my girl," Claire said.

When Cady started away slowly, Ciel put her arm around her shoulders and moved her along a little quicker. "She was so alert," Cady said, daring to view it as a positive sign. "She hasn't been that coherent in almost a week."

"It goes like that, Cady," Ciel said. She stepped out of Claire's room as the partygoers left. "Take it as a sign that you're meant to have a good time tonight. No worries, okay?"

Cady gave her sister a half nod before being dragged off to the elevators by Kyla and Renyatta, both of whom enjoyed the admiring stares and compliments they got from the patients and staff. Cady barely noticed. The elevator was taking a long time to come, and the longer she waited, the more she wanted to run back to Claire's room and take her post at her grandmother's side.

What if she wants water? Cady wondered to herself. Ciel and Clara don't understand her like I do. What if she's too cold or too hot? What if they don't put her detective show on at nine? What if she codes again?

Just when Cady felt as though her head and heart would explode, the elevator doors opened. "Finally!" Kyla bellowed. She stepped into the elevator and almost collided with Keren, who was exiting the car.

"Excuse me," he said, catching Kyla by the shoulders. He seemed not to even see her as he ushered her and Renyatta into the elevator. "Cady?" he said, his eyes fixed on her.

"We're on our way to the Corazon Ballroom," Cady said. Kyla grabbed her wrist and pulled her into the elevator. They heard Keren gasp aloud as he caught a glimpse of Cady's rear view. "Please check on Claire tonight," Cady called to him.

"I'm on my way now. I was just paged to her room," he said as the elevator doors closed in response to Kyla's impatient jabs at the lobby button.

During the descent, Cady anxiously twisted the short handle of her beaded palm purse. By the fifth floor, she noticed Renyatta staring at her with a big smile.

"What?" Cady asked.

"Did you see his face?" Renyatta said.

"Keren's?"

"No, Eddie Murphy's," Renyatta said sarcastically. "Yes, Keren's."

"What about it?" Cady asked.

"You're going to see it again tonight," Renyatta said.

"Why do you say that?" Kyla asked.

"Because there ain't no way in heaven or hell that Dr. Bailey is going to let her get too far out of his sight tonight, not after Clara paged him to make sure that he saw your sister in that dress," Renyatta said.

While Kyla blistered the dance floor with Zweli, Cady fended off invitations. They came at her so quickly, she barely had time to say no to one before she was being offered another. She found sanctuary in the company of Abraham Raines, the 83-year-old former neurology head and son of a co-founder of Raines-Hartley. Once Cady and Dr. Raines were engaged in conversation, none of her admirers dared to attempt to lure her from the hospital's grand benefactor.

Dr. Raines was a fascinating man, but he wasn't the one with whom Cady had hoped to spend her evening. The doctor himself was surprised to be her choice of companion and said, "You flatter me, Zacadia, but tell me, why are you wasting your time with me instead of one of the handsome young fools who've been staring at you all night?"

Cady managed to look sultry, voluptuous and shy all at once as an all-over blush warmed her skin. "I didn't really want to come here tonight," she said. "I certainly didn't come to lead the Soul Train line, like my sister." Cady tipped her head toward Kyla, who was in the middle of the dance floor shaking her groove thang to Marvin Gaye's *"Got To Give It Up"*.

"She is rather high-spirited," Dr. Raines said, adjusting his spectacles on the bridge of his nose. "I dare say that Dr. Randall will have his hands full with that one."

"If you don't mind me asking, sir," Cady said, "where's Mrs. Raines this evening?"

"Millicent should be along shortly, my dear," he said. "She had to attend a fundraiser at the art museum earlier this evening. It's the season, you know. Why do you ask?"

"I noticed that you keep glancing at the door," Cady smiled. "I assumed that you were expecting someone."

A knowing smile graced the weathered brown parchment of the doctor's 83-year-old face. "After fifty-three years of marriage, it still makes my heart leap to see her enter a room," he said fondly. "We first met almost sixty years ago, at a function similar to this. Her father was the only black surgeon at the old St. Ursula's Hospital, and every year he threw a big holiday party at the Parkmoor Hotel in Clayton for the hospital's African-American doctors, nurses and orderlies. This was years before the Parkmoor would even allow people of color to stay as guests at the hotel. I literally saw Millicent from across a crowded room. She came in on her father's arm and I couldn't take my eyes off her. Her father introduced us, and we spent the rest of the night talking. She had graduated from

Morehouse that summer and was still looking for work as a journalist."

"Like me," Cady said. "I'm a journalist."

"That's right," Dr. Raines said. "Only Millie couldn't get a job at a paper in St. Louis for another five years. She worked at St. Ursula's in the meantime. We saw each other every day. I don't think we've spent more than a week apart in all the years we've been together. She's the love of my heart. So if you catch me watching the door for her, it's only because I never get tired of seeing her enter a room and make a line straight for me."

"Dr. Raines, you're a romantic," Cady said.

"Indeed I am," he said. "Now it's your turn. Tell me why *you* keep watching the entrance to the ballroom."

"Have I been that obvious?" she asked.

"Well, given that you've spent all your time talking to me and watching the entrance, I can only assume that you're hiding from someone or expecting someone. Which is it?"

"Neither," she said somberly. "I sort of hoped that Dr. Bailey would come, but it's almost ten o'clock. If he were coming, he would have been here by now."

"That Dr. Bailey is a strange one," Dr. Raines said. "He's one of our best doctors. I handpicked him for the Raines-Hartley staff. But he's a peculiar man. Not particularly forthcoming."

"I think that's one of the things I like best about him. He surprises me." She stared into the ice melting in her cocktail glass. "I thought he would surprise me tonight. I guess I was wrong."

The doctor's silence made Cady raise her face and look at him. "Guess again, my dear," he said.

Cady followed the doctor's gaze and turned toward the ballroom entrance. The whole room had gone a bit quieter as many of the partygoers stared at the same thing Cady saw: Dr. Keren Bailey.

He walked into the ballroom and through the crowd as though the room were empty. To Cady, he seemed to move in slow motion, to the rhythm of the Alicia Keys love ballad filling the room. From head to toe, he looked magnificent in a handsome, understated tuxedo. Women stared at him hungrily, as if he were calorie-free chocolate mousse. Even Kyla paused in her wild gyrations to eyeball Keren, who proceeded directly to Cady.

He never took his eyes off her. When he'd first arrived and scoped her out, he'd offered a silent prayer of thanks to find her with Dr. Raines. The last thing he'd wanted was to have to steal her from someone else. But he would have done it. He'd gotten a brief look at her in the elevator, and that look hadn't been enough. He wanted to gaze upon her at his leisure.

He wanted to study each strand of her glossy, upswept hair. He wanted to bask in the silvery shimmer of her beaded black mini-dress. With his eyes he wanted to trace the long, sensuous lines of her sexy legs. He wanted to infuse himself with her scent, an inviting blend of jasmine, bourbon vanilla and white amber. Most of all, he wanted to make sure that no other man had access to the expanse of silky, coppery-gold skin exposed by the dangerously low-cut back of the dress.

"Good to see you here, Dr. Bailey," Dr. Raines greeted when Keren stopped before Cady.

Keren was deaf to all but Cady's nervous breathing. He offered her his right hand and said, "Would you dance with me?"

She held his intense gaze as she gave him the only answer she could. She raised her right hand and slipped it into his. Keren took a step backward, leading her to the dance floor. Cady reached behind her with her left hand to set her cocktail glass on a table. The glass would have crashed to the floor if Dr. Raines hadn't caught it.

"Thank you, Doctor," she said absently.

"Congratulations," Dr. Raines called after her.

Cady barely heard him as Keren turned and led her through the crowd of dancers. His shoulders looked impossibly wide in the tuxedo, but she knew enough about sewing to tell that it was all him and not shoulder pads sewn into the jacket. When he stopped, turned and took her in his arms, her knees nearly went weak. She didn't speak. She didn't even look at him. She closed her eyes and reveled in the feel of his chest against hers, his warm hand on the bare skin at the small of her back. She wrapped her right arm around his shoulders. He held her left hand, tucking it between them, close to his chin. She rested her head on his left shoulder and let his body guide her movements.

The Corazon Ballroom sprang to life for Cady. She finally noticed the warm glow of muted light from the three golden chandeliers hanging from the cathedral ceiling and the way her high heels glided over the checkerboard pattern of the marble dance floor. She suddenly wanted to taste the marinated baby crab claws offered at the gourmet buffet and to guzzle champagne straight from the bottle. When Keren's chin nuzzled her cheek, her world shrank to the two of them.

Keren was concerned only with the silky whisper of her legs against his and the way her fingers teased his nape. Nothing existed, other than Cady.

When a man tapped his shoulder, to cut in, Keren shrugged him off, barely aware of him. Other men tried to cut in twice more only to be shunned. A fourth took a more dangerous approach. He tapped Cady on the shoulder. When she didn't acknowledge him, he loudly cleared his throat.

"Gosomewhere!" Cady hissed all in one word as she whirled on him. The interloper successfully scared off, Cady returned her head to its comfortable perch on Keren's shoulder. Her eyes were drowsing shut in utter contentment when she noticed Dr. Raines and a lovely elderly woman in a red gown dancing nearby. Dr. Raines winked at Cady, and she smiled with her whole body.

"Dr. Raines seems quite fond of you," Keren said.

"He was my date. Sort of. He invited me to this little soirée."

Keren tipped her face up to look at her. "Abraham Raines? How do you even know him?"

"I barged in on him before I barged in on you when I first came home for Claire. He was very helpful. He asks about her every time I see him."

Keren's eyes brightened, and he almost smiled. "Is there anyone in this hospital that you don't know?"

"Yes," she said. "You."

He looked away from her, then pulled her closer, placing his mouth near her temple. "I'm just a man, Cady." He sought her gaze. She was taken aback by the sadness in his eyes. Never before had he shown her so much. "Do you really need to know more than that?"

"No." She smiled softly and gently cupped his face. "Not tonight."

Kyla was at the head of a conga line snaking rapidly toward Cady and Keren at one of the buffet tables when Cady decided that she wanted to check on Claire. "It's almost midnight," Cady told Keren as she set aside a small plate of artichoke-stuffed mushrooms. "Grandma won't get mad at me for going back. I came, I had a good time, and now it's time to leave before Kyla can catch me."

"I'm with you," Keren said, just as eager to avoid the conga line. "You lead the way."

Cady hadn't worn a coat to the party, since she was only going across the street, so Keren draped his tuxedo jacket over her shoulders before they exited the Plaza's lobby. She pulled the jacket close about her as they crossed the street. She caught his scent on it and it hit her like a blast of winter air, making her blood rush. Her face was still flushed when they got to Claire's dimly lit room.

"Did you have a nice time?" Claire asked as they entered.

"Yes," Cady said. She smiled at Keren as she took Claire's hand. "What are you doing up? And where are Clara and Ciel?"

"They went to the cafeteria, for coffee," Claire said. "You two look so nice together."

"We do?" Keren said as he perused Claire's chart. His brow wrinkled. Cady made a mental note to ask him later if everything was okay.

"Lord, yes," Claire said. "I don't think I've ever seen a handsomer couple."

"You're just stirring up trouble now," Cady said. She tucked Claire's blankets more comfortably around her.

"You started the trouble," Claire said. "By wearing that dress. I'll bet she got some looks tonight, didn't she, Dr. Bailey?"

Keren joined Cady at Claire's bedside. "Yes, ma'am, she did. She was the most beautiful woman in the room."

Cady was embarrassed by the unexpected compliment. A dizzying thrill shot through her when Keren moved behind her and put his hands on her shoulders, which relaxed as her head tilted back toward him. When she felt his breath on her neck, her own breath caught in her chest.

"I'm glad you went to the party, Dr. Bailey," Claire said. "I think it did you some good."

"It certainly did, ma'am," he said.

His words were hot puffs of air on Cady's skin. He was standing so close to her, and she impulsively opened her left hand behind her and clasped his outer left thigh. His hands tightened briefly on her shoulders before leaving her completely. Before she had time to miss them, she felt his fingertips lightly stroking her back, from her nape to the pair of dimples above her buttocks, leaving a trail of goose bumps.

Cady would have turned and kissed him if Clara and Ciel hadn't entered the room. Keren tucked his hands into his pockets and stepped away from her. A guilty blush colored Cady's cheeks.

Ciel raised a telltale eyebrow. "Hello. Did you two have fun?"

Cady nodded. Keren picked up his jacket and slung it over one shoulder.

"I think they're still having fun," Clara said. She went and sat cross-legged on Cady's rollaway bed. "The night's still young, you know. Ciel's going home now, but I'm staying the night with Grandma. If you guys want to go back to the party, you can."

Cady turned to her grandmother. Claire had dozed off. Her breathing seemed strong and even. Sure that she was out for the night, Cady said, "I don't really want to go back to the party."

"Neither do I," Keren said. "Your sister probably has everyone doing the bunny hop by now."

"So walk Dr. Bailey out," Clara said. "Maybe you can find some mistletoe somewhere."

Ciel snapped her fingers, drawing Cady's attention. She pointed to the tiny bunch of mistletoe that had been affixed to the top of Claire's doorframe.

"You guys don't give up, do you?" Cady said. "Did Grandma put you up to that?"

"Nope," Clara said, sipping her coffee. "We did that all by ourselves."

"Excuse me, ladies," Keren said as he left the room.

"Keren and I are just friends," Cady said firmly. "Now I'm going to walk my *friend* to his office. I'll be back."

"When?" Ciel asked.

"Very funny," Cady said. She kissed her grandmother. "I love you, Grandma," she whispered. "And thank you for making me go to the party."

Cady hurried from the room, hoping to catch Keren.

He caught her instead. He was standing just outside Claire's room, waiting for her. He took her by her upper arms and leaned her against the wall. He stood close to her, toying with her neckline and a loose tendril of her hair. "I don't want to be your friend," he said before clamping his mouth to hers. He left her weak and breathless with a devouring kiss, proving that he indeed was not her friend.

Her beaded purse fell to the floor as she wrapped her arms around him and let him mold her body to his. He kissed her until she couldn't breathe. When she tore away for air, his lips moved to her throat and shoulders. She arched her body into his when his hungry lips closed around her earlobe. She was tugging his shirt from his pants when he took her wrists, stopping her. He knew that she was capable of some outlandish acts and didn't doubt for a second that she would make love to him right there in the corridor if the impulse struck her.

"Not here," he said, his hands playing in her hair.

"Your office," she whispered.

"You deserve better than that," he gently murmured in her ear.

"I have a room right across the street."

"Your mother," he reminded her. He would never go to the Plaza anyway, not after what had happened the first time they were together there. And with the hospital party being there, someone would surely see him going up to her suite. Being seen going to her suite would be the star on the Christmas gossip tree.

"Your place," she suggested. "You're only three blocks away."

He took her hand and started for the elevators.

CHAPTER NINE

The taxi ride to Keren's apartment took exactly four minutes—including a stop for condoms at the Raines-Hartley pharmacy—which gave Cady no time at all to cool down and gain a measure of self-control. Neither of them spoke as Keren opened the main door of his condo complex. They maintained their silence as they waited for the elevator, as they groped and kissed in the elevator, and as Keren let them into his condo.

Cady still had nothing to say to him when he went into the kitchen and she gave herself a tour of his apartment. She took the clip and the pins from her do and shook her hair free in his spacious living room. She left one of her dangling black pearl earrings on the polished teak of his dining room table, and another on the spotless marble countertop in his bathroom. She slipped her dress off in the master bedroom and left it draped over his pillows. Dressed only in thigh-high black stockings and her high heels, she met Keren in the living room.

He almost dropped the wine glasses he carried. He froze, nearly overcome by her beauty. She was so perfect, it hurt to look at her. He had never had a problem meeting or being with beautiful women, but Cady touched him deeply in ways no woman ever had. He wanted her. There was no doubt about that in his mind and certainly not in his body, which suddenly had a mind of its own. As much as he wanted her, though, he held back. He had no faith that he would be able to control himself once he touched her. After their first kiss he had felt as though she owned him. Even now, he risked total surrender just by gazing upon her as he did.

As if she realized her power over him, she went to him and stood behind him.

"Cady...are you sure this is what you want?" he asked in a voice choked by desire.

She reached around him and began unbuttoning his shirt.

"I can't promise you anything," he rasped. His hands tightened around the wine glasses.

"Have I asked you for anything?" She slipped his shirt from his shoulders.

"No. Not yet."

She pulled his ribbed tank over his head, making him splash wine on his shoulder and chest. "When I want something from you, I'll tell you. I won't ask." She ran her hands over the defined muscles of his bare torso, then she moved around him, to face him.

"I don't take orders from anyone," he said. "You know that."

She raised her eyebrows. "Kiss me."

"That's not fair."

She lightly grazed her fingertips along his sides as she tasted one of his nipples. "Kiss me," she purred into his torso. "Now."

He gritted his teeth.

"I won't tell you again, Dr.—"

He grabbed her about her waist and kissed her madly, passionately, pressing her body into his, slightly bending her backward to make her fit him. She returned his kisses, overwhelmed by his ardor. It was more than she'd bargained for. She hadn't expected so much fire or imagination from him. No wonder he didn't take orders. He didn't need to. He knew exactly what to do.

Keren backed her onto the damask sofa and kneeled as she languorously spread herself over the cushions. Cady lightly caressed his face, drawing him in for a kiss. He leaned over her, returning her kisses, which grew more ardent as his right hand moved over her ribcage and waist until pausing on her lower abdomen. He planted kisses along her throat and collarbone while his fingers parted the copper curls between her soft thighs. When his mouth found the plum rose cap of her caramel breast, Cady gasped, arching her back. Her thighs parted farther, granting him full access as he brought her close to the peak of exhilaration.

His mouth left her breast, but it was only to join his skilled fingers between her legs. She cried out at the first taunt of his tongue against her eager and oversensitive flesh. In the farthest recesses of her mind, she laughed at herself. How could she have accused this man of being made of ice? He was heat and fire and his touch was melting her.

He kissed his way up her body, pausing to lovingly nibble her nipples as he shifted her on the sofa. He sat her up against the back of it, settling between her legs as he suckled her left earlobe. Cady's shaking fingers went to his waistband and hastily unfastened his trousers, and she slid them from his narrow hips, deliberately passing her palms over the firm mounds of his backside as she did so.

He retreated just enough to kick off his trousers and to peel off his black silk boxers. Cady's eyes briefly widened and she drew in a quivering breath at the sight of his nude form. The man was too perfect to be real. He had the chiseled pectoral and abdominal muscles of a professional athlete. His legs were long and sleekly muscled. The dim track lighting cast golden highlights on his deliciously dark skin.

He looked good enough to eat.

For the second time that night, he offered his hand. "Come with me."

She laced her fingers behind her head, crossed her legs and lay back on the sofa. "Would you help me with my shoes?"

Keren dropped to one knee before her, keeping his eyes on hers as he lifted one of her feet to his knee and unbuckled the slender velvety strap that snaked around her ankle. He removed the shoe, then peeled her stocking from her leg. With agonizing slowness, he did the same with the other shoe and stocking.

He stood, and again offered his hand.

"I just remembered," she said, her voice a sultry growl. "I don't take orders from anyone."

With one arm under her shoulders and the other under her knees, he easily scooped her up. Cady laughed and wrapped her arms around his neck. "You'll take orders tonight, and you'll like it," he said. He sat in the matching oversized armchair adjacent to the sofa and draped her over him. Taking her hand, he kissed each of her fingers, leaving her to silently wonder what he would do next. He eased her hand along his body until it closed around the rigid length of him. Cady sat up and shifted her right leg, curling it around his hip. Her head fell back when he brought his masterful lips to her bosom. She rose on her knees to better align the heat at her center with his.

He thrust his fingers into her hair and tilted her face to his, to catch her mouth in a furious kiss that stole her breath. She wrapped her right arm around his shoulders and raised herself enough to accommodate his swift and powerful entry.

Clamping his eyes shut, he grimaced in exquisite relief when he entered her and felt her weight come down to rest upon him. He braced her, cradling her smooth bottom as she wrapped both arms about his neck and shoulders and both legs around his waist. Her strong, supple thighs found a rhythm that pleased them both.

Her heated panting filled his ear, her hair caressed his shoulders, and the soft skin of her cheek pressed against his forehead. Keren held his breath, wishing, praying that time would stop, that this moment with her would last forever. This was where he was meant to be. This was heaven on earth and far more than he deserved. It was all he could ever want as every sadness and disappointment he had ever known diminished in the shadow of his love for Cady Winters.

Cady broke her embrace to reach behind her and grab his lower thighs. She maintained her undulating motion, making him groan at the sheer loveliness of her body displayed before him. He placed his thumbs at the juncture of her thighs, to knead the hooded kernel of her passion. She shivered as she reached the pinnacle of her pleasure. Her darkness closed around him, bringing him to a shuddering climax along with her. Even after she had wrought every bit of his essence from him, she continued to move upon him. He sat up a bit and placed his hands at her lower back. He brought her to him. A sheen of perspiration sealed them together as Cady kissed him, tasting the fine beads of sweat covering his forehead and upper lip. Keren took her breasts, kneading them in rhythm to her movements. When he took a dusky bud gently between his teeth, Cady squealed in pleasure and tossed her head back. Passion took hold of her again and her body spasmodically clenched around him, bringing him to readiness once again, and wrenching a climax from him that seemed to stretch into forever.

Spent, at least for the time being, Cady's limp body slumped onto him. She cradled his head and covered his face with satisfied kisses. Keren's hands moved all over her. From the nape of her neck to the tip of her littlest toe, he left no part of her uncaressed or unkissed. Cady completely gave herself over to his careful ministrations. She had never felt so cared for, so treasured. She lay in his embrace, goofy with contentment, listening to the lullaby of his heartbeat. If she could have found suitable words, she would have told him how much this moment meant to her, how thoroughly happy she was at having shared herself completely with him, knowing that he had given totally of himself.

What they had just shared should have seemed like an ending, like the final act of a play they had written as they went along; but it didn't. To Cady, it felt like the beginning of a whole new life. She looked at him, trying to see if he had been similarly affected.

Keren kissed the end of her nose and held her closer. Though his need for her had been satisfied, he wanted her again already, even more than he had before. When her fingertips grazed the nest of curls between his legs, then moved a bit farther down, he knew that she was ready for him, too. He moved her to the sofa, this time positioning her on her back. She smiled at him, easily reading his desire in his eyes. Instead of the victorious smirk of a satisfied conqueror, her smile was soft and sparkling, the smile of a woman who had earned her lover's total and unconditional surrender. Keren moved to kiss her and realized that in surrender, he had actually won more than he ever imagined possible.

She guided him atop her and kissed him deeply, fully. Just by stroking his buttocks and the sensitive skin just below them, she made him moan. Already she had him straining and eager for her. Though his desire for her was keen, the urgency was gone. He would take the time to make love to her so well and so thoroughly, it would banish any thoughts she had of returning to Boston.

He carried her to his bed and set her on it, flattening her on her back as he laced his hands through hers and pinned them above her head. He devoted himself to her left breast, his artful tongue dancing around the puckered skin capping it, then flicking over the pebbled tip high at its center. He nibbled, using the right balance of teeth and lips. He ignored her writhing and mewling, and her soft pleas for more. She felt the long, strong muscles of his arms flex when she tried to liberate her hands to touch him. Held in place, she was captive to the maddening pull of his lips and tongue as they closed around her flesh and leisurely suckled.

"Keren," she gasped. "Please…"

He took mercy on her by taking her right hand and cupping it where her thighs met. With his long fingers aligned over hers, he guided her movements over her slick flesh. Her knees fell open wider as his mouth at her breast and his synchronized explorations farther down made her sweat with desire. When he slid his longest finger into her aching darkness, she began to sizzle at her core and grabbed his wrist, holding his hand in place as her hips rose to meet each thrust of his finger. He stroked her to the brink of ecstasy, then replaced his finger with a part of him far more filling and far more satisfying. She wrapped her legs around him, taking him deeply with each powerful thrust of his hips. She took his ears and guided his mouth to hers, kissing him so voraciously his teeth clacked against hers.

When he stiffened upon her and filled her with his heat, she drove her head back into his pillows as her insides convulsed over and over. Afterward, Keren's light kisses and caresses returned her to her senses. He lay on his side, his right leg bent possessively over both of hers, and Cady lay nestled in his embrace, drowsy with contentment.

He laid his hand on her cheek, tracing her lips with his thumb. She smiled as sleep took her, and that made Keren smile, too. The smile felt odd because he smiled so rarely, but it was an outward sign of his inner happiness.

"That's it," he muttered to himself. He pushed his face into Cady's hair and breathed deeply of her scent. "I'm happy." He chuckled and held Cady closer. She turned her body more into his and a satisfied hum escaped her. Happiness moved through Keren's system like a drug. For the first time in his life, he felt totally at ease. He felt peace.

Damn, he thought to himself. Who knew that happiness would come in the wild, beautiful and passionate form of Zacadia Winters?

The absence beside her roused her from sleep. Cady woke up on her stomach in a tangle of whisper-soft sheets to see Keren kneeling on her side of his king-size bed. The room was dark but the light from the corridor beyond Keren blinded her. With one eye squinted shut and the other open but unable to focus, Cady said, "What t'hell time is it?"

Keren's fingertips danced over her exposed shoulder blade. "Five o'clock."

"Did I scramble your brains last night?" she asked, her voice raspy with sleep. She took him by the lapels of his white coat and tried to tug him to her. "Get back in this bed."

He took her wrists and kissed her hands. "I have morning rounds. I can't stay, Cady. No matter how much I want to."

She sat up on her elbows. Her hair was a sexy tousle that made her look like a 1960s ingénue. The bed sheet slipped down, exposing the sweet flesh he had sampled so thoroughly the night before. It sorely tested his resolve, and Cady knew it. She grinned and ran her hand through her hair. The sheet slipped down even farther. "Get in this bed," she demanded.

He cupped her face and kissed her. "I can't. I have to see my patients." She tossed the sheet away entirely and lay on her side, her back to him. "I took all of your orders last night," she said. "It's only fair that you take mine today."

"You're not making this easy for me, although you have a point," he acknowledged. She had been more than cooperative in their intimate time together, so much so in fact, that he seriously contemplated leaving rounds in the hands of a resident.

He eased onto the bed, moved her hair aside, and he began dotting sweet kisses along her spine. She tried to ignore him, but when his lips reached her tailbone, she rolled over and hugged him to her, kissing him full on the mouth. Keren wondered how she could look so wonderful and taste so sweet. He was fast losing the battle between what he wanted to do and what he needed to do. Cady was working at his belt when he started backing off of the bed.

"Okay, Dr. Bailey," she sighed. "I guess I'll just have to come with you."

"Cady, the sun's not even up. Stay here and sleep. I'm sorry I woke you. You were sleeping so soundly."

"I was," she said. She fell back flat on the bed, tugged his pillow to her side and hugged it to her body. It smelled of him, which made her skin tingle.

He covered her with the top sheet and lingered long enough to kiss her once more. "I'll try to come back after rounds. You get some more sleep."

"Okay," she mumbled. She was drowsing off again already. "Would you call me and let me know how Claire is? I saw the way you were looking at her chart last night. Was something wrong?"

"No," he said. "Her heart rate was a bit erratic, but it was probably because of all the party excitement you and your sisters subjected her to."

Cady's eyes were closed. Her words slurred sleepily as she said, "I should go with you, to see her. I should bring her some donuts…some cherry-filled…since…I'm…awake…"

Keren kissed her exposed shoulder before he left the room. He turned off the light in the corridor and smiled at the soft snoring he heard from his room as he left for the hospital.

"Good morning, Mrs. Winters," Keren greeted brightly. "How was your night?"

"Fine," Claire managed. She smiled. "You look like the cat that swallowed a full dish of cream this morning."

Keren bowed his head to hide his close-lipped smile and studied Claire's chart. "You're not usually up this early," he said. "Did you sleep well? Is your pain being managed?"

"I feel good, Keren. I sent Clara off to the donut shop to get me a cherry-filled. They open at four A.M., and the best ones are the ones that come out first."

"You know you can't eat donuts, Mrs. Winters," Keren said. She had called him Keren. For the first time in their seven-year acquaintance, she had called him by his name. He took out his stethoscope to listen to her heart.

She raised a frail hand to stop him. "Did Cady have a nice time last night?"

"Yes ma'am, I think she did," he said. Claire smiled at him, her dark eyes shining happily. She seemed to be waiting for more details, but he couldn't exactly tell her that her granddaughter was curled up asleep in his sheets after making love to him too many times to count. The two times in the living room had been capped off by a marathon session in his bedroom. He should have been exhausted after only an hour of sleep, but his body still hummed in remembrance of Cady's touch.

"Love is a funny thing, Keren," Claire said. "Sometimes it comes out of nowhere, like summer lightening. It hits you where you stand and goes right through you, and you're never the same again."

How did she know? Keren wondered. She had perfectly described his experience with Cady.

"You know what they say about lightning, don't you?"

"That it never strikes in the same place twice," Keren said.

"Words to live by," Claire said sagely.

"Actually, the hospital had a 40-year-old patient last summer who had been struck by lightning six times in his life," Keren said.

"I guess some people have all the luck." Claire tried to laugh, but no sound issued from her wasted body. She winced in pain. As Keren checked her monitors, her heart rate spiked erratically, but quickly settled.

"You have to keep calm, Mrs. Winters," Keren said. "I'm concerned about your heart."

"That's fair," Claire wheezed. "I'm worried about yours, too."

"Why?"

"You don't listen to it." A choppy breath escaped Claire. Keren took her hand in his. "Sometimes your heart knows what you need better than your brain does. It did my heart good to see you and Cady last night, Keren. I love my grandbabies so. It ain't for me to say how Cady feels about you, but I can speak for myself. I love you, Keren. You're a better man than you know. As for Cady, you need to think of something real nice to say to her, to let her know how you feel about her."

Claire smiled wanly at him, shaming him with her pure love for her family and the tender way she had encompassed him in it. "Thank you, Mrs. Winters," he said as her heart monitor screamed out an alarm. Her left hand clenched into a weak fist as Keren launched into action. He called the code and put oxygen on Claire. Even as she struggled to breathe, she smiled at him. When the code team arrived eighty-six seconds later, Claire was holding Keren's hand, as if to comfort him.

Keren sat in his dark office, watching the falling snow collect on the trees and playing fields of Forest Park. Claire's chart and folder were behind him, on his desk. He knew that he should be preparing for her chart review, as he had done so many other times after so many other cancer-related cardiac arrests, but he couldn't seem to get started.

Death was a part of medicine, particularly oncology. He lost patients on a regular basis. But this one was different.

This loss wasn't the end of a series of symptoms and treatments. This one was personal. Every beat of his heart drummed the pain into every cell of his body as he stared at the piece of paper bearing Cady's cell phone number.

Despite the cold, Cady's step was light as she walked the short distance from Keren's condo to her hotel. Although the sun was bright, it offered no warmth on this brisk December morning, and Cady was wearing only Keren's tux jacket, which had turned out to be half of Zweli's "emergency" tux. Thoughts of her night with Keren warmed her far more than the jacket did. Cady hummed as the Plaza's doorman held the door for her. Passing the Corazon Room on the way to the elevator, she hid a smile behind her hand. By the time she used her keycard to let herself into her suite, she was giggling to herself.

"Ab—" she started before switching mid-syllable to "Mama?"

There was no answer. Cady quickly slipped into the bathroom, started the shower and undressed. Wherever her mother was, Cady wanted to shower and change before she ran into her and was forced to explain where she'd been for the past nine hours.

Cady luxuriated in the warm water and the froths of lather that coursed over her body. The only thing that would have made the shower better would have been sharing it with Keren. She had to cool the water when her imagination ran wild with images of rich clouds of pale lather sliding over the planes and angles defining the muscles beneath Keren's dark, velvety skin.

She tilted her head back and let the water buffet her neck and shoulders. She wasn't virginal, never had been, even when she was a virgin. But she had never known a touch like Keren's, had never felt the intensity and variety of sensation he had introduced her to. He had shown her what she could only describe as…"Utter bliss," she sighed.

He hadn't said that he loved her, but he hadn't needed to, not after showing her so powerfully with a language far more ancient and binding than the spoken word.

That he had invited her into his most personal space made her feel special. The thought that he loved her made her heart do happy back flips. "I'm an idiot," she told herself. "It's like I got drunk on him last night and have a hangover from it this morning."

She suddenly realized she was thirsty. Turning off the water, she grabbed a thick towel from the warming rod, wrapped it around her, and leaving a trail of wet footprints, padded into the kitchen. She opened the fridge and saw that Abby was keeping it well stocked. She grabbed a half-gallon of orange juice and drank right from the carton until her thirst was quenched. Then she realized the room was dim, that Abby hadn't opened the living room drapes.

Cady started for the tall, wide windows, but got distracted by the tux jacket she'd draped over the back of a dining room chair. Biting her lower lip, she forced back another delighted giggle before she picked up the jacket and held it to her nose. It still smelled like him, like sandalwood and musk. As she ran her hand over Zweli's expensive wool jacket, she wondered if Kyla's evening had been as good as her own.

Cady doubted it. Kyla, for all her male admirers, was more tease than temptress. She had never known her little sister to have any lasting or substantial relationships, although she'd have to admit that her own track record wasn't much better. She set down the jacket and went to the window, convinced that her record was about to improve. With her left hand clutching the towel wrapped around her, Cady used her right hand to pull open the drapes. The sun burst into the room, filling it with light and radiant heat. Cady stared at the clear sky and shook her damp curls out. She was using her fingers to fluff her hair when she looked into Claire's room.

Her left hand involuntarily clenched more strongly around the towel. She exhaled, but couldn't seem to inhale as she read the scene before her. A woman in a dark blue R-H housekeeping tunic was removing a bundle of sheets from Claire's bed. Renyatta was taking items from Claire's nightstand and putting them in a white box. Cady snatched the drape cord and violently pulled it. The drapes rushed together, enveloping the room once more in darkness as a chill settled into Cady's bones.

Renyatta and Zweli were among those sitting around the large oval table in the conference room on fifteen when Cady burst through the door. At the head of the table, Keren stood at the projector, where he used a laser pointer to indicate a particular section on the chart they were all there to discuss.

"Here you'll see the first noted occurrence of Mrs. Winters' severe tachycardia," Keren said tonelessly. "Seven more notations were made in the course of the next thirty-six hours, clearly indicating that the patient's demise was imminent."

"Why didn't you call me?"

Keren turned sharply from the projected page of the chart. He'd recognized the voice, but at the same time he didn't. This version of her voice was deeper, sharper, and slightly menacing.

"Cady, you shouldn't be here for this," he said. He reached for her shoulders, but she knocked his hands away.

"Why didn't you call me?" she repeated.

He could only stare at her, at her shower-damp curls and her clingy t-shirt, which she'd pulled on braless over her damp skin. She wore her leather jacket and jeans, and looked so much like she had the first time he'd seen her furious beauty.

"Let me get through this, Cady," he said softly but firmly. "Wait for me in my office."

Her fists opened and closed. She held his gaze, pleading with him to give her a good reason for not having called her to tell her about Claire. When it didn't come, he watched her fury become disappointment, then desolation. Her shoulders slumped under the weight of her despair. Keren would have preferred her wrath to the exquisite sorrow that dulled her lovely eyes and made her chin quiver. He would have preferred anything to the look she spent on him before turning away and walking from the room.

For a long moment, Keren stared at the space she had occupied. Renyatta began to weep openly, unable to hold back any longer. Zweli, his face stony with grief, uttered one word: "Go."

Keren raced down the corridor. When the elevator didn't come fast enough, he bolted for the stairwell and took the stairs three and four at a time, hoping to beat Cady to the lobby. He exploded from the stairwell on the ground level and almost flattened a man recovering from an appendectomy. He sprinted past the gift shop, the parking validation station and the metal detectors. He leaped into the revolving door, but an elderly woman in a wheelchair had slowed it. Keren squeezed out of it as soon as he could and he trotted down the hospital's front driveway.

"Cady!" he shouted once he caught sight of a multicolored tousle of untamed curls at the end of the driveway. He chased her, barreling past a row of wheelchairs and people getting in and out of taxis and cars. "Cady!" he shouted once more as he lost sight of her hair.

He reached the end of the driveway just in time to see the back of Cady's head in the rear window of a taxi heading far away fast.

CHAPTER TEN

Cady sat in the attic window of her mother's house. The familiar perch gave her an eagle-eye view of the front yard and the neighborhood beyond it. She had logged years of "window time," the hours she'd spent sitting cross-legged in the window, scribbling in her spiral-bound notebooks, spinning tales of star-crossed lovers, swashbuckling pirates or homicidal maniacs. Sometimes, the hero and heroine represented all three themes.

Cady was an artist whose medium had always been words. Her spiral notebooks had given way to a state-of-the-art laptop, and her experience as a reporter had made her immune to writer's block. But as she sat staring vacantly at the cars lining the street in front of the house, her words and her ability to shape them deserted her. The obituary had been easy, just a simple statement of facts from which she'd detached herself completely. But this second thing was the most important and most personal piece of writing she would ever have to do, and it was turning into an impossible task.

She touched her forehead to the cool glass and watched as a furniture rental company truck double-parked in front of the house. Abby was having dozens of extra chairs and two tables delivered. The service was tomorrow, a full week after Claire's death, which had given out-of-town friends and relatives a chance to get to St. Louis. Abby was expecting a huge turnout for Claire's service and repast.

Tearing her gaze from the window, Cady squinted her eyes shut and tried to make the first word come. "One word," she whispered. "Just give me one word."

"Cady?" came a voice from the doorway.

She opened her eyes to see Clara and Kyla moving past dusty boxes of old clothes and unused furniture draped with old bed sheets. Clara coughed as she and Kyla stirred up clouds of dust and cobwebs with their movements.

"I figured you'd be up here," Clara said. She sat on the very edge of the windowsill to keep from getting the seat of her trousers dirty.

"Yeah, after you'd looked everywhere else," Kyla said. She peeked under a pale drape covering an old rocking chair. "Ooh, *Antiques Roadshow*, here I come," she muttered.

"Scavenger," Clara said.

"I was just looking." Kyla joined her sisters at the window. "Cady, Mama wants you to write something for me to read at Grandma's service."

"That's what I'm working on now, and I'll read it myself," Cady said.

Clara covered Cady's hand with her own, concerned by the odd tone of her voice.

"You faint when you have to speak publicly," Kyla reminded her.

"Not this time," Cady said.

"What do you have so far?" Clara asked.

Cady shrugged a shoulder. There was so much she wanted to say. Everyone already knew how special Claire was, but Cady wanted to give them something more, something that would show them the woman that she had known and loved so well.

"Remember the time we made parachutes and we got trapped dangling out of the window, and she wouldn't cut us down until we asked her for help?" Kyla suggested.

"Cady's writing a eulogy, not a stand-up routine," Clara snapped. "If you're not going to be helpful, why don't you just go away?"

"Fine." Kyla turned on her heel and left.

Clara returned her motherly attention to Cady. "Have you eaten today? Did you sleep last night?"

Cady shook her head to both.

"Grandma told us what she wanted for tomorrow," Clara said. "She wanted to wear powder blue, she wanted two hymns, two psalms and she wanted you to write her obituary and speak at her service."

"I know," Cady said. The two words were scratchy and raw, as if they'd had to claw their way past the lump in her throat.

"You need to get some rest. Every bedroom and sofa here is packed tight and the kids are keeping everyone up. But you're paid up through this week at the hotel, right? Maybe you should go back there, just for tonight. Some quiet might help you think."

"It's quiet up here," Cady said.

"At the hotel—"

"I won't go back there," Cady said, cutting her off. The last thing she wanted to do was spend another second looking into Claire's empty room.

"Is it because of Keren?"

"I haven't given him a thought." And she hadn't. He had disappointed and wounded her so thoroughly, she had blotted him from her mind completely. At least during her waking hours. The nights were different. That was when she felt her losses most keenly. She missed Claire so much more so in that surreal transition from drowsiness to actual sleep. She missed Keren then, too, and the comfort he could have given her. If only he'd tried.

"He called about a half hour ago," Clara said. "That's what brought me up here."

Cady swung her legs to the floor and closed her laptop.

"He didn't leave a message," Clara went on. "Cady, we tried to call you and tell you when Claire passed, but you weren't in your suite. I'm sorry you found out the way you did."

"Keren knew where I was." Cady stood up and struck the attic dust from the seat of her jeans.

"Don't stay mad at him," Clara said.

"I'm not," Cady said sharply. "I have no feeling for him at all."

"Don't say that," Clara said sadly. "Don't close him out. Call him."

Cady laughed bitterly. "I'm supposed to do for him what he couldn't do for me?" She picked up her laptop and tucked it under her arm. "Tomorrow, I'm going to spend the day, Christmas Eve no less, with my family, rejoicing in the life of the woman I loved more than anything else in this world. The day after that, I'm flying back to Boston. I'm going back to work, and I'm going to forget that I ever met Keren Bailey."

"That was very convincing, but I know you better than that, Cady." Clara stood to face her sister. "If you leave like that, without settling things one way or the other, I promise you will regret it for the rest of your life."

"Everything's settled," Cady insisted. "Keren settled it for me." She started for the door.

Clara used her secret and most powerful weapon. "Grandma was happy to see the two of you together. She told me so."

Though Clara's pointed statement sent a barb of guilt through Cady's heart, Cady returned fire. "Grandma's not here now, is she?"

Cady crossed her left leg over her right and clasped her hands over her knee to stop her right foot from jumping. She sat in the front pew of Mt. Tabor Baptist Church, packed in shoulder-to-shoulder and hip-to-hip with her mother, Kyla and three of Claire's siblings.

Cady's jaw ached, and she realized that she was grinding her teeth. She forced her face to relax, but when the sounds of soft sniffling and weeping reached her ears, she gritted her teeth again. For the past week, misery had lived in her like a hungry parasite. It fed on her, stealing her ability to concentrate, to laugh, to even smile. It was so big and so deep, she hadn't been able to move tears around it and cry out her sorrow the way her mother and sisters had.

Kyla sat on her right, for once stoic and calm. Abby was on her left, quietly sobbing into a saturated handkerchief.

In the pew directly behind them, Clara and Ciel sat with their husbands and children. Ciel's six-year-old, Clarence, sat on his mother's knee. That brought his mouth on a level with Cady's ponytail. The riot of curls was too much for the boy to resist, and while a soloist from the choir sang "Let the Work I've Done Speak for Me," Clarence began sucking one of his Aunt Cady's curls.

"Stop it, boy!" Ciel angrily hissed.

Cady felt the tug as Ciel removed her child from her head. Cady would have offered a smile, if her misery hadn't claimed it. Grandma would love this, she thought.

There were at least a dozen children at the service, and they were doing the loud, annoying, restless things children do. Prior to the service, Clarence had led his younger cousins in a game of chase, running them around the pews, then pausing at Claire's casket so each of the children could wave at her. Claire was surrounded by grand flower arrangements and laughing children, and Cady knew that Claire wouldn't have wanted it any other way.

Cady's remarks were curled in her hand. While going through some of her old things stored in the attic, she'd found one of her spiral notebooks from her junior year of high school. A story about a man who became psychic after swallowing a 9-volt battery occupied the first dozen or so pages. The blank pages after her inane fiction had drawn her in, and inspired that first word she had been hunting. Her pen had moved across the pale blue, college-ruled lines, filling them with one word after another. When she set the pen down, Cady knew that she had done the best, most fitting job possible. She never edited or even re-read what she'd written, not until the pastor called her to the podium.

But when she opened her mouth to speak, she felt a wail of grief rising within her and stood mute, bracing a hand on either side of the podium.

"God bless you, sister," someone called from the assembly.

"You go on, Cady," called someone else.

Cady looked out over the pews. There were so many people and so many faces, yet her eyes were drawn to one. Keren's. He sat with Zweli in one of the middle pews. Though his somber gaze held hers, Cady couldn't read his expression. But her anger at him gave her the power to push back her grief just enough to begin her remarks.

Keren bowed his head as Cady's voice captivated the congregation. She spoke simply, though eloquently, and used her words to paint a joyous and loving picture of a woman who loved children and gardening, and who'd dedicated her life to her family. Cady's words pulled at his heart as her voice broke and she had to stop speaking. She looked at him, mutely conveying her pain, and Keren wanted to run to her, soothe her hurt and take away her sorrow any way he could.

The pastor approached her and placed a reassuring hand on her shoulder, and Cady continued. "She always wanted a parcel of land, and I think she has it now. The earth is dark and moist beneath her feet, and it molds to the shape of her strong hands. She grows the fruit trees she always wanted, alongside the roses she coddled and cherished. There are dandelions, because you can't have the good without the bad, but their roots are not deep. She tends her garden, knowing that her work here is done, and that it was done so very well."

"Amen, sister!" someone shouted.

"That's right, that's right!" shouted someone else.

Keren followed her with his eyes as she returned to her seat. Her remarks were the last, so the service was ending. The immediate family stood and started the procession past Claire. Each granddaughter lingered, saying farewell in her own way, but Cady was the only one who leaned over Claire, spoke to her and kissed her forehead. Her face was rigid with grief when she straightened and turned toward the aisle. Her mother and sisters followed her, sobbing. Keren noticed that Cady's eyes were glassy and dry.

"It still doesn't feel like goodbye," trembled from Abby's lips once the limousine began to pull out of the Mt. Tabor driveway. "I feel like she's away on one of her church trips and she'll come back to us just before we really start missing her too much."

"She's not on vacation this time, Mama," Kyla said, earning a sharp elbow to her ribs from Clara.

With her crumpled tissue, Abby dabbed at her moist eyes. "Cady, your remarks were just beautiful. Claire would have been so pleased."

Cady stared at the tinted windows. As if the day weren't difficult enough, Abby had gone and invited Keren and Zweli to ride with them in the limo to the cemetery.

"I'm amazed that you didn't faint," Kyla said. She leaned over Cady to open the mini-fridge. "Is there any water in there? I haven't had anything to drink all day."

Cady took out a bottle of spring water and handed it to Kyla, along with an empty champagne glass. As she poured the water, Kyla began dancing in her seat, singing Madonna's "Music."

"You are so not funny," Clara said, although they all chuckled at Kyla's foolishness.

All except Cady, who was lost in her own world, and Keren, who couldn't stop looking at her.

"I know it sounds strange to say, and I mean no disrespect, but this is the best funeral I've ever been to," Zweli said. "It doesn't feel like a funeral."

"Claire wanted a celebration of her life, not a mournful farewell," Abby said. "She wanted to be remembered with laughter, not tears."

Cady listened to the cool, clipped syllables of her mother's speech as she spoke to Zweli. Abby always sounded like the teacher she was. A little on the heavy side for her five and a half foot petite frame, Abby always dressed with the casual elegance of a presidential executive assistant. As Claire wished, none of her immediate family wore black. With her silver and black hair styled in an elegant chignon, and wearing a dark navy, double-breasted suit dress with imprinted silver buttons, Abby looked like a Supreme Court justice.

Keren looked from Cady to Abby. Cady had her mother's beautifully shaped mouth and slender hands, but the similarities ended there. Where Abby was calm and cool restraint, like Ciel, Cady was fire and emotion. Where Abby was regal and sturdy, like Clara, Cady was free-wheeling and lithe, like a dancer. From what Keren had seen, Abby and Cady were as different in temperament, demeanor and opinion as a mother and daughter could be.

Cady cast her eyes at him, catching him looking at her. He shifted in his seat, but he didn't say anything. She fixed her gaze on the window again.

"There were a lot of people in the church," Ciel said. "I wonder how many of them are going to the cemetery?"

Twisting in her seat, Cady looked out of the rear window. What she saw gave her goose bumps and made her mouth drop open. "All of them," she said, answering Ciel's question.

The Winters sisters crowded the back window. As far back as they could see, there were cars with bright orange stickers marking them as part of Claire's funeral procession. Cady bit her lip to stave off tears. She had never seen such a long processional for someone who wasn't a public figure. But, given that practically everyone Claire had ever met had called, sent cards and flowers or attended the service, Cady supposed that her grandmother was a public figure after all.

"Thank you for such a nice tribute, Rev. Kurl," Cady said, although she hadn't really paid attention to the short sermon he'd given at Claire's interment.

"Your words at the church far surpassed mine," the old preacher said. He gave her hand a warm squeeze. "Sister

Claire would have been so pleased to know how much she will be missed."

When the reverend turned to greet other family and friends, Cady joined her sisters, who were clustered just outside the tent covering Claire's interment site.

"Mama put flowers on Grandpa Hank's stone." Clara nodded toward the big bouquet of white winter lilies on the black granite headstone that Claire would soon share. "We're going to put some flowers on Daddy's grave and then go home for the repast. Mama's already gone over to Daddy's with some poinsettias."

The sisters accepted hugs and condolences from the mourners that passed them. Each teary-eyed face started Clara and Ciel weeping again, but Cady maintained her composure. Keren stood at a distance with Zweli, watching as Cady stonily consoled one of Claire's sisters.

"I expected Cady to be the one falling apart," Zweli said.

"She will," Keren said softly. *Her grief has to climb a little closer to the surface before her tears can find their way out,* he thought to himself. He stared after her as she put her arm around her great-aunt's shoulders and walked her farther away from the tent. Keren couldn't hear Cady's voice, but whatever she said brought a hint of a smile to her elderly relative's face. Cady kept talking and holding her hand until a full laugh escaped the old woman.

"Cady, Kyla, are you going with us?" Clara called as she and Ciel headed for their father's grave.

"No, thanks," Kyla said. She picked her way carefully over the frozen ground to protect the fine heels of her

shoes. "Why should I visit his grave? I never knew him."
She held her faux fur coat closer about her as she went in
the opposite direction and approached Keren and Zweli.

"I'll be right there," Cady said, speaking loudly enough
to mask the name Clara called after Kyla.

"Don't you two look handsome?" Kyla said cheerfully.
She stood between Zweli and Keren and linked her arms
through theirs. "Let's go wait for the graveyard shift in the
car. It's freezing out here."

Keren let Kyla lead him to the waiting limo, but he
didn't climb into its warm interior with Kyla and Zweli. He
waited outside and watched Cady's cloaked figure grow
smaller as it ventured farther away from him. He jogged a
few steps in place to keep warm. The black wool of his
Burberrry Chesterfield was impenetrable to the below-zero
wind chill, but the cold stung his face and numbed his feet
and gloved hands.

Keren squinted into a blindingly bright sky that held no
warmth. It was a gorgeous day, far too pretty for putting a
loved one in the ground. The Winters women were in
dresses and he wondered how they could stand the bitter
cold for so long. But then he realized that they probably
weren't even feeling it. Grief had a way of numbing you to
everything. Keren knew that better than anyone.

Cady, predictably, was the last to leave. Her mother and
sisters were halfway back to the limo as Cady leaned against
the side of her father's headstone. Her gloved hand absently

caressed the top of the black marble stone that Claire had chosen twenty-five years ago. Abby had been too distraught to handle any of the arrangements following Zachary's death.

Though Cady's memories of that time were few, they condensed, coming into sharp focus for an instant before dissipating, like her breath in the cold air. She remembered how her mother's grief had taken the shape of a dazed silence that no one, not even baby Chiara, could penetrate. Claire had fed, clothed, cleaned and comforted all of them, including Abby. Grandpa Hank had been able to function, but he was never the same after his son's death. Grandpa Hank had joined his beloved son ten years ago, and now Claire was with them, too.

"I miss you, Daddy," Cady whispered. "Show Grandma the ropes."

She abruptly started away before her thoughts turned from nostalgic to crippling and reached the limo in time to see Kyla popping out of it.

"People are on their way to the house for the repast, you know," she nagged. "I want to get home before cousin Sharonda gets there. You know she'll be picking through Grandma's things."

"Shut up, Kyla!" Clara yelled from within the limo as Ciel said, "You just want to beat her to it."

"Sharonda's a damn jackal and you all know it," Kyla countered.

Cady stayed out of her sisters' tensions as she ducked past Kyla and got into the limo. The driver was holding the door for Kyla, who was transfixed by something in the distance. "Miss?" the driver said, prompting her to get into the vehicle.

"I'm not ready," Kyla said quietly.

Cady glanced at her sisters and her mother, wondering if they'd heard what she had. Kyla's voice was too soft, too shivery. When Kyla started away from the limo, Cady went after her.

"Ky?" Cady called. She had to move fast to catch up to Kyla, who was rushing back to Claire's tent.

"I'm not ready," Kyla repeated, and this time the rising hysteria in her voice drew everyone from the limo. "Stop that!" Kyla shouted, reaching an arm forward as she began to run to Claire's grave.

Cady drew up short when she saw the source of Kyla's emotional charge.

Claire's coffin was being lowered into the grave.

"Don't do that!" Kyla screamed. The frozen earth caught the heel of one of her stiletto shoes and she tumbled to the ground. Zweli raced past Cady and Keren and caught up to Kyla. He took her in his arms and pressed her head to his chest, facing her away from Claire's grave. Kyla fought him, sobbing wildly as she kept saying, "I'm not ready!"

Cady wanted to comfort her sister, but didn't know how to do it without dropping her own defenses. Kyla hadn't fooled anyone with her devil-may-care attitude. Cady had known that the reality of Claire's passing would hit each of them at some point. And since Kyla cloaked so many of her feelings, Cady had known that reality, when it came, would hit her like a ton of wet sand.

"Don't look, baby, don't even think about it," Zweli soothed as he pressed his lips to the top of Kyla's head.

"Let me go," Kyla cried. "They're putting her in the ground…"

"Let's go back to the car," Zweli said, holding her closer.

"No! I have to stop them," Kyla insisted.

Zweli gripped the sides of her head and forced her to look at him. "Let them finish taking care of your grandmother, Kyla. There's nothing you can do for her now."

Cady clutched a handful of her cloak over her heart as Kyla's utter heartbreak gleamed in her maple eyes. "No," Kyla moaned. "This shouldn't be happening. If she hadn't eaten so much fried food and if she had taken better care of herself—"

"Don't blame Claire," Zweli said. He gripped her shoulders and pulled her closer to him. "She didn't do anything wrong. Her cancer was age-related, not behavioral."

Cady appreciated Zweli's attempt to ease Kyla's heart and mind, but she knew that what he said wasn't completely true. Claire had never gone to the doctor until a pain went just past unbearable. She once tore her Achilles tendon while playing kickball, and she limped around on it for two weeks before she bowed to Abby's demand that she see a doctor. When the lump in her breast was discovered, it was the size of a deck of playing cards.

"Stop being so greedy, Kyla," Zweli gently chastised. "You had Claire for almost thirty years. I got her for only a few months. Do you know how much I envy you and your sisters, that you had such a great lady in your life? What would she say if she saw you carrying on this way?"

Kyla buried her face in Zweli's coat front and sobbed. Cady dropped her eyes to the ground. Her shoulders rose and fell heavily as she struggled to keep her own tears at bay. One messy display at Claire's gravesite was enough. Cady was about to succumb when a hand on her shoulder steadied her and calmed her. Her breathing became more rapid as a band of heat drew her toward the body to which the hand belonged.

Keren inched a step closer to her, hungry to give her whatever solace she would take from him. He envied the ease with which Zweli lovingly comforted Kyla, and Keren wished that he could give Cady what she needed now.

Cady's shoulders relaxed. All she had to do was turn around and open his coat and climb into the warmth of his body. He would shield her from the cold. He would be the buffer between her ears and the sound of dirt thumping against Claire's coffin. He might not have been there for her a week ago, when Claire passed, but he was here for her now...if only she would forgive him.

A heavy clod of dirt struck Claire's coffin, startling Cady out of her reverie. No, she thought to herself. I can't forgive him. I needed him then. I don't need him now. She bowed her head and turned, avoiding his imploring gaze as she circled around him and started back to the limo.

CHAPTER ELEVEN

"I know what that's called."

Keren, who had thought he was alone on the enclosed back deck of the Winters house, looked down to see a child. A small one. A little boy in a navy blue suit and a plaid bow tie stared up at him from behind a pair of round, wire-rimmed glasses. "You know what what's called?" Keren asked.

The boy touched Keren's kneecap. "That's your pateller."

"Patella," Keren corrected as he uncomfortably eased away from the child.

The boy got on his hands and knees and touched Keren's shin. Keren jumped as though he'd been bitten. Which was a possibility, if this child happened to be Clarence, Ciel's six-year-old. "This is your ulnar."

Keren touched his forearm. "The ulna is here."

The boy smacked his palm into his forehead. "Oh, you're right," he said with a goofy roll of his big brown eyes. "Down here is your fibiar and tibular."

"Tibia and fibia, Clarence," Ciel said as she stepped out onto the deck and scooped her son up. She set him on his loafered feet. "He's been interested in bones lately," Ciel explained apologetically. "His sitter reads to him from a book about the skeleton. She's from the boot hill, right on the Missouri-Arkansas border, and she adds an 'er' sound to every word that ends with a short 'a.'"

"Rebbecar talks good," Clarence said in defense of his sitter.

"Boy, go somewhere," Ciel ordered. Clarence scampered off.

"He's smart," Keren said. "Cute."

"Why, thank you, Dr. Bailey." A smile brightened Ciel's tired face. "That was the closest we've ever come to having a regular conversation."

Keren felt the heat of a blush creeping across his cheeks.

"C'mon," Ciel said, taking him by the wrist. "Come back inside and meet some of the folks."

"Actually, I was on my way out. I have to get back to the hospital."

"Zweli says you aren't on until tonight." Ciel led him into the crowded kitchen and through to the living room. Zweli was surrounded by women, but he had eyes for only two: Kyla and Clara's daughter, eight-year-old Danielle. Zweli allowed the little girl to drag him into the dining room, where she began to introduce him to each of the dolls she had set on the chairs. Danielle, who was old enough to understand what was going on, had taken comfort as Kyla had, in the generous care and attention of Dr. Zweli Randall.

"Dr. Bailey, have you eaten?" Abby asked. With a regal wave of her arm she guided his eye to the dining table, which was covered by a wide assortment of food. There was food all over the house, with ham being the dominant item. There were three hams on the dining table and four more on a counter in the kitchen.

"I'm not hungry, ma'am," Keren said.

"I'll fix him a plate," Ciel offered.

"Thank you," Abby said. She took Keren's arm. "You and I can talk while Ciel gets you something to eat."

Abby led him to the foyer, to the rows of photos that began near the front door of the old Victorian. "This is Enid Winters, Cady's great-great-great-grandmother," Abby said as she lightly touched the frame of a small daguerreotype.

Keren peered at the beautiful, dark-skinned woman in the picture. She smiled, a rarity in Civil War-era photographs. The woman was tall and had straight black hair.

"This picture was taken a year before she died," Abby said. "She was killed in 1868 in Juniper Falls by men who wanted her land. They burned her house and she and her mother died in it. She saved her children, though." Abby pointed to two more framed portraits lining the walls. "Her son Jacob and her daughter Zacadia grew up and both went to Wilberforce University in Ohio. They became doctors and practiced in Juniper Falls until the day they died.

"From Jacob Winters down to my husband Zachary, the Winters family has always stuck together, through thick and thin," Abby went on. "Claire's death is the biggest blow we've had in a very long time. When Claire married her husband, she caused quite a scandal when she made him take her name. She was an only child and a girl, and she was determined to have the Winters name survive her. Zachary and I had five girls, so the Winters name has likely died with my husband.

"I'm a Winters by marriage. My daughters are Winters women from scalp to sole. Claire was their rock. Mine, too. But I'll get past this. Clara and Ciel have families of their own to help them through. I worry about Kyla and Chiara because they're alone, but I know they'll come through okay."

Abby turned to Keren and took both of his hands. "I fear for my Cady," she said. "She has such a hard time letting go of what she loves, and her love for Claire is fierce."

She let go of me easily enough, Keren thought. He wanted to kick himself for even remotely entertaining the possibility that Cady loved him.

"Why are you telling me this, Mrs. Winters?" he asked.

Abby cupped his cheek and chuckled sadly as she shook her head. "Because you're family now, Dr. Bailey. Claire took you for one of her own. And if I'm not mistaken, my stubborn daughter has, too."

Eating from the plate Ciel had prepared for him, Keren managed to keep to himself, despite the number of people filling the house. It seemed that half of eastern Missouri had turned out for Claire's service and repast. Abby's fellow teachers, past and present students, and her brothers and sisters were there. Clara's husband Christopher and their sons, Chris Jr. and Troy, circulated among the guests as did Ciel's husband Lee and their daughters, Abigail and Ella. There were friends from the neighborhood and their church, and merchants from Soulard Market, which probably explained why the fruit baskets lining the foyer were among the best Keren had ever seen.

Teenagers Claire had once babysat had come to pay their respects along with half of the Raines-Hartley medical, maintenance and cafeteria staff. Adele Harrison made an appearance, along with Rosina Ippolito and Gloria Williams.

Claire had wanted a joyous remembrance, not a sad, weepy affair, and she got what she wanted. People were laughing, talking and eating, and the children were playing around the brightly lit Christmas tree. It was more family reunion than funeral.

Keren glanced about the rooms, easily picking out Cady's family members despite their varied personalities, colors and lifestyles. The Winters women were beauties, from the ebony complexion of Claire's sister Enid to the cashew hue of Clara's daughter, Danielle. Tall, short, slim or stout—they were captivating women. But Cady stood out from the rest.

From his corner in the living room, Keren watched her serving the guests, making small talk, cleaning up spills and offering comfort. He marveled at how effectively she masked her own feelings to care for others, but he was particularly interested when Cady went to a young man standing alone in the crowded room.

"John Mahoney?" Cady said, touching the shoulder of the well-dressed young man.

"No more Mahofro?" he said, gazing at her with the prettiest eyes Cady had ever seen.

Cady gave him a warm embrace, then took him by the shoulders as she looked at him. John Mahoney— "Mahofro" as she'd nicknamed him because of the short, curly afro he'd sported in high school—had grown up. He had shoulders now, nice ones, judging by the cut of his tailored suit. The cute boy with the hazel-grey eyes and pecan-brown skin who had been Chiara's high school sweetheart had become a very handsome man.

"Chiara told me about Claire," John said. "I had to come and pay my respects. She was a very, very special lady."

Cady gave him a somber smile of thanks. "I'm glad you came, John." Cady's face hardened a little. "I wish Chiara had come, too."

"She's in Thailand," John said, rushing to Chiara's defense, as always.

"She could have come, if she'd wanted to."

"I'm not so sure about that," John said pensively. He lowered his voice and spoke closer to Cady's ear. "I haven't seen or heard from her much since she went to public relations and was sent overseas."

Both John and Chiara were seven years out of high school and had attended George Washington University. They were subsequently employed by U.S. IntelTech, Inc., a global computer software corporation based in Chicago. Cady assumed that it was just a matter of time before John became her brother-in-law. If anyone knew of Chiara's comings and goings, it was he.

"She's in Thailand? She didn't tell me that when she called today," Cady said. "I thought she was still in Hong Kong."

"She doesn't say much at all about what she does on all those trips U.S.I.T.I. sends her on," John said. "I miss her in Information Technology. I suppose Public Relations had to have her when they saw how smart and beautiful she is, not to mention that she speaks four languages and can charm—"

"When are you going to marry her and get it over with?" Cady asked. "It's obvious that you're still in love with her."

"It doesn't matter," he said. "U.S.I.T.I.'s got her."

Cady's brow knitted at John's curious phrasing. "You probably see her and hear from her more than we do."

"Used to," John said. "Not anymore."

Cady gave John another hug. She had no idea what the status of Chiara's relationship with John was, but he clearly missed her. "Maybe you should transfer to Public Relations," she suggested. "You two could share a desk again."

"No, thanks. Public Relations has the highest turnover at U.S.I.T.I. People burn out quickly."

Abby spotted John and joined them. "John, I loved the flowers you sent. That was so thoughtful. "Be sure to take a ham with you when you leave."

"No one wants a death ham, Mama," Cady scowled. Abby had offered whole hams to just about everyone, and Cady was tired of hearing people search for polite refusals. When Ciel came over and introduced "Mahofro" to her husband, Cady left John safely in the care of her sister. She took an empty potato salad bowl into the kitchen to steal a moment of quiet. Keren's eyes tracked her.

She stood at the sink, washing the large red serving bowl, which was shaped like overlapping cabbage leaves. She wore a mid-calf length knit dress, sheer black hose, and calf-high suede boots. The charcoal-colored form-fitting dress had a turtleneck collar that emphasized the pretty length of her neck. Her hair was styled in a single ponytail that left a bouquet of wild curls at the back of her head and she wore gold stud earrings. Knowing better, yet still unable to stop himself, Keren couldn't help feeling a twitch in his loins at how sexy she looked. Her face was brittle and hard and he longed to soften it with kisses and caresses. He wanted to go to her, embrace her and share the weight of her sorrow.

She glanced up and saw him watching her.

"Doctor, may I take your plate for you?" Abby asked, appearing from nowhere.

Keren held Cady's gaze, mutely begging her to open up to him.

"Doctor?" Abby repeated.

"Ma'am?" Keren said, finally noticing her. "I'm sorry, I was...thinking."

"We've all been caught thinking around here lately," she said. She glanced at Cady and back at Keren. "Why don't you take your plate in and see if Cady needs any help?"

That was all the encouragement Keren needed. He shouldered his way through the crowd and into the kitchen. Glad to find Cady alone, he closed the door behind him.

She didn't look at him or remove her hands from the hot, soapy water in the sink as she said, "I don't want to do this now."

"Do what?" he asked.

"Whatever it is you came in here for." She angrily pushed a pile of dishes into the water, sloshing suds onto her rolled up sleeves.

"I want to fix this thing between us," he said.

Cady propped a wet hand on her hip and glared at him. "What 'thing' would that be, Keren?" she snapped. "And how do you propose to fix it? With an apology? Would you even know what you're apologizing for?"

"I didn't come in here to upset you or to start a fight." He took a drying towel from the rack attached to the cabinet door under the sink. "Your mother thought you'd like some help with the dishes."

Cady didn't move. "You didn't answer my question."

He took a crystal serving bowl from the drying rack and gave it a once-over with the towel. "What do you want from me, Cady?"

She balled her fists and almost gave in to the urge to pop him one right in the stomach. "Not a damn thing!" she spat. She snatched the towel from him and the bowl came away with it. Keren tried to catch it, but it tumbled to the Congoleum floor and broke into several pieces. Drying her hands as she went, Cady started for the kitchen door.

"Cady, don't hurt him!" Abby fretted, rushing into the room and fearing the worst.

Cady moved past her without a word.

"I'm sorry about your bowl, ma'am," Keren told Abby. He stooped to pick up the pieces of glass.

"I got this old thing at a yard sale," Abby said, pushing him toward the door. "If you want to fix something, go talk to Cady."

Keren went after her, calling her as he followed her through the crowded rooms. Cady ignored him as she grabbed her cloak from the coat tree in the foyer and walked out the front door. "Cady, calm down and talk to me," Keren demanded as he caught her by the arm and stopped her on the front porch.

"Why are you even here?" she groaned in anguish. "You didn't care enough about Claire or me to call me last week when I specifically asked you to. Why do you need to talk to me now?"

"I need to make you understand something."

"I understand all I need to." The fight left her as misery began to wear her down. "I asked you to do one thing for me, and you didn't. What I don't understand is why you won't just go away and leave me alone."

Though Cady's relatives crowded at the windows to watch the heated exchange on the porch, Keren was oblivious to them. He was determined to find a way to keep her from pushing him out of her life. She could give him dirty looks, she could yell at him, cuss at him or hit him, but he couldn't allow her to leave him. He took her by her shoulders and pulled her to him. "I can't leave you alone because I love you, Cady," he blurted. "I love you."

Her eyes widened and glistened as they filled with shimmering tears. Her mouth worked to find words but failed.

"I love you," he said once more, touching his forehead to hers.

Cady jerked from his grasp and took a step back. She blinked and tears rolled down her cheeks. She swiped them away, smiling bitterly as she said, "Only you could find a way to make me feel worse when I already feel as bad as I thought I possibly could."

"What does that mean?" he asked. "I didn't say that to hurt you."

"Well, you did," she said. "But you won't get a chance to do it again." She went back into the house, closing the screen door when Keren tried to follow her. "Go to the hospital, Keren. Or go home. Go anyplace. Just please go."

The house had emptied and the children were long in bed by the time Abby made it up to the attic, presumably to say goodnight to Cady. When Abby lingered, Cady knew that her mother had something else on her mind. "What is it, Mama?" Cady sighed wearily.

Abby crossed her arms over the bosom of her velour robe. "You're too hard on people, Cady," she said. "You expect too much from the people you love. Loving someone doesn't automatically turn that person into what you want him to be. You have to give a little. Or a lot, in Dr. Bailey's case."

Cady kicked off the ratty brown house slippers that had once belonged to Clifford Williams and climbed into the narrow twin bed set between the dormer windows. "You have no idea how much he hurt me," she said. "All he had to do was call me. He didn't. I can't forgive him for that."

"Why the hell not?"

"Because he did wrong." Cady lay on her side and pulled her blanket up to her chin. "What if he really does love me, Mama, what then? How can he justify his failure to make a simple phone call? I expected more from him. Can't I expect everything from someone who claims to love me?"

"Of course, but within reason. None of us could reach you after Claire died," Abby said. "Renyatta called me at the Plaza and told me. I told her that you'd been out all night and I had no idea where you were."

Cady ignored the pointed comment.

"You'd give him another chance if Claire asked you to."

Cady sat up. "What's that supposed to mean?"

"I gave birth to you, but Claire mothered you. She's the one you went to when you got in trouble in school or needed a dress for a dance. I didn't mind. She understood you, and you needed that, Cady. But I love you, too. I was your mother first and I'll always be your mother. When I tell you to talk to that man, it's for your own good."

"Why can't you let it go? I have."

Abby set her mouth in the stubborn line that always prefaced their best battles of wills. "No, you haven't. You couldn't if you wanted to, and *you don't want to*."

"Is this grief talking?" Cady asked. "Because you aren't making any sense."

Abby sat on the edge of the bed. "The second you let go of your anger at Keren Bailey, you're going to have to face the fact that you love that man. You love him so much that you can't see past your anger to forgive him. You're spinning your wheels in a vicious rut of your own creation."

Cady flinched from a sudden burst of longing for Keren. He loved her. He'd said so. Yet the admission had further damaged her already broken heart. "You can't fall in love with someone in five months," Cady said.

"You're right. You fall in love in an instant." Abby snapped her fingers. "Like that. You can know someone for twenty days or twenty years, and suddenly, in one fleeting beat of your heart, you know that you've found someone to whom you want to give everything."

Cady stared at her mother in amazement. "Is that what it was like for you?"

A visible peace settled over Abby as she gazed inward and spoke of her late husband. "I fell in love with your daddy the first time I met Claire," she said. "She and your Grandpa Hank treated me like I was gold, and they were so happy together that I knew that Zachary Winters came from good stock. That he came from a home filled with love.

"I'd been dating your father for two months. We were having coffee after my first dinner with Claire and Hank, and I knew right then that I loved Zachary. If I'd known then that I'd only have him for fourteen years, I still would have married him. He gave me five splendid daughters and the best in-laws a wife could want."

Cady pulled her knees to her chest and hugged them. She hid her face as she asked, "Don't you hate him, Mama, just a little?"

Abby jumped. "Hate…? Who? Your father? Why on earth would you even suggest such a thing?"

"He left you alone to raise five children. Even if you had wanted to find someone else to love, how could you, with Grandma and Grandpa living right here with us? How can you forgive him for disappointing you?"

"Cady, my husband was killed performing a job he loved," Abby said firmly. "He didn't set out to be blown up. He could have been killed anywhere, even right here in our own backyard. If God meant to take him, distance, place and my preferences wouldn't have stopped it from happening. Your father died too soon, but I don't hate him for that. I can't. I love him too much, even after all these years."

Cady nodded, and wiped a tearing eye on her shoulder.

Abby gathered her daughter into her arms and held her tight. "Each day brings its own happiness and heartbreaks, Cady. You're so busy nursing a heartbreak that you can't see that there's joy out there for you. All you have to do is pick up the phone and give Keren a call."

Renyatta was waiting for Keren in his office when he returned from the cafeteria with a cup of coffee. She was still wearing the fire-engine red dress that she had worn to Claire's service, which led Keren to believe that she had come straight to the hospital from the Winters house.

"Is there something wrong at Cady's?" Keren asked, concerned. "Is Cady alright?"

Renyatta smiled. "They're all fine. Wore out, but fine. It's nice seeing you care about someone, Dr. Bailey. Claire might have been right about you all along."

"Right about what?"

"Claire once told me that a good woman could turn you into a whole new man." She set a tiny white box on his desk as Keren sat down at it. "I think she was right. Claire gave that to me a couple of weeks ago and asked me to pass it on to you on Christmas Day, if she couldn't do it herself." Renyatta bowed her head and grabbed a wad of tissue from her pocket. She hastily blotted the tears that sprang to her eyes. "Christmas is still a few hours off, but I don't see the harm in giving this to you now, especially since I won't see you tomorrow."

Keren hesitated before picking up the box. "What is it?"

Renyatta shrugged. "I didn't ask, and she didn't tell." She grinned through her tears as she stood to leave. "I can keep a secret when I want to."

"Thank you, Renyatta," Keren said. "Enjoy the holiday."

"You, too." At the door, Renyatta turned and said, "I'll be expecting you to tell me what was in that box."

The left side of Keren's mouth almost lifted into a smile as Renyatta left the office and quietly closed the door behind her. Keren turned the box between his fingers. It was light enough to be empty, but when he shook it, he heard a soft scratch within it. He opened it and found a folded square of paper with a lump in the center of it. When he unfolded the paper on his desk blotter, two rings glinted in the lamplight.

There was writing on the paper, and he had to study it closely to make out the words. He knew the labored writing was Claire's and understood the incredible effort it must have taken for her to write it:

I wanted these to stay in the family.
Please see that they do.
All my love,
Claire Winters.

Pinching the gold wedding band and the platinum band of the diamond engagement ring between his left thumb and forefinger, Keren's chest tightened as he gazed at them. The rings represented so much history and love. He closed them in his hand, leaned his elbows on his desk and pressed his fists into his forehead as his anguish welled within him.

It was bad enough that he'd disappointed Cady. Now he had to disappoint Claire, too.

Keren lay in bed, restlessly moving beneath his flannel sheets. Rolling onto his back, he tucked one hand under his pillow and stared at the swirled plaster ceiling. His Christmas Eve shift was complete and he had a four-hour break before he had to return to Raines-Hartley for a tour of duty in the ER. Since he had no family obligations, every year he volunteered to take an ER shift, to allow someone else to spend that time with family.

Every time he closed his eyes, he saw Cady. Every time he moved his nude body against the soft sheets, he thought of her, and how big his bed was without her in it. Every part of him missed her and seemed to groan in frustration as he thought of her.

He had become familiar with the Winters clan in the course of Claire's illness. Claire had treated him like family and made him want to become a part of that family. He had seen how her people interacted, how they fought, defended and loved each other. The funeral and repast had shown him exactly what he was missing and exactly what he wanted most in his life. He wanted children of his own, a family of his own, and he wanted them with Cady.

He wanted Clarence to show him his "scapular" and "vertabrer," and for Danielle to introduce him to her dolls. He wanted to sit with the rest of the husbands, talking about sports and mortgages over coffee after dinner. He turned onto his side and his eyes fell on the little white box sitting on his nightstand. Claire had wanted it, too. She hadn't exactly spelled it out in her note, but her meaning was clear. But he couldn't even get Cady to talk to him, let alone marry him. And there was one more little problem: the fact that she didn't love him.

"Do I even want to know what that is?" Keren said. He stared at the oddly shaped object Zweli had propped on the ER dispatch counter. The gift was covered in gold foil wrapping and satiny brown ribbon. Zweli began composing a message in a Christmas card as Keren attempted to figure out what the gift was by lifting it.

"It's a Christmas present for Kyla," Zweli said. "I'm on my way over there now."

"How was she when you left the house last night?" Keren asked.

"Better," Zweli said. "It just sort of hit her all at once, you know?"

Keren nodded. "This thing must weigh at least ten pounds. What is it?"

Zweli, grinning, picked up the gift and held it by its narrowest part. With exaggerated humility, he said, "I'd like to thank the Academy, and everyone who supported my career…it's an Oscar. It's a fake, but a great copy."

"Man, Kyla will love this."

"That's the plan." Zweli returned to his gift card. "On her website she says that her ultimate goal is to find a good man and to receive an Oscar. I can handle the Oscar part."

"Kyla has a website?"

"All the actresses do these days. Kyla actually makes money off hers. She's popular. Yesterday she told me that she's received over one thousand hits on her site from the *St. Louis News-Chronicle* alone. The more hits she gets, the more advertisers pay to appear on her site. She's a smart business lady."

"When is she going back to Los Angeles?" Keren asked.

"She was planning to leave after New Year's, but I'm going to persuade her to stay longer. Maybe even for good."

"Really?"

"I know it'll be a crying shame for all the lovely ladies I'll be abandoning, but I'm not one to pass up a golden opportunity."

"Wait a minute," Keren began. "You're not…"

"Yes, I am," Zweli laughed. "I'm going to ask Kyla to marry me."

Stunned, Keren took a half step back.

"She's smart, she's hot, she's got a great sense of humor and a great family," Zweli said. "She's the only woman I've ever met who plays the game better than I do. I can't imagine spending the rest of my life with any other woman."

Keren was speechless. He didn't know whether he was more shocked by Zweli's impassioned confession or the fact that Zweli felt about Kyla the same way he himself felt about Cady.

"I know," Zweli said. "It surprised me, too."

"When are you going to ask her?"

"At my New Year's Eve party, to which you have a standing invitation," Zweli said. "I'm inviting Abby, Clara and Ciel, and their husbands, too."

"What about Cady?"

Zweli stared at him for a second. "She's leaving for Boston. Today. I thought you knew."

Keren cast his eyes downward and shook his head. "I don't know much about Cady lately. Not much at all."

"She should be stopping by fifteen soon," Zweli added. "She wanted to drop off some presents for Mrs. Ippolito and Mr. Millbrook and some of the other patients and nurses."

Keren took up a chart. Rather than assigning the patient to a resident, he decided to take the case himself. "Give my best to Abby and the rest. I have a patient to see."

Zweli wasn't fooled by Keren's cloak of professionalism. "Don't let her leave without talking to her, K.," he warned. "She's mad now, but she can't stay mad forever."

"I don't know about that, Zweli," Keren said. "After yesterday, maybe some distance would be a good idea."

"Maybe," Zweli agreed as he buttoned his jacket and picked up the fake Oscar. "But I doubt it."

Cady stood at the reception desk on fifteen, an empty plastic sack dangling from her right hand. She had delivered her Christmas presents, along with felt stockings she had made and filled with Lindt chocolate truffles and gourmet jams and jellies for the doctors that had cared for Claire. Renyatta sat at the reception desk, hugging her gift to her sturdy bosom.

"Girl, you know red is my color!" She stroked the fuzzy mohair of the sweater Cady had ordered especially for her from a boutique in Boston. "You must have spent a fortune spoiling us with these nice gifts."

"It's the least I can do," Cady said. She spoke to Renyatta although her eyes were trained on the corridor leading to the doctors' offices. "You took such good care of Claire."

Renyatta slightly stood, to see what Cady was looking at. The corridor was empty, so Renyatta sat back down. "What time does your plane leave?"

"In two hours," Cady said.

"So why are you still hanging around here?" Renyatta asked. The nimbus of fluorescent light at the desk cast odd shadows on Renyatta's face, making her look like a gypsy from a black and white movie. "Are you rethinking your decision to leave?"

"Absolutely not," Cady said.

"Well, I think that maybe you're hanging around to give Keren one more chance to get on your nerves."

A blush borne of guilt warmed Cady's skin. "Is he here today?"

"He's here every Christmas," Renyatta said. "He's got no family and it doesn't seem like he's got any friends. Your mama invited him and my family to your house for dinner. I'm on until nine, so I can't make it, much as I'd like to."

"Is Keren going?" Cady picked at the cuticle of her right thumb as she waited for Renyatta's answer.

"Don't know."

"Is he in his office?"

"No, he's covering the Emergency Room. He always works the ER on Christmas to give some parent the day with his family."

Cady's heart thawed a bit at his consideration. For others. She heartily wished that he'd shown her half as much concern the day Claire passed. Cady reached over the low counter and hugged Renyatta. "You take care of yourself, hear?"

"You too, Cady," Renyatta said. "And come visit us soon. Okay?"

Cady cast another longing look down the corridor. "We'll see," she said.

CHAPTER TWELVE

Cady stared at the blank document on the computer monitor in the center of her desk. She had come back to the office the day after Christmas, and was surprised and flattered by the round of applause her co-workers had given her. The idea for a story had come to her in the course of her visits to Raines-Hartley, and since returning she'd spent three straight days in the newspaper's library gathering research. Now she was ready to turn her notes into easily digestible information. Or so she thought. The harder she stared at the blank screen, the easier her words eluded her.

She'd thought going back to work immediately was the best thing to do. She'd gathered her mail, two U.S. Postal Service bins full of press releases, invitations, announcements, tear sheets, magazines, departmental memos, union newsletters and guild updates, and had spent three hours listening to her voice mail messages before they had started to blur into just so much electronic noise. She had logged onto her company e-mail account only to log right back out rather than read the hundreds of new messages that had been sent to her over the past five months.

She had thought she was fine, or close enough to it, until she had begun organizing the clutter that had mounted on her desk in her absence. She had lifted a pile of newspapers and found a framed picture of herself and Claire. The picture was small, only 2" x 3", a tourist shot taken at the end of a Duck Boat Tour during Claire's last visit to Boston. Cady had held onto the photo, smiling at Claire, who was literally the picture of health. Her silver hair and her smile gleamed in the sunlight. A 35mm camera she'd bought specifically for the trip hung from her neck and sat snugly in the middle of her ample bosom. She wore a denim jacket that she had picked up for pocket change at Filene's Basement and a pair of pink Nikes that had logged miles in the Common, the Public Gardens, Fenway Park and the Franklin Park Zoo.

The memory of Claire's visit had made Cady nauseous with longing for her grandmother. Even though she had shoved the picture into her desk drawer, it had worked its spell. Cady's thoughts turned to Claire and they stayed there.

She had accepted condolences from her friends and co-workers without hearing them and listened to five months' worth of gossip, nodding and saying "Uh huh," in the appropriate places without really understanding or caring what was said.

When Sean Murphy, her editor, called her into his office on New Year's Eve to run down potential stories, Cady couldn't muster her usual enthusiasm.

"The weather's fairly mild tonight, so there should be a substantial turnout for the First Night festivities," Sean said. "You could do a reaction piece, interviewing the man on the street about what he thought was hot and what wasn't. It's a fluff piece, but you could balance it with a crime report. Good weather and holiday booze always lead to an attempted murder or two."

"Sure," Cady said vacantly.

"If you feel like getting dressed up, there's a shindig at the World Trade Center." Sean used a ballpoint pen to tap his notepad. "The governor will be there to do the count-down and toast in the New Year. The event is a fundraiser for the Josiah Hugh Children's Fund, and as you know, there's been an internal investigation as to how the Fund has been using their donations. This would be a great story for you, Cady. You're good at getting people to talk to you about things they'd rather not talk about."

"Uh huh," Cady mumbled.

Sean left his chair and rounded the front of his desk. He leaned his heavy frame against the desk and crossed his arms over his chest. "The Castle Beach Polar Club is having their annual skinny dip at midnight. I thought you could join them this year. I'll send a photographer and we could run a front page photo of you in the buff, jumping into the harbor with a bunch of naked geriatrics." Cady didn't respond. "We'd sell a million papers with that cover."

"I'm sorry, Sean," Cady said, snapping out of her fugue. "You said something about the weather?"

Sean took a few quick steps and closed his door. Then he pulled a chair up beside Cady and sat down. As he looked her in the eye, he asked, "Are you ready to come back, kiddo?"

Cady wanted to say that she was fine. That she was fired up and ready to tackle dishonest politicians, convicted drug lords, disgraced businessmen and deceitful lawyers. Sean had been her editor for ten years and had taught her just about all she knew about being a reporter, particularly how to tell when a subject was lying. Cady could hide her personal tells from most people, but not Sean. His blue eyes could read the truth in her face, no matter what her mouth said.

She shook her head.

"You haven't been the same person since you came back, Cady." Sean patted her shoulder as he stood. "I knew something was up when you came back to work and didn't park your car in the publisher's reserved spot. You know, that's how I always know when you're in the newsroom. Rex Wrentham calls me, cussing and spitting about your car."

Cady mustered a weak smile.

"I know you were close to your grandmother," Sean said. "You still have a month of your leave left. Why don't you take it? Spend some more time with your family."

"I can't go back to St. Louis," Cady said. The last thing she needed was to be in the same time zone with Keren Bailey.

"This isn't just about your grandmother, is it?" Sean asked knowingly.

Cady didn't answer. Sean was a good editor and a fair boss, but his question bordered on a line she didn't want to cross. She had fought too long and too hard for Sean's respect to let him see that in a moment of weakness, she had let a man get under her skin. Standing up, she shoved her hands into the back pockets of her jeans. "I think I will take the rest of my leave," she said, offering her hand. He shook it. "Thanks, Sean."

"You *are* coming back in a month, aren't you?" Sean said. "You're making it seem like this is goodbye forever."

"I'll be back," Cady said, dropping her eyes. *I think,* she added to herself.

First Night took on a new meaning for Cady as she sat on the wrought-iron fire escape outside her bedroom window. In a way, this felt like the first night of the rest of her life; a life that seemed far less full, now that she was actually spending some time thinking about it.

People lose people all the time, she thought. Mama lost Daddy, Claire lost Grandpa Hank...Keren lost me.

She felt the heat of tears behind her eyes. She couldn't think of Claire without thinking of Keren, and vice versa. She had known Claire all her life and Keren for only a few months, yet the loss of each hurt equally. The pain was fast becoming too much to bear. She pulled her hands inside the sleeves of her mohair sweater. The night was mild as Sean had predicted, but mild for First Night in Boston was still only thirty-nine degrees.

Cady was out on the fire escape because she felt she didn't have anyplace else to go. But that wasn't completely true. She had been invited to at least ten New Year's Eve parties, including Rex Wrentham's. Though he hated her parking in his reserved space, he never tired of seeing her in an evening gown. Cady had contemplated going for a half second, maybe wearing the backless mini she'd worn to the Raines-Hartley holiday party.

Thinking of the dress had stirred up emotions and memories that she still struggled to suppress. She had worn that dress on the most perfect night of her life, a night when she had both Claire and Keren.

Tonight, First Night, she had neither. New Year's Eve revelers laughed and talked four stories below her as they moved to and from parties and pubs in anticipation of the new year to be born in a few hours.

Cady's one-bedroom apartment was small and over-priced, even for Boston. But the exorbitant rent was worth every cent twice a year: on the Fourth of July and on New Year's Eve. Boston celebrated each holiday with grand fireworks displays on the Charles River at the Esplanade. People came from all over New England and began lining up at dawn to get a view that was only half as good as the one Cady had from her wide living room windows. In past years, Cady would start New Year's Eve at a party or restaurant, and then retire to her apartment with a small, select group of friends to watch the fireworks over the Charles as they popped open a bottle—or two or three—of Cristal.

This year, Cady's drapes were drawn tight when the fireworks began to fill the night with sound and color and the scent of gunpowder. Drunk on her own tears, Cady had retreated from the rousing celebrations below her and climbed back into her dark bedroom. Since the New Year came to her before it reached her family in St. Louis and California, Cady usually rang them no later than 12:05 Eastern Time, to wish them a happy New Year.

But this year, Cady lay on her neatly made bed and pulled a corner of the duvet over her head. Her tears spilled forth all at once, with no sniffling preamble. "I miss you!"

she whispered urgently, mourning Claire and Keren equally.

Keren stood alone on the terrace of Zweli's penthouse, watching moonlight shatter upon the dark waters of the Mississippi River just behind the gleaming Gateway Arch. On the warm side of the glittering wall of French doors behind him, Zweli's annual New Year's Eve party was fast becoming an historical event. The women outnumbered the men three to one, and each woman was prettier than the last. Zweli's female guests had plagued Keren all night, slinking up to him in their five-inch heels and brushing their body parts against him. Keren hid out on the terrace in the frigid air to escape the brazen, boozy, buxom women.

Bodies writhed in orgiastic dances to pounding music in the penthouse while Keren lost himself in quiet thought outside. He pondered why Cady had reacted so extremely to his failure to call her about Claire. When he wore out that chain of thought, he began wrestling with his memories of the moments in his office, right after Claire's death, when he could have made the call.

Why didn't I? he wondered.

The answer came easily: because he hadn't wanted to be the one to hurt her. With that, the error of his decision hit him. It was the *message* that would have hurt Cady, not the messenger. Even so, he adamantly believed that the news should have come from one of her sisters, her mother or even Renyatta.

"Why should I have been the one to tell her?" he asked aloud.

Yes, they had shared an incredible night of intimacy, on all levels, but still…he wasn't family.

Keren thought back to his mother's last days, and how angry he'd been at his father, who hadn't told him that his mother had died. Keren's Great Aunt Bernadetta had come into his room, crushing his Hot Wheels into the wood flooring and filling the room with the scent of mothballs and lavender toilet water. Bernadetta was a big woman. She had grabbed him and smothered his head in her marsh-mallowy bosom when she'd said, "Your mama's with the angels, Keren. It's just you and Sammy K. now."

"Sammy K." was what she'd always called her nephew, Keren's father. The adult Keren recalled how even at nine years old, he had hated Great Aunt Bernadetta for telling him that his mother was gone. And he'd been furious with Sammy K.

"He should have told me himself," Keren muttered, feeling the old hurt anew. "Something like that should always come from someone you love, not some…"

Keren slapped a hand over his face as understanding washed over him. Cady loved him. She was mad at him because he had disappointed her by not being there for her the one time she truly needed him. But none of it would have mattered if she didn't love him.

He should have put it all together at the repast after Claire's service, when Cady got so upset at Chiara's absence. Cady could take disappointment from anyone, except the people she loved.

"That's it," he said. "Cady loves me."

Keren hurried back into the penthouse to find a phone.

Keren was still trying to work his way through the packed room when Zweli, dressed to thrill in his Armani tuxedo, leaped onto the dais-like elevation that led to the French doors of the terrace. He made a slashing motion with his hand at his throat, cueing the DJ to stop the music, and pulled Kyla up beside him. Together, the two of them led the countdown of the final ten seconds of the old year.

"Ten! Nine! Eight! Seven!" the crowd chanted along with them, drowning out Keren's 'Excuse me's' and 'Pardon me's.'

"Six! Five! Four! Three!" they went on as people settled comfortably into twosomes in preparation for their New Year's kisses.

"Two! One! *Happy New Year!*" Zweli's party culminated in an ear-splitting cheer accompanied by horns, whistles, kissing and hugging. Keren was pinned among a group of kissing couples. He caught sight of Zweli and Kyla locked in a passionate kiss against sunbursts of red, blue, gold and green blurred by the condensation on the French doors as fireworks exploded over the Mississippi. Streamers, confetti and metallic-colored balloons floated about them as Zweli broke from the kiss and pulled a ring box from his inner breast pocket. Still embracing Kyla with one arm, he handed the box to her. She took it, her expression curious.

She said something, but Keren couldn't hear a word over the noise. When she opened the box, her jaw slowly dropped and she froze, the silvery-red fringe of her skintight dress shimmering around her.

From his vantage point halfway across the large room, Keren could see the blinding glint of light off the rock in the box just before Kyla snapped it shut and handed it back to Zweli. Though Kyla smiled and spoke all the while, Zweli's face fell as he let her lead him away from the French doors and into another room.

The crowd dispersed as most of the partygoers went out onto the terrace to watch the fireworks. Free to move, Keren doubled his efforts to find a phone. He didn't want his New Year to begin the way Zweli's obviously had.

Every phone, including the one in the shower, was being used. Keren borrowed Zweli's cell phone and then stepped into a utility closet in the kitchen to give himself a measure of quiet and solitude. He called long-distance information to retrieve Cady's number. As the automated operator searched for it, he made a New Year's wish, hoping and praying that she wasn't unlisted. He allowed the automated connection, and then anxiously waited while her phone rang.

Although he had hoped she would pick up herself, she didn't and he inwardly chastised himself for expecting her to be in on New Year's. He took it as a sign of her emotional healing that she had gone out and celebrated the New Year.

After a long series of short beeps and one long beep, Keren cleared his throat and began a message.

"I owe you an apology," he started. "That's not true. I owe you so much more. I'm sorry for letting you down and for not recognizing the trust…and love…you placed in me. I should have been the one to tell you about Claire. I know that now, and I know why. I wish I didn't have to do this by phone, but I wanted to talk to you as soon as I could. I wanted to apologize. Call me when you get this message, Cady. I'll be waiting."

He hadn't known what he would say until after he had said it. He ended the call, hoping that he had said enough.

Cady awoke uneasily from a restless sleep. The phone had become an unwelcome intruder, ringing almost incessantly from midnight on. The New Year was only a few hours old as Cady stood over her telephone, in the dark, pressing the MESSAGE button on her answering machine. Her machine had a Caller ID function, so she could see who the call originated from before deciding whether or not to listen to the message.

The first several calls were local, from friends at the *Herald-Star*. The next several numbers were from Clara, Ciel and her mother, and from relatives and friends in St. Louis. The name attached to the last number generated a weak spark of interest: Randall, Zweli. But then Cady remembered Zweli's New Year's Eve party, and that Kyla had planned to attend. Figuring that Kyla had made the call from Zweli's phone, Cady erased that message without listening to it, along with all the others.

With only the light of the moon through her sheer curtains to guide her, Cady went to the bathroom before returning to bed. The nest she had made atop her bed within her duvet had cooled in her absence, and Cady shivered inside it, too numb with despair to make the effort to go into the living room to raise the temperature on the thermostat. She was on the fringe of sleep, in that drowsy twilight between wakefulness and oblivion, when she had a flash of regret at not having listened to her messages, or at least saved them.

They probably just wanted to wish me a happy New Year, she told herself. With that, she was glad that she had erased them. There was nothing happy about this particular New Year, and the last thing she wanted was to be subjected to someone else's good cheer.

Her tears began all over again when she thought of her mother and her sisters, and especially of Kyla. They of all people should have known that there wasn't a damn thing worth celebrating.

CHAPTER THIRTEEN

By Martin Luther King Jr. Day, Zweli was ready to discuss what had happened between him and Kyla on New Year's Eve. As Keren and Zweli sat in the Raines-Hartley cafeteria, presumably to discuss a patient over lunch, talk invariably turned to two of the Winters sisters. Keren placed a dark red apple sideways on a paper plate before slicing it in half as he listened to Zweli spill his heart.

"The player got played," Zweli said with a pained sigh. "My proposal caught her off guard, I know. That was the whole point—to surprise her. But she surprised me. We went into one of the bedrooms, she sat me down, and damned if she didn't give me my own speech. And since she's an actress, she delivered it better that I ever did."

"What's the speech?" Keren asked. His relationships seemed to die of mutual boredom rather than end as a result of a calculated act on one part or the other.

"The 'I'm not ready for such a major step in our relationship, let's just be friends, why ruin what we've got, blah, blah, blah, etc.' speech." Zweli had a full meal before him, spaghetti with turkey meatballs, corn on the cob, lemon whip gelatin and a hot buttered roll, yet he'd touched nothing but his coffee.

"You only knew each other for a few weeks," Keren said. "What would you have done, honestly, if she had said yes? Would you be planning a wedding right now?"

Zweli pinned him with a wounded stare. "We would probably be finishing up our honeymoon if she had said yes. I would have flown us to Las Vegas and we would have been married on New Year's Day. I had the plane tickets, the chapel booked and a suite at the Venetian reserved." Zweli leaned forward in his chair and rested his elbows on the table, hooding his face with his hands. "I was so sure that she would say yes. There was something real between us, K. But she walked away from it."

"Maybe it's for the best that she said no. You two are so much alike, you would have ended up hating each other."

"Ain't that the pot trash talkin' the kettle," Zweli said, dropping his hands. "You and Cady are practically the same person."

Keren laughed. "Cady and I couldn't be more different."

"You're both intense. Stubborn. Inflexible in your ways. Picky."

"Picky?" Keren spat. "I'm not picky."

"I can't remember the last time you spoke to a woman, let alone hooked up," Zweli said. "And Kyla told me that Cady hasn't had a serious, long-term relationship in years."

"Claire told me that Cady dated an attorney named Cornrow for almost two years," Keren volunteered.

"Cornrow?"

"Claire couldn't remember his real name, so she called him Cornrow. She didn't like him."

"Whatever his name was, Kyla said that Cady dated him, but refused to *date* him. Cady's wild but she's cautious. Apparently she never completely trusted Cornrow."

"I wonder why she put up with him for so long," Keren said.

"Maybe she needed an escort for those newspaper events she gets sent to," Zweli guessed. "Who knows why women put up with men that are wrong for them."

Keren absently swirled his spoon in his bowl of beef lentil soup. "I suppose she's back with him now."

"They broke up for good in August, right before Cady came home."

"If Cornrow has half a brain, he'll be trying to get her back," Keren said.

"Cady doesn't want him back. She wants you. That's two more things you two have in common. You want each other, and you're both too stupid to do anything about it." Zweli looked up as an attractive woman, an administrative assistant that had been eyeing Zweli for some weeks now, passed by in a beige business suit. The blouse was low cut, the jacket was too snug and the skirt was too high—just the sort of business Zweli was accustomed to. With a flip of her dark hair she smiled over her shoulder at the two handsome doctors.

Zweli sat up straighter and answered her smile, but it didn't quite reach his eyes. "With Kyla back in California to stay, I guess I'm back on the market," he said. "Excuse me, Dr. Bailey."

Keren watched as Zweli half-heartedly pursued the woman. She made it easy for him, slowing her pace. They spent a moment talking before the woman, with another flip of her hair, withdrew a pen from the breast pocket of Zweli's white coat. She used it to write something, Keren assumed it was her phone number, on the heel of Zweli's hand before they left the cafeteria together.

Keren sat alone, wondering how Zweli could attach himself to another woman so soon. His heartbreak had seemed genuine. Usually Zweli talked nonstop about a woman after he'd been dumped or dumped someone, but he hadn't mentioned Kyla at all until this lunch date. Keren supposed that was just Zweli's way, to cloak his hurt and disappointment by going after the next pretty thing.

Keren knew that he couldn't do that. Several of the women from Zweli's party had called him since then, to invite him to dinner or for drinks or to skip both entirely and go straight to the intimate frolicking drinks and dinner could lead to. Cady hadn't returned his call, and thinking she was still mad at him, he hadn't tried to reach her again. Even if he never spoke to her again, he was sure of one thing: no other woman would ever captivate him as Cady had.

As he went about his day to day activities, going to work, to the market, jogging through the park and working out at the gym, he noticed other woman but saw only how they came up short when compared to Cady. The cashier at Dierberg's had beautiful eyes, but they seemed dull, lifeless and lopsided against his memory of Cady's eyes. The woman who had volunteered to spot him on the bench press at the gym had gorgeous legs, but she might as well have had rickets when he compared them to the poetic beauty of Cady's legs. One of his patients had a young daughter with a head full of multicolored curls, and looking at her, all Keren could think of was how wonderful it would be to make a daughter with Cady, a daughter with Cady's magnificent hair.

He saw Cady's smile in the sunrise. He felt the whisper of her caresses in his dreams, when he tossed and turned in his big, empty bed. Cady had moved into his life and into his heart, and nothing short of a surgical procedure could remove her. Keren stood up with his tray and decided that he didn't want her removed. He acknowledged that Zweli had made some valid points, but he hotly disagreed with one of them.

Cady's not stupid and neither am I, Keren told himself as he ditched his tray of half-eaten food. I want her back, and I'm going to find a way to get her back.

Abby's kitchen was a chaotic mess of dirty mixing bowls, steaming pots, sizzling pans and the sweet and savory aromas of all the dishes she was cooking for a family dinner that night. As cool and elegant as always, Abby stood at the cluttered table in the center of all that chaos. She had been cooking for hours, yet not a hair was out of place, and she hadn't even broken a sweat. Keren's unexpected visit had come as a welcome surprise rather than an inconvenience. Setting him to work snapping and stringing a small hill of fresh green beans, she spoke to him while she measured out the ingredients for cornbread.

"Clara and her brood are coming tonight and so are Ciel and her people," Abby said as she poured cornmeal into one bowl, and milk into a separate, smaller bowl. "This will be our first dinner together since Claire passed. I'm using Claire's recipes, but I've never been as good at duplicating them as Cady is. Claire always cooked with her senses instead of measuring things out. It was like pulling teeth, getting a recipe out of her. I have yet to successfully duplicate her cornbread." Abby propped her hands on her hips as she said, "When I first married Zachary, I once called her, to ask how much milk I should put in her recipe for cornbread. You know what she said?" Abby didn't wait for an answer. "She said, 'I don't know. Put in enough so that it looks right.' " Abby laughed as she shared the fond memory. "Claire would have a set list of ingredients, but she relied on how a dish looked, smelled or tasted to determine how much of something she would use."

Keren enjoyed listening to Abby and watching her move from the table, where she mixed her cornbread, to the stove, where she stirred her pots of mustard and collard greens, and to the oven, where she basted her ham and her eye of round. The succulent aromas made Keren's stomach rumble. He marveled at the way Abby seamlessly moved from one task to the other and he derived sublime pleasure from sitting in the hot, sunlit kitchen with her. All at once he understood what it meant when people referred to the kitchen as the heart of the home. The meaning of it was right there in front of him, as he watched Abby slavishly prepare a big dinner for her family.

"I should get a doctor to snap and string my beans all the time," Abby smiled, noting Keren's quick and efficient work. She took the colander full of the beans he'd snapped and shook it. "I bet if I measured each bean, they'd all be the exact same size. And no strings hanging off the ends, either." She set the colander back down. "You're going to make some woman a very helpful husband someday, Dr. Bailey."

"That's sort of what brought me here this afternoon, Mrs. Winters," he said. "I want to...court...Cady."

Abby stopped stirring the wet ingredients into the dry ones for her cornbread. "You want to what her?"

"Court her. Woo her. I want her to be a part of my life on a more long-term, permanent basis."

Abby resumed her stirring. "Are you asking for my blessing to pursue my daughter? You already have it. I gave it to you on Christmas Day."

"I need more than your blessing, ma'am. I need your help."

"You could start by calling her. She can't stay mad at you forever, and it's been about three weeks since she fell out with you." Abby pulled a heated cast-iron skillet from the oven and poured the cornbread batter into it, using a rubber spatula to scrape down the sides of the bowl.

"I called her on New Year's," Keren said. "She never called back."

Abby squeezed the cornbread into the oven, between the ham and the beef roast, and turned back to Keren, her brow drawn in concern. "Clara and Ciel and I called her, too. I didn't get through to her, and I don't think they did, either. No one's heard from her since she left."

"I'm worried about her," Keren said. "I love her and I know that she's still hurting."

"I wish I knew what to tell you, Dr. Bailey. This is more Claire's area than mine."

"Maybe I should send her some flowers," Keren suggested.

Abby shook her head. "Ciel's the flower person. She'll forgive anything if the apology comes with plantings for her garden, or two dozen red roses."

"I could send her one of those baskets from the hospital gift shop," he said. "They have a stuffed animal and chocolates and jelly and things like that. The patients seem to really enjoy them."

"That's Kyla's thing," Abby said. "She's like a ferret when it comes to gift baskets. She likes the little goodies all piled up."

"Maybe I should just write her a letter." He'd already written her letters. He just hadn't had the courage to send them.

"A letter is just a phone call on paper. Too easy for Cady to ignore." Abby fell deep into thought as she removed the ham from the oven. Keren's eyes widened at the size of the thing, and the strength Abby must have to heave it onto the countertop. The ham was garishly decorated with pineapple rings, maraschino cherries and cloves. Abby maintained her thoughtful silence as she began to brush the ham with an orange and brown sugar glaze. "I've got it," she said abruptly. She hastily finished glazing the ham and stuck it back in the oven, rounded the table and took Keren by the hand. "Come with me."

Abby pulled him into the finished basement, to the storage rooms in the farthest corners. Keren helped her move boxes neatly labeled with names, dates and contents before she finally dragged out a box with CADY'S TREA-

SURES neatly lettered on it. She coughed as she stirred up a cloud of dust when she removed the lid. She sorted through Nike rollerskates with orange wheels, rainbow suspenders, a worn, dog-eared paperback copy of *To Kill A Mockingbird*, a collection of baseball cards bound by a rubber band, a blue first place spelling bee ribbon, several spiral-bound notebooks covered with doodles and boys' names, a handwritten play titled *Disco CinderFella* and a host of other things that reminded Abby so much of Cady that she couldn't bear to get rid of them. At the bottom of the box she found what she'd been looking for.

She handed her discovery to Keren. It was a cassette tape, the heavy black plastic kind with metal screws, and it was so old and worn, the title and the names of the songs had been rubbed off.

"Cady listened to this tape all day, every day, the summer she turned eight," Abby said as she covered Cady's treasures and slid the box back into place. "You'll find a way to reach her with it."

Cady couldn't remember if she had eaten or not, nor did she care. She sat at the small circle of her kitchen table and picked at a blueberry muffin. When she'd returned to Boston, she'd gone food shopping, but little thought had gone into her selections. Chicken had gone into her freezer and was still there. Lettuce was shriveling in her crisper, and the cucumbers were now a bag of green goo. The wonder of preservatives had kept the muffins palatable, but for the most part, Cady was living on canned goods straight from the can.

Six months ago, Cady could have counted on one hand the number of times she had eaten in during the year. She ordered lunch out every day at the paper and she sometimes grabbed dinner on the fly in the course of covering a story. More often than not, her stories took place at events where she could eat all the rubber chicken and cheese cubes she could hold.

She often ate out with friends, or with Courtland. She was a regular at Legal Seafoods, which served the wood-grilled scallops she could eat by the handfuls, and at Bob the Chef's Jazz Café, which had the best soul food on the East coast. And then there was Magnolia's in Cambridge, which offered Cajun-style Southern cuisine that was so good, Cady had once actually licked her plate.

But Cady had no cravings for any of her favorites as she plucked a crumb from the muffin and put it in her mouth. Food had no flavor to her, and her body seemed unable to digest anything anyway. All she wanted to do was sleep. She padded about her apartment in old sweatclothes, changing them only when she remembered to bathe. She didn't phone anyone, and it scarcely registered in her brain when the phone rang. She didn't collect her mail or answer the door when a deliveryman rang to leave a package. She didn't turn on the television, stereo or the lights, or even open her curtains. At night, when it became too dark to see, she closed her eyes and slept in her bed or on her sofa, whichever was closest when she wanted to drop.

Cady was lost in her bereavement, and deep inside she knew it. But she didn't care. When the pain of Claire's loss became too much to bear, she retreated inside her memories of her grandmother, closing her eyes tight and envisioning Claire in the kitchen. Cady gasped as she suddenly smelled Claire's biscuits, light and warm and fluffy, the way they always smelled when Claire first pulled them open and served them to her with a dollop of sweet cream butter. Cady breathed deep, afraid to open her eyes and not see the sunny kitchen with the fruit-patterned curtains she and Claire had made, and the old yellow and brown Congoleum tiles Claire scrubbed mercilessly, as if there were an eleventh commandment against waxy build-up.

Cady wallowed freely and deeply in her memories. It could have been an hour ago or a week ago that Sean Murphy had stopped by her place and knocked on her door, telling her that he was worried about not having heard from her in so long. He'd slipped a note under the door, but Cady never read it. She never even noticed it lying there on the hardwood floor of her living room. It was too easy to shut out the misery of the real world when she had the comfort of Claire stored within her heart and her head.

As she infused her lungs with the scent of Claire's biscuits, another memory surfaced. She could almost hear Claire's voice, hollering "You're driving me to distraction with that music!" as she carried her portable tape player through the house, blaring a cassette tape Claire had given her for her eighth birthday. Cady's eyes teared as her memory took a cruel turn and delivered a scratchy tune to her ears.

She wiped her eyes and that gesture chased away the image of Claire clapping her hands over her ears in mock agony while Cady sang along with the tape at the top of her lungs. The image fled but the song remained. Cady stopped breathing as she turned her head toward her living room, where the answering machine was doing what her old portable tape player used to…It was playing a Jackson 5 song.

Cady drew her knees up and set her heels on the edge of her chair, weeping as she recalled how she and her sisters spent the summer of her eighth year dancing and singing to the Jackson 5 cassette tape she had gotten for her birthday from Claire. They'd matched themselves up by birth order to the five Jacksons. Clara got Jackie because he was the oldest, same as she was; Ciel had gotten Tito; Kyla had Marlon; baby Chiara had Michael; and Cady, the third, had gotten the handsome, mellow-voiced man of her dreams: Jermaine.

No amount of Ciel's begging, bullying and bribery had forced Cady to trade Jermaine for Tito. A weak, nasal laugh erupted from Cady as she remembered how Ciel had offered her forty-six pieces of red shoestring licorice and a *MAD Magazine* for Jermaine, but in the end, Tito had grown on Ciel.

Shuffling stiffly over to her answering machine to see which of her sisters had sent her such a sweet keepsake, Cady laughed through her tears. She had to read the name in the digital display panel twice before it registered. Bailey, Keren.

The words of the song, *"Got To Be There,"* took on a whole new meaning, one her eight-year-old heart had never considered, and one her woman's heart couldn't ignore.

There was no message at the end of the song. There was only Keren's phone number.

"Which one was your favorite?"

Keren sat back in his chair, too weak with relief to speak. He had hoped that she would respond to his message, but he never imagined that she would do it so quickly. He had just ejected the Jackson 5 tape from his office stereo when his phone rang. He gripped the receiver, silently thanking God for Cady's call.

He fought to keep his voice even. "Which what was my favorite?"

"I liked Jermaine," Cady said. She sat in the dark, curled up cross-legged on the floor, her back to the bureau supporting her bedroom phone. "I liked his voice. It was like…warm honey. Michael was a singer but Jermaine was a crooner."

"I was always partial to Tito." Keren closed his eyes and savored the sound of her voice. Starved of it for so long, he cherished every word she spoke.

"I…" Her words caught in her throat. She wouldn't have thought she had any tears left, yet a fresh batch clogged her throat. "I miss you."

"I wish you had returned my call." He spun his chair toward the window and sat forward, resting his elbows on his knees.

"I called as soon as I got the song."

"Not this call, the one on New Year's."

"I erased all my calls without listening to them," she admitted.

"Then you never got my apology," he said. He slumped back in the chair and put his feet up on the window ledge. "I know what I did was wrong, Cady. You're absolutely right. I should have been the one to tell you about Claire. I let you down. I'm so sorry for that, and please believe me when I say it won't happen again."

"It's okay." She quietly wiped tears from her cheeks with the cuff of her sweatshirt. "It doesn't matter now."

He abruptly stood and began to pace at his desk. "Yes, it does. Nothing has changed for me, Cady. I still love you. And I think you love me, too."

She covered her eyes with one hand and brought her knees to her chin. He was saying all the right things, but nothing that could change the way things were. "I have to go, Keren."

"Cady, don't hang up," he pleaded. He could tell that she was weeping.

"I don't know what else to say to you," she insisted.

"The writer is at a loss for words?" he gently teased.

"It happens," she sniffed.

"Come home, Cady."

His plea wrenched at her. "I can't. The thought of going back to St. Louis, and knowing that Grandma is gone, just…really hurts."

"Your family is here, Cady," he said. "I'm here."

"They'll just remind me of her even more. They miss her, too. I'm having enough trouble with my own feelings."

He knew how hard it was for her to admit that she was having problems coping with her loss. The fact that she had openly admitted it made him realize how bad off she really was. "It's still fresh," he said. "It's going to hurt. That's natural. But you know, one day it won't."

"It doesn't feel that way," she said. "It hurts deep in my bones. I feel it in my skin."

"I know," he said tenderly, aching to do something to help her. "Do you still have Carmen Ortega's card?"

"Yes," she said.

"Call her. Right now. Or I could talk to her and have her call you."

"I can call," she said over a rush of stinging tears.

"You need to talk to someone, Cady."

"I am talking to someone."

"Who?" he asked.

"You."

He sat back down and ran a hand over his bald head. "I'm not trained in grief management, Cady. I can't give you what you need."

"I don't need a trained counselor!" She didn't bother to mask her tears or her frustration. "I don't need Mama or my sisters or anyone else. I need you!"

"I have some accrued vacation time." He hit a button on his intercom and quickly asked Renyatta to call up his calendar on the computer. "I have about eight months' worth, since I never take vacations. I can schedule a visit to Boston. Would you like that?"

"Yes." With both hands she held the receiver to her ear, as if it were a lifeline. "How soon can you come?"

Renyatta scurried into the office with a printout of Keren's schedule. He stopped her with a raised index finger when she started to leave. He flipped through the pages as he spoke to Cady. "I'll have to arrange for coverage on fifteen, and I have to cancel two speaking engagements and lectures at Washington University, Northwestern and MIT, and a conference in Tucson—"

"When can you come?" Cady asked weakly.

"The end of March looks good."

Renyatta's mouth popped open, then snapped shut at the look Keren gave her. She left the office.

Cady loosened her grip on the phone. *I should have known better than to expect more from him,* she thought dismally.

Her silence began to scare him. "Cady? Is that okay?"

"Sure," she said flatly. "It's fine."

"I'll set the wheels in motion," he said.

"Okay."

"March isn't that far off," he tried to assure her. "January is half over and February's the shortest month. The time will fly by."

Renyatta zoomed back in and said, "Dr. Bailey, we need you for a code."

"I have to go, Cady, it's a code," he said. He hung up.

Cady lowered the receiver and stared at it, her melancholy bleaker than ever before. "See you in March," she whispered.

Keren raced past Renyatta, but doubled back into his office when she didn't follow him. "Nurse, are you coming?" he demanded.

"There's no code," Renyatta said. "I made it up."

Keren faced her, staring down at her with his hands on his hips. "Are you insane, Renyatta?"

"No, but you must be. You're the only person who's heard from Cady since she left. Abby was so worried about her after you talked to her on King day, she sent her boss at the paper to check on her. If you really cared about Cady, you'd go up to Boston and see how she's doing."

"I have patients that need me, remember?" Keren argued. "I can't just pick up and leave."

"Your patients need you because they're sick. Don't confuse that with the way family needs you."

Keren backed away from Renyatta, ashamed that she knew him so well. In the absence of a family of his own, he had attached himself to his work and his patients. He had the luxury of always being surrounded by people, even if their presence was fleeting, impersonal and professional. His patients didn't give him birthday cards or holiday gifts. They didn't cook for him or invite him into their homes and hearts.

But Cady had. Both Claire and Cady had loved him like he was family. They had loved him better than family. And if nothing else, Cady had taught him that when family needed you, you went to them without hesitation.

"Renyatta, I apologize for asking you to do this, and I know you're not a secretary, but—"

Renyatta clapped her hands gleefully as she finished his thought. "You want me to make like a travel agent and book you a flight to Boston?"

"No," he said, temporarily dashing Renyatta's rosy hopes. "Clear my schedule. Effective immediately."

When the phone rang an hour after she had hung up, Cady picked it up on the first ring, hoping it was Keren. It was Kyla, and she started having a conversation whether Cady participated in it or not.

"Zweli asked me to marry him," she began excitedly, as if this were the continuation of a conversation they had already been having. "On New Year's Eve. Can you believe it? At the stroke of midnight he pulls out this little white velvet box and I thought it was a joke. I figured spring-loaded snakes would pop out as soon as I opened it. So I open it, and sitting there on a bed of white satin is a three-karat marquis cut pink diamond—with a platinum band—and he goes, 'Will you be my wife?' Cady, girl, I didn't know what to say, much less what to do. I took him aside and told him that I was flattered but that it was too sudden, there was too much going on in my life and I didn't want to burden him with it. You know, the company line. He should be out here in L.A. He's a natural born actor with a definite flair for the dramatic."

Cady lay on her side in her bed with the receiver balanced over her left ear. "You could do worse than marry Zweli."

"He wasn't serious, Cady," Kyla panted. Cady realized that her sister was calling her on a cell phone while she worked out on a treadmill or a LifeCycle. "He was just having fun at his party, making me a part of the entertainment. He gets bored with women quickly. He told me so. The proposal was something he could do to drum up some excitement."

"I don't know, Ky," Cady said dispassionately. "He seemed to really like you." Cady would never forget how Zweli had comforted Kyla at the cemetery, how he hadn't hesitated to give Kyla what she needed when she needed it most.

"Zweli and I had some good times, in spite of the circumstances," Kyla huffed and puffed. "We didn't connect the one time I made a direct move for him, but he was really there for me when I needed someone at Christmas. But you don't marry someone after knowing him for only six weeks. Well, out here you do, but not in St. Louis. You don't fall in love in six weeks."

"You're right," Cady agreed, the pit of her stomach filling with fresh misery. "You fall in love in an instant." Even though she knew it was futile, she closed her eyes and wished for Keren.

"Zweli loves himself too much," Kyla said. "He's got no room left in his heart to love anyone else."

"Zweli's a good man," Cady said. "You underestimate him."

"Are you on his side or mine?"

"Yours. I understand why you turned him down, but I hope you haven't made a mistake by not taking him seriously."

"Cady, the ring wasn't even real," Kyla insisted. "It couldn't have been. A diamond like that would cost a fortune."

"What if it *was* real?" Cady asked. "What if Zweli really wanted to marry you and to live the rest of his life with you? What if he truly loved you?"

"I'd think that I'd fallen into a really bad script," Kyla said. "That sort of thing is for the movies, not real life."

"You should have given him a chance."

"You gave Keren a chance, and look how that turned out."

That was Kyla. She always knew how to turn the knife to cut a little deeper. "I'm sorry, Kyla, but I have to go," Cady said.

"You don't sound so good," Kyla said, ignorant of the injury she had caused. "Are you alright?"

"I have to go, Ky," Cady said, and she hung up the phone.

CHAPTER FOURTEEN

Keren booked his own flight to Boston and was standing before Cady's door less than eight hours after she'd called him to discuss the finer attributes of Jermaine Jackson. He had knocked three times already and was about to knock a fourth time when the heavy, old-fashioned door opened as wide as the thick brass security chain would allow.

Keren spoke into the dark gap. "Cady," he said. "It's me, Keren. I know it's late…or early, rather, but I couldn't wait until March to see you. I should have called before I came, but there really wasn't time once I booked the earliest flight out of St. Louis, and there was so much turbulence during the flight, passengers weren't allowed to use their cell phones."

He lightly touched his fingertips to her door. "Cady, if you're upset with me, I understand. I'll go away, if that's what you—"

The door swung wide open and Cady flew into his arms as though magnetically drawn to him. Her arms went around his neck as she put as much of her body as she could in contact with his. He hugged her tight as she wept, and wondered if he would ever be able to let her go.

Carrying his bag over one shoulder, he held onto Cady as he backed her into the apartment. He used his foot to kick the door shut with Cady still plastered to him and let his bag slide to the floor so he could kiss her properly. He kissed her tear-stained cheeks and her puffy eyes before claiming her lips to kiss her deeply, thoroughly, making up for all the kisses he hadn't given her since their night together.

Her body was lost within the massive volume of her sweats, but he sought contact with her flesh by slipping his hands beneath her sweatshirt. Cady's tears evaporated in the heat of her love for this man who had dropped everything and come to her. His hands moved over the unobstructed skin of her back and sides. He relished the satiny feel of her, but cringed when he felt the prominence of her spine and ribcage.

Grief had taken a lot out of her, far more than he had thought possible. Cady broke the kiss to look at him, to begin healing herself with the real-life visage she had craved.

"You look terrible," Keren chuckled sadly, taking her face in his hands. Her hair was wilder than usual. There were dark pockets under her tired eyes and her cheeks were gaunt. Grief had ravaged her, yet she was still the most beautiful creature on Earth.

"You look wonderful," she sighed tearfully. "I'm glad you came."

He hugged her to him, wrapping her body around his. "Oh baby, so am I."

Cady's apartment building was already one hundred years old when Keren's condo complex had been built, and he appreciated the quaint architectural details of her apartment. The place was small, by St. Louis standards, but had plenty of room for one person. A short foyer led into the spacious living/dining room, which reflected Cady's tastes and personality. A long, deep, overstuffed sofa covered in black chintz was the dominant fixture in the room. There was a matching armchair with an ottoman, a glass-topped coffee table and a standing console that hid a television and stereo system. The kitchen was a tiny nook off the dining room area, which was almost overwhelmed by a dining table that had once been a barn door in Vermont. Cady had bought the door cheap at an estate sale and had refinished it herself.

Six chairs surrounded the table but Keren guessed that it could accommodate twice that many. He assumed correctly that the table had seen its share of dinner parties with Cady's good cooking covering it.

One of Keren's favorite features in the Beacon Street apartment was the deep bathtub. The lion's claw feet of the tub marked it as a true relic of a bygone era. When he learned that Cady had bought the tub at a hotel auction, Keren complimented her on her savvy purchase. Now Cady sat in her tub, up to her shoulders in warm, softly-scented lather. Keren had drawn the bath for her and lit the candles she kept on the back of the toilet and the windowsill.

By design, he was keeping the lights low and the talk light. He had spoken to Carmen Ortega before he left St. Louis, and her advice to him had been to keep stimulation to a minimum and to follow Cady's lead. If she wanted to talk about Claire, he was to listen. The worst thing he could do was to push her into talking, or even eating or sleeping, before she was ready.

Keren sat on a footstool at the edge of the tub. The sleeves of his white shirt rolled up, he used a natural sponge to squeeze warm water over her exposed knee. He helped her rinse her hair after she washed it with an apple-scented shampoo, then he looked at her, unsure if the moisture on her face was tears or water from her hair. She blinked and he saw new droplets trail down her cheeks. Her pain fast became too much for him to stand, and he reached into the tub and hugged her, half lifting her from the water.

Though the bath seemed to have washed away a layer of misery, Cady's nerves were exposed and raw. She couldn't suppress the wail of sorrow that climbed from her throat as Keren held her. Shivering from the force of her grief, she clung to him with all her strength. She had been strong in St. Louis, unwilling to let anyone see her shed useless tears as she helped her family prepare for Claire's funeral. But alone in Boston, she had allowed herself to cry. In Keren's arms, she allowed herself to bawl. She couldn't hold it in any more and she wet his shirt with tears and scented bathwater.

He rested on his knees, holding her cold, quivering body against the warmth of his chest, smoothing her hair from her face and pressing kisses to her head as she gave voice to the one thing that made it impossible for her to move past her sorrow.

"I should have been there," she admitted woefully. "All the times in my life that she was there for me, and I wasn't there the one time that she needed me. I just can't forgive myself for that."

She wriggled from his embrace and sank back into the tub. She covered her eyes with her hands and sobbed. Keren grabbed a thick towel and used it to dry her face.

"You *were* there," he reminded her. "You were there every day and every night."

She shook her head, dripping tears into her bathwater. "I wasn't, not when it mattered the most. I was with you."

"Cady," he said, "Claire was ready to go. You have to trust me on that."

"You didn't know her!" she cried angrily. "Did you hear a word I said at her service? I told everybody that she loved life, and she did." Cady stood, sending a wave of sudsy water over the edge of the tub. Keren was shocked anew at the sight of her nude body. She couldn't afford to lose all the weight she had. He wrapped a towel around her as she stepped onto the damp bath mat. "Did you know that she had a green thumb?" Cady went on. "She could plant a toothpick and grow a pencil. She could cook like you wouldn't believe. Every barbeque we had was like a block party because our neighbors would come out by the dozens with their plates in their hands, and wait by the grill for a taste of my grandma's ribs and chicken. She could sing, too, but she hardly ever did. When I was little, she would sing to me." Cady winced at the bittersweet memory. "She would sing to me and I always felt better."

She bowed her head into Keren's chest, framing her head with her fists. Her shoulders shook as she cried. "She was my best friend. I was so stupid. I knew she wouldn't be here forever. She told me that, every time I had a fight with my mother or one of my sisters, or had a problem at work and called her to complain about it. I should have found another emotional safety net to give me what she gave me, but I didn't because I didn't think anything else could ever be as good or as reliable as she was."

Keren held her as she spilled her feelings. It was all he could do, for now.

She raised her face and placed her cheek against his shoulder as he began to dry her. "I was so selfish. And the height of my selfishness was me not being there when she died."

Keren took her by the shoulders and held her so he could look into her eyes. He didn't know if Carmen would approve of what he had to say to Cady, but he needed to say something to ease her guilt. "She left when she could, Cady. You wouldn't let her go. She was ready, but she *couldn't* leave, not with you there. The day before you came to St. Louis, Claire asked me about a DNR."

Cady's mouth worked, but no words came out. A DNR, a Do Not Resuscitate order? Signing one would have meant that Claire didn't want heroic measures performed if her heart or breathing stopped.

"That doesn't make sense," Cady said. "She wanted to fight it. She wanted to dance at my wedding and see my children."

"Yes," Keren said. "Your arrival gave her the strength to try to fight it again. You made it impossible for her to leave. She had to go when you weren't there to stop her."

"I miss her!" Cady cried. "I didn't say goodbye and she never said goodbye to me. I left her all alone."

He couldn't hold her closely enough. "She wasn't alone," he told her gently. "I was with her. And her last words were for me, not you." Stunned, Cady searched his face with red-rimmed eyes. "She was ready to go. She knew that you would be cared for. She knew that you would be loved. That's all she wanted for you, Cady, to know that you wouldn't be alone."

"Is that all she said to you?"

"She said that it made her happy to see the two of us together." He cleared the lump that had formed in his own throat when he added, "She said that I was a better man than I knew."

Cady wept and Keren held her until her tears ran dry, until the candles burned down, and until the water in the tub was cold and still. Her exhausted breaths hitched in her chest when Keren lifted her in his arms and carried her into her dark bedroom. He laid her on her bed and spread out beside her, nestling her into his body. He pulled the damp towel from around her and drew the duvet over her.

Just when he thought she was asleep, her voice came to him like a part of the night. "Claire loved you, Keren."

He nodded, the only thing he was certain he could do without shedding tears of his own for Claire Winters.

Cady woke up convinced that she had been asleep for at least a week. It was just after six A.M., but with her bedroom curtains drawn, she couldn't tell if the sun was even shining. She braved the cold morning air by crawling out of Keren's embrace and padding to the windows on her tiptoes, opening the curtains, filling the room with the bright light of morning. The light bathed Keren's sleeping form and Cady's heart surged. She still felt weary in body and mind, but she felt a thousand times better than she had the day before.

Keren was the reason for her renewed spirit. She climbed back into bed and snuggled into the warm hollow beside him, resting her head on his chest and trailing her fingers over the expanse of his chest. His dark skin was as beautiful by day as it was by night. His chest was naturally hairless, but there was a thin trail of curly dark hair on his lower abdomen. Cady couldn't remember him taking his clothes off, but she was glad he was lying nude beside her. She hadn't eaten regularly in weeks, but now, gazing upon the bare physique of the man who had pulled her from the depths of despair, she didn't want food. She wanted Keren.

The radiant heat of the sun or Cady's rising body temperature made her immune to the cold room as she flattened her breasts against Keren's chest and tenderly kissed his earlobes. He stirred and moaned, curling an arm around her, but he didn't wake up. Cady ran a hand over his torso, traveling lower and lower until her fingers found the dark whorls of crisp hair at the place where his thighs met. Her hand moved a bit farther as she kissed his throat and his lips.

Every part of him seemed to awaken with a start. His arms clapped around her, dragging her atop him. He bent one leg, settling her hips against his reaching manhood. His hands roamed over her, reacquainting themselves with the lines and curves and textures of her. He returned her kisses, deepening their intensity.

"Cady," he breathed huskily. "Maybe we should wait…"

She took him in her hand, stroking the rigid velvet of him as she kissed him. "Do you really want to wait?"

He answered her by rolling onto his side, which turned her onto her back. He thrust his fingers into her hair and studied her face. It was more relaxed after her good night's sleep, and the bags under her eyes had faded. Her curls covered the pillow and gleamed in the sunlight. She cupped his face and a slow, easy smile bloomed on her face.

He dropped his face and kissed her. That smile, that lovely, wonderful smile…he hadn't seen it since the night of the Raines-Hartley holiday party. He kissed her, wordlessly thanking her for the gift of her precious smile. Cady returned his kisses, welcoming the taste and heat of his mouth upon hers. His mouth moved lower, peppering her collarbone and her chest with kisses. She gasped and violently arched into him when he took the tight peak of her left breast into his mouth. He used his hands to caress and tease her to the brink of fulfillment as his mouth deliciously tormented her breasts.

She returned the attention by working her hand between his legs, caressing and stroking him until he grunted and grabbed her wrist, stopping her from taking him too far, too fast. He raised her hands over her head and kissed the length of her left arm, from her elbow to her armpit, then kissed his way to her breast. Her breathing became deeper and louder as he drew on her nipples, pleasuring one and then the other, as he moved between her legs. He brought his mouth to hers for a long, penetrating kiss as he pressed the center of his passion to hers, and began a gentle friction. Cady shuddered, forcing her head into the pillow. Keren nipped and kissed her exposed throat, teasing one of her most sensitive areas.

He ran his hand over her right thigh, lifting her leg to his waist. She wrapped both of her shapely legs around him as he slid into her heat in one magnificent thrust. He moved slowly, powerfully, relishing every second of their union. Cady cupped the back of his head with her right hand and draped her left arm over his shoulder as she met his thrusts, creating a sensuous rhythm of her own that heightened their pleasure. She held his gaze as his face tightened and his pace quickened. He felt himself spiraling to unmatched heights of bliss as her hips bucked and she constricted around him again and again. He exploded within her, his eyes never leaving hers. Convinced that his soul had fused with hers in that moment of climax, he stayed with her, nursing more pulses from her with the gentle grind of his body against hers.

When she cupped his face in both hands and pulled him in for a kiss, he lay beside her, never breaking the kiss. He tasted her lips, tenderly suckling the lower one. She teased his tongue with her own, showing him all over again how delightful a kiss could be. Their hands moved restlessly over each other, stilling only when Keren opened his mouth to speak, but then said nothing.

"What is it?" Cady asked tenderly.

He sat up and pressed a hand to his head. He had just shared an amazing experience with the woman he loved, yet there was something on his mind that he couldn't shake. Loving Cady had unleashed a full range of pent-up emotions that left him slightly confused. He swung his legs to the edge of the bed and set his feet on the cold hardwood floor.

Cady sat behind him, framing him between her legs. She hugged him, pressing her chest to his back. "Tell me what's wrong," she said, placing a kiss on his right shoulder blade.

"It's Claire."

His tone scared Cady a little. He always sounded serious, but now he sounded anxious and serious. "Tell me," she said, almost afraid of what he would say.

"Before she died, she told me that she loved me." He sighed and it was the saddest sound Cady had ever heard. "Claire is the only person I remember ever telling me that."

Cady shifted to his left side, to better comfort him. She kneeled on the bed and hugged his head to her chest. "Didn't your mother and father ever tell you that they loved you?"

"I think my mother might have," Keren said. "Right before she died. She was at home in her bedroom. I knew that she was sick, but I never knew how bad it was. I just thought she was tired all the time, because every time we played games or read books, she was in bed. She got weaker and weaker to the point where she couldn't even sit up any more. One day, my father took me into her room. She looked like a ghost. She took my hand and said something to me. All these years, I've hoped that what she said was 'I love you.' "

"Tell me more about your mother," Cady said.

"I have two really vivid memories. I remember one snowy day when I was in kindergarten. School was closed and I was tearing up the house out of boredom. My mother got an apple and some paint, and she taught me how to make apple prints. She cut the apples sideways, so the star showed, and we dipped them in paint. We made apple stars all over the kitchen wall."

"I saw the star," Cady said. "You shared it with me."

"There was another time at Thanksgiving. I was in the first grade and had just learned about wishbones, and I forced my mother to let me pull it with her. She got the big part, but she gave it to me. She gave me her wish."

"How can you doubt that your mother loved you?" Cady said. "She gave you stars and wishes. Whether she said it or not, she loved you."

"I know," he said, his voice breaking. "I wish I'd told her, just once, that I loved her. I don't think I ever told her."

"She knew," Cady said. "You were a kid. Kids show, they don't tell. She knew that you loved her."

"I wish I had more memories of her," he said sadly. "She died of cancer when I was six. Cancer took my father three years later. I never really understood that my parents were sick. Dad, he coughed all the time. They both slept a lot. But my mother…she would read to me. When I was really little, I remember that she used to blow bubbles during my bath time. Then one day, I came home from school and she was just gone. All her clothes were there, her books, her pots and pans, but she had just disappeared."

He clenched his jaw to bite back a rush of emotion. "My father died at New Baptist Hospital. I didn't get to say goodbye to him, either. I was in foster care by then, and he'd been dead for a week before anyone told me."

Cady held him closer, sharing the strength he'd shared with her. "Was the cancer caused by something at the chemical company they worked at?"

Keren lifted his head from her chest. "How do you know about Gerritson?"

"I'm a good researcher, remember?"

He lay back down in the bed. He took Cady with him, holding her close. "Yes. They both worked there. They met there. The whole time they were there, they were exposed to carcinogens. They were part of a class action lawsuit, but both of them died before a settlement was reached. Their share of the award was put into a trust for me."

"Who took care of you?"

"No one. I was sent to the Lindenwood Center for Boys. I lived there until I was fourteen, when I was recruited by Warwick Country Day School."

Cady was impressed. "Warwick is an excellent school. People start trying to enroll their sons there while the kids are still in the womb."

"I was a good student," he said. "I studied hard and worked hard to be polite and well mannered. I thought that would make someone want me. I have a great-aunt and some third or fourth cousins on my father's side, but they fell out of sight when my parents' award was put in a trust.

They didn't want me unless the money came with me, and I couldn't touch it until I was 25. My Great Aunt Bernadetta wanted a monthly stipend of $2,000 plus expenses for me before she would agree to take me in. I won't ever forgive her for abandoning me to the boys' home."

Cady took on the role of caregiver and soothed Keren's festering hurt with kisses and soft caresses. "How long were you at the center?"

"Four years. Warwick took guardianship of me upon my acceptance. That meant I could board at the school during the academic year, through holiday and summer breaks and that upon my graduation, they would receive an endowment equal to the cost of my four years of tuition, room and board. It's called the Keren S. Bailey Scholarship and every four years it's awarded to a qualified minority applicant. At least the money is being put to good use."

"When you were at Warwick, did you ever go home with friends? Or spend a holiday with a teacher?"

Keren uttered a dry laugh. "Friends…My friends were books. I was the richest poor kid at Warwick. The only clothes I had were my school uniforms. The school gave me a fifty-dollar a week allowance, but I didn't have a car to go anywhere to spend it."

"Warwick had a sister school, Shelby Institute," Cady said. "Didn't you go to any of the mixers?"

"How do you know so much about Warwick?" he asked.

"I went to Hamilton-Foxx," Cady said.

"Ah," said Keren. "The alternative hippie prep school."

"And one of Warwick's academic rivals," Cady pointed out. "You were about to tell me about the mixers."

"I met a few girls, here and there," he said. "A couple of them left an impression, but I couldn't really relate to them beyond the physical. That's been a problem in every relationship I've ever had."

"Even me?" Cady asked.

"With you, it's the opposite." He turned her face to his and planted a kiss on her forehead. "I can't seem to hold anything back. I don't want to hold anything back."

"Keren, it means so much to me that you came here and helped me get control of myself, but what do you want from me?"

He didn't want to scare her or burden her needlessly with too much too soon, but he knew exactly what he wanted from her. He wanted a wife. He wanted a mother for the children he hoped to have. He wanted someone to grow old with, and to come home to at night. He wanted someone to love who would love him right back. Basically, he wanted…"Everything," he finally told her.

Cady was moved by the naked honesty of his admission. "Claire was determined to make you a part of the family."

"I love your family," he said.

"Keren…"

"Yes?"

"Are you sure that you still love me?"

He was sorry that she even had to ask as he took her face in his hands and kissed her. "Yes," he said before suckling her sweet lips. "Yes," he repeated after kissing the corners of her wondrous smile. "God, yes," he murmured, the words distorted by the movement of his tongue against hers.

The duvet fell away as their limbs and bodies twined on the bed. Lying on their sides face-to-face, Keren eased her leg over his hip. The brush of his crisp dark fleece against the softer, lighter floss between her own legs sent an erotic charge through her. Still, she had the presence of mind to ask, "What happens now, Keren? I love you. You love me. What comes next?"

He held her questioning gaze and smiled as he said, "You do."

Cady's heart thumped hard at the minor miracle. Keren was a handsome man, but when he smiled, he was divine. His rare smile was as arousing as his touch as he shifted her weight onto his right leg and slid into her, leaving her dizzy with pleasure. He palmed the weight of her breast, teasing its burnished-rose bud into a taut pebble with the pad of his thumb. He allowed her to roll onto her back, pulling him on top of her without separating from him. Keren had freer access to her breasts and he brought his mouth to them, suckling and nipping each in turn until she cried out and clapped her hands over his buttocks. Her dark channel tightened around him. She used her hands to help drive him deeper and deeper with each rhythmic pulse of pleasure. Sweating from the strain of trying to hold back, Keren joined her at the zenith of their lovemaking, adding his heat to hers.

Afterward, as they recovered from their exertions, Cady asked him a question. "When did you know for sure that you loved me?"

He readily answered. "When you noticed the star the day we shared an apple in the cafeteria. Do you know when you fell in love with me?"

Her hair tickled his chest as she nodded. "It was when you banned me from the oncology ward and forced me to talk to Carmen Ortega."

Keren was surprised. "I thought you hated me for that."

She placed her small hand along his cheek. "You helped me when I couldn't help myself. I loved you for it then just as I love you for it now."

"I'm here for two weeks, if you'll have me," he said. "I booked a room at The Copley Plaza. It's nearby and—"

"You're staying right here," Cady insisted. "If I've only got you for two weeks, then I want you right here."

"What happens after the two weeks are up, Cady?" he asked.

"Ask me again then," she said. "Let's just enjoy what we have right now. I can't think about the future just yet. Okay?"

He made himself smile again. "Okay," he agreed. But in fourteen days, he would definitely be asking her about the future and praying that she wanted what he wanted: to build a future together.

CHAPTER FIFTEEN

Ten days into Keren's visit, eight inches of snow blanketed Boston and there was no sign of a let up. Keren and Cady stood looking out her living room windows after breakfast, watching erstwhile commuters fight their way down the slippery, snowy sidewalk.

Keren stood behind Cady, his hands clasped over her middle and her hands resting over his. She leaned her head on his shoulder. "I guess we'll just have to stay in until the streets are plowed."

"I wanted to go to a barber," Keren said.

"I could shave you," Cady offered.

"You wouldn't mind?"

"I like bald men."

He turned her so that she faced him. "Is that so?"

She set her hands on his shoulders, close to his neck, and teased the back of his head. "Not many men have the confidence to carry off the bald look. I've always thought of a bald head as very…sensual. All that exposed skin…All that heat."

"That's it," he said. "I'll never grow hair again."

Cady backed a chair up to the kitchen sink while Keren got his shaving kit and a towel. After he removed his T-shirt and sat, she draped the towel over his broad shoulders, admiring his muscled "V" shape. With a giggle she squirted a big glob of shaving cream onto her palm and very slowly smoothed the cool cream over his head, both of them enjoying the slick softness of the shaving cream against his warm skin. Her body brushed his as she moved around him, very carefully shaving his head. Every time she flicked the razor in the sink, wicking off the shaving cream, her breasts shook within her camisole. The garment was made of cotton, but was as soft and sheer as silk.

"Ready to rinse," she said. Keren hung his head back in the sink and Cady used the sprayer to remove the last traces of shaving cream. The warm water coursing over his head heightened the pleasant sensation of Cady's strong fingers as they massaged his scalp. He watched as water splashed on her camisole and spread, making the garment transparent. The sight of her dark nipples rising against the see-through wetness of her top started him on a path he couldn't travel alone. When she leaned farther over him to rinse behind his ear, her breast aligned perfectly with his mouth and he seized the opportunity. His hands went to her waist, holding her in place as he teased her nipple through the thin fabric.

Rapid, shuddering breaths issued from between her teeth as she rested her elbows on his shoulders and cradled his head to her bosom. Her breasts had always been sensitive, but they were particularly responsive to Keren. She whimpered when he slid his hands under her camisole and thrilled her nipples simultaneously with his hands. Cady straddled him, grinding the damp center of her passion into the hardness at the apex of his thighs.

She placed her hand on his cheek. Her thumb grazed over his full, luscious lips. "I can't get enough of you." Her voice was a husky whisper. "You touch me, and I turn to lava inside."

He cupped her neck, brought her mouth to his and he kissed her luxuriantly, using his tongue to taste and trace every texture of her mouth. She was so sweet. He wondered how a woman could be so delectably sweet, and it wasn't confined to her mouth. The caramel cream of her shoulders, the satiny sugar of her breasts, the silky nectar between her thighs…every part of her stirred his most carnal appetites.

He placed his hands on her upper thighs. Sliding aside the moist triangle of cotton hiding her feminine center, his skilled thumbs kneaded the aching tip of her womanhood, teasing her into a frenzy. She clapped her chest to his, hugging him to her as she covered his mouth with kisses. Her hips rode his thumbs and when she could stand no more, her pleas filled his mouth.

"Now." Her breath mingled with his. "Now. Please."

He gave her what she wanted. She locked her legs around his waist, and in one effortless motion, he lifted her, used his free arm to clear the kitchen table, and pressed her onto it. She pulled his pants open, tugged them down, and drew him to her by imprisoning him within the circle of her strong legs. He plunged into her snug darkness and sent them rocketing to the height of pure sensation. Lacing his fingers through hers, he buried his face in her neck as he gritted his teeth and groaned out his pleasure. Each thrust of his strong, trim hips made Cady cry out in heavenly fulfillment.

Even when her breathing and heart rate had returned to normal, her skin continued to quiver and jump when Keren moved along her body, kissing her most sensitive places. She ran her hands over his smooth head and smiled lazily at the ceiling. "Now this," she giggled, "is what a snow day should be."

"The streets are cleared," Cady said as she brought in her mail. "It's cold but we can't spend another day cooped up in here."

"Yes, we can." Keren drew her down onto the sofa where he was having a cup of coffee and reading the morning *Herald-Star*.

She tugged the paper from his hands and crawled onto him. "Look at you. You're on vacation and you look like…a doctor."

"That's for obvious reasons."

"Don't you ever get tired of being the poster boy for Brooks Brothers?" She flipped his perfectly knotted tie over his shoulder.

Keren looked at what he wore. It was what he always wore: starched and pressed white shirt buttoned up to his throat, pleated wool trousers and a black leather belt with a beeper clipped onto it. "I suppose I do look a little…"

"Stiff." A devilish twinkle appeared in her eyes. "I know. I'm taking you to Newbury Street."

They bundled up, Cady in an oversized parka and striped alpaca hat and mittens, and Keren in his "doctory" Chesterfield, and walked three blocks to Newbury Street. The narrow streets, narrowed further by heaps of plowed snow, were congested. Frustrated drivers honked madly, as if that would make the traffic magically disappear. Despite two close calls with psycho taxi drivers, Cady and Keren made it safely to Boston's strip of premier clothing stores.

They visited half a dozen of the expensive, trendy designer boutiques before Keren stopped and refused to go any farther.

"Given your incredible wardrobe, I should have known that you were a shopaholic," Keren said.

"I hate shopping. I usually go to just one store."

"K-Mart?" he suggested.

"Ha, ha, Doc. Come on." She grabbed his hand and led him down Berkeley Street to Boylston Street. In keeping with Boston tradition, they crossed against the light.

Keren froze. "Not…"

"This is the perfect place." Cady opened the glass doors. Keren's blood froze in his veins as he slowly passed beneath the giant GAP sign and entered the store.

"Abandon all hope, ye who enter," he mumbled under his breath.

They were greeted by an ear-piercing shriek.

The screamer, a tall, thin African-American man dressed in black, grabbed Cady and hugged her, his straight black hair swinging back and forth as he chastised her loud enough for the whole store to hear. "Shame on you for stayin' away so long and makin' me worry. I thought you'd got yourself laid off at the paper or something. It ain't like my baby not to call or write or pop in and buy one of everything."

"I'm sorry, Guy," Cady said. "I had a family emergency to tend to."

Guy planted a saucy fist on his hip. "You been gone five and a half months, Peaches. What kind of emergency takes…" Guy's eyes went wide as he slapped one hand to his mouth and the other to his 30-inch chest. "Grandma?" he squeaked.

Cady looked away as she nodded.

"Oh, honey, I'm so sorry," Guy said, using his normal speaking voice and not the stage one he used to work the floor. "Are you okay?"

Cady nodded. Keren stepped closer to her. Guy studied him from heel to head. Keren looked at him from the corner of his eye. "Now who do we have here?" Guy asked with a sly smile.

"This is Dr. Keren Bailey," Cady said, glad to steer the conversation away from Claire. "He was my grandmother's doctor."

"Charmed." Guy offered his hand, fingers pointing down. Keren tipped his head in a nod. "Baby's playin' doctor with a doctor! Shoot, I would have dived head first into that, and never come up for air."

"Keren needs jeans," Cady said. She cut Guy off before his engine got too warm. "And some shirts."

"Straight leg, wide leg, boot cut, relaxed fit, regular fit, adjustable waist, stretch or distressed," Guy said. "Blue? Or black?"

Keren had no idea what Guy had listed. The last time he'd worn jeans they were just called jeans. "Uh…could you repeat that?"

Cady and Guy studied Keren's frame. "How about…blue straight leg," Cady said.

"In a 32 waist and a long, long, *long* inseam," Guy said.

"And an oxford," Cady added as Guy skipped off. "A white button-down."

Cady browsed with Keren while Guy retrieved the jeans and shirt. She picked up a burgundy sweater with a navy design running through it. "Too Bill Cosby," Keren said.

Cady held a pair of leather pants to his waist. "Too P. Diddy," Keren said.

"Try on this jacket." Cady slipped it from a hanger. "It's fake fur."

Keren passed. "Too pimp daddy."

Cady grabbed up a cashmere cap with a giant pom pom on top.

"That's too...*too*," Keren said.

Guy brought Keren a neat stack of clothes and aimed him toward the fitting rooms. "I took the liberty of bringing you some of our sports briefs," Guy said. "They're a comfortable change from silk boxers. Enjoy!" With a wiggle of his fingertips, Guy vanished.

"How did he know I wear silk boxers?" Keren whispered.

Cady shrugged. "Same way he knew that I preferred cotton bikinis when I first came into this store. He's good at what he does."

"Would you wait outside while I change?" Keren asked at the fitting room door.

They had spent most of the past three days naked, so Cady was surprised by his request. "Why the sudden shyness?"

"I'll be 65 before I let you see me in just my boxers and socks. And by then my chest will be where my stomach is."

"Then we'll be a perfect match. I'll be 61 and when I'm naked, I'll look like I'm melting."

He kissed the tip of her nose. "And I'll love you just as much as I do right now." He chuckled. "I can't believe I let you bring me to the GAP. What's next? Shopping for skateboards?"

"Change, then see if you still want to make fun."

Cady waited on the main floor of the store while Keren tried on his ensemble. When he cautiously emerged from the fitting rooms, Cady saw that he was just as tucked in and buttoned-up as he was in his doctor's clothes.

Guy propped his right elbow in his left hand and tapped his chin with his right index finger. "Well," he sighed, "it's a start."

Cady studied Keren as she slowly circled him. She pinched the fabric of his shirt between her thumbs and forefingers and loosened Keren's tucking job. She unbuttoned his cuffs and loosely rolled the sleeves halfway up his forearms. She unfastened the top two buttons of the shirt, and stood back to look at her work.

Guy kissed his fingertips and said, "Voilà!"

Keren shifted uncomfortably from foot to foot. "How do I look?" he asked Cady.

Cady glanced at the nearby salesgirl. She was stacking V-neck knit tops, but she stared so hard at Keren that she dropped shirt after shirt onto the floor instead of on the display table beside her. A female shopper licked her lower lip as she hungrily stared at Keren. Cady had known that Keren would look good in jeans. The button fly, the seat, the legs— the denim pants flattered his natural gifts and wrapped them perfectly.

Oblivious to the cat-like stares of the female onlookers, Keren concerned himself with only one opinion. "Cady? How do I look?"

She took his sleeve and stood on tiptoe to whisper in his ear. "Like I want to follow you into the dressing room and take those jeans off you with my teeth."

Keren's eyes held Cady's heated gaze as he spoke to Guy. "I'll take five pairs, please, exactly like these."

Keren's new jeans were a pool of denim on the living room floor and Keren and Cady lay tangled together beneath a colorful afghan on Cady's sofa. True to her word, she had used her teeth to bare the contents of his new jeans the minute they had returned to her apartment. Her talented mouth hadn't stopped there. She had peeled his new grey sports briefs from him with her teeth and had used her mouth to slip a condom on him before tantalizing him in ways that introduced him to dimensions of ecstasy he had never imagined. Touching him with only her lips, tongue, teeth, eyelashes, cheeks and hair—anything but her hands—she had wrought a climax from him that made him feel as though the soles of his feet and the top of his head had blown off.

"Jeans," he'd panted afterward, "are the soundest investment I've ever made."

Her spirits high, Cady slipped on Keren's new briefs and a T-shirt before she scampered into the kitchen to start dinner. Keren pulled on his jeans and followed her. Going to the fridge, he took out a 24-oz. bottle of water, which he heartily gulped down.

"Thirsty?" Cady took the bottle and sipped.

"I need to replenish my bodily fluids." They had gone to the grocery store and her fridge was well stocked. Cady gathered a bunch of fresh asparagus, a head of red leaf lettuce and a package of tuna steaks and set them on the counter adjoining the sink. A small paring knife made easy work of slicing through the thick blue rubber band securing the asparagus. Cady took one of the knitting-needle thin spears and bit its spiky blossom.

"I've never seen anyone eat raw asparagus," Keren said.

"Claire taught me to always taste it before cooking it. That way I know how to serve it. This bunch is fairly sweet and very fresh. I'll blanch it for a minute or so, and whip up a spicy onion vinaigrette for it." She filled a plastic bowl with cold water and plunged the lettuce into it, leaving the stem end up.

"Won't the lettuce wilt if you leave it in the water?"

Cady lifted the head and let the water drain into the bowl. "The cold water makes it nice and crisp." She shook off the excess water before showing the head to Keren. "Look at these colors." Her fingers danced over the ruby and violet tints edging the emerald leaves. "No wonder artists paint vegetables in their still lifes." She began pulling the leaves apart and dropping them into the cold water. "Claire taught me that you should never use a knife on lettuce. You should always tear it to keep from bruising it. Claire—"

"Cady?"

She turned. Keren looked pensive as he screwed the top back on the water bottle. "I've had a wonderful visit."

She wrinkled her brow and gave him a nervous smile. "It's not over yet. We still have a few more days."

"I know." He studied her closely as he said, "I was wondering if I could take you into Cambridge tomorrow, to show you some of my old college haunts."

"Okay," she smiled. "I'd like that. But before we do that, I want to take you to Bob the Chef's Jazz Café. They do a Sunday brunch that is out of this world, and the music is incredible. Claire and I spent three hours there one Sunday, and she even went back to the kitchen to compare biscuit recipes with their cook." Cady began unwrapping the tuna steaks from their waxy white paper.

Keren took her shoulders from behind. "You can't keep doing this, Cady."

"Doing what? Making dinner?"

"The Claire Winters Memorial Tour of Boston," he said gently.

She turned. "What are you talking about?"

"You have stories and anecdotes about Claire for every place we've gone in the past week and a half. I feel like Claire's been with us the whole time."

She returned to the tuna steaks and began seasoning them. "She has been. She's always with me and she'll always be with me."

"I'm glad that you aren't despairing any more, but I'm worried that you've overcome the pain of sorrow by anesthetizing yourself with memories of Claire."

Her shoulders fell. She rubbed the heel of her left hand across her forehead hard enough to leave a red mark. Her voice became low and tense. "Why are you doing this to me?"

"I'm only trying to help you, Cady."

He hadn't scratched deep to find that her sadness and hurt were still there, just under the surface. "Why can't you just let me be happy? Just for this two weeks. Please…" For the first time in a week, she felt like crying.

He took her hands and kissed them, and then pulled her to him. "I'm telling you this because I won't be here forever."

"Claire used to tell me that all the time."

He held her face in his hands and spoke very slowly and deliberately. "You have to find a way to let go of her."

She tried to shrug out of his grasp, but he wouldn't let her. "You don't know what this is like for me!"

"Don't I? I lost two people I loved very much when I was too young to fully understand what was going on. It left scar tissue around my heart that kept me from getting too close to anyone, and risking that kind of loss again. Then suddenly, you came into my life like a force of nature. Until you, I never realized that people were worth holding on to, no matter how little time you have with them. Until you came along, I never believed that I could love someone and that I could be loved in return. You showed me that love is worth holding on to. I need to show you that sometimes, you have to let it go, too."

Cady tore from his embrace and backed into the stove. "Are you telling me to just forget about her? To move on as though she never mattered to me? Until last week you never spoke to me about your parents. I can't file Claire away in some emotional vault the way you did with your parents."

"Don't hear words I haven't said. I would never tell you to forget Claire. I expect you to hold on to every memory you have of her, so that our…*your* children will know about their amazing great-grandmother."

"Then why is it so wrong for me to talk about her, and to retrace some of my best moments with her here in Boston?"

"I'm scared that you're trying to shape your life to fit your memory of your grandmother, instead of fitting your memories of Claire into your life. You can't just revisit the places and things you did with her. You have to find some way to carry Claire into your future. You can't dwell in the past. It's not healthy."

She impatiently wiped hot tears from her eyes. "Everything reminds me of her. Sometimes, I smell her face powder or hear her laugh…"

She let him take her in his arms. He tucked her head under his chin and rocked her. "I carry my mother in the star of an apple. I see my father every time I look in a mirror. Find a symbol of your love for Claire. That's all you need, love. I promise."

"I didn't want to go back home because I didn't think I could stand the strength of my memories of Claire, but she's just as much a part of my life here in Boston. I love her so much."

He stroked her back, and she melted into him. "A long time ago, I realized that death is not the opposite of life," Keren whispered. "The opposite of death is love. When you love someone, they live within you forever."

Cady sat in the windowsill, watching the outline of Keren's slumbering body shift beneath the quilt on her bed. Claire had made the quilt, stealing moments here and there to piece it together, combining so many odds and ends to cover her in love and warmth. When she and Keren had changed the bedclothes, Cady had drawn the quilt from its storage bag in her hall closet.

Cady had spent two hours telling Keren the stories behind each square of fabric. The blue chambray with the embroidered trim was the dress she'd worn for her second-grade school picture. The magenta moiré taffeta with the white lace overlay was from the senior prom dress she had made under Claire's direction. The petal pink polyester with the tulle flower came from the leotard she'd worn in her first dance recital. Claire had even pieced in a square from the scuffed and scarred black leather of the motorcycle jacket Cady had worn as she'd delivered the valedictory speech at her Hamilton-Foxx graduation.

As Keren slept, Cady's eyes bounced from square to moonlit square. Orange and black striped fur from a favorite stuffed animal. Brown chenille from a favorite blanket. There was even a square made from one of the anklet socks Cady had worn the first time she'd won a college tennis tournament.

With love and patience, Claire had hand-stitched a treasury of Cady's best memories. Beneath it lay Keren, Claire's last and best piece.

Only he's not so square anymore, Cady chuckled inwardly, now that I've got him wearing jeans.

Keren had made a good point about how she was managing, or rather, not managing, her grief. She knew that she couldn't wrap herself in a mental quilt fashioned of her memories of Claire. But if she didn't… "I might forget something," she fretted.

At that moment she accepted that her greatest fear had come true. Claire was gone and Cady knew she couldn't do a thing about it, other than accept it. But I can't lose any more of her, she told herself. She placed her hands over her heart. All I have is what's in here, and I can't let it go. I can't.

She gazed longingly at the quilt, wondering if her sisters had dug theirs out, too. Were they looking at them and missing Claire so much that it physically pained them? Had they found ways to do what Keren had suggested? Had they found something that could truly symbolize their memories and love for Claire?

All Clara had to do was look into her daughter's face, for Danielle had Claire's deep, dark, knowing eyes. Ciel had only to look out of her bedroom window and into her garden, for she had inherited Claire's green thumb. And her garden, like her grandmother's, always had something lush and green growing in it. On Christmas Day, Kyla had rooted through Claire's jewelry box and had taken a pair of black pearl earrings Claire had bought for a song in Tahiti. Kyla had always wanted them, and Claire had promised them to her. Kyla had put the tiny earrings in the locket she always wore. Like Claire, Chiara liked to travel, and did far more of it than Claire ever had. Chiara had once told Cady that no matter where she was in the world, all she had to do was think of Claire, and she'd be home.

Cady wished that it were that easy for her.

Her father was the only person she had ever loved and lost, but she had been so young when he died. She had memories of him, but time had blurred the line between which ones were her own memories and which ones had been given to her by Abby, her older sisters and Claire. She had no memories of her father that were truly her own.

Yes, you do.

A strange sensation traveled along Cady's spine. The voice had sounded within her head, but she still looked around to see if Keren had spoken. He slept soundly, his dark chest rising and falling evenly, his beautiful lips parted in a soft snore.

"No, I don't," Cady argued with herself.

You have your words.

Cady went limp under the wave of understanding that washed over her. Leaping off the windowsill, she went to the kitchen pantry and got on her hands and knees and cleared out a 5-pound bag of russet potatoes, a 2-liter bottle of lemon-lime soda, a six-pack of cola and a sack of old practice tennis balls from beneath the bottom shelf. She used her fingers to dust off the dial of the safe mounted in the wall. She tried the combination twice before the lock popped and the door opened.

She drew out her jewelry box, which was simply an old Nike shoe box containing a pearl necklace, a pair of opal earrings and a diamond ring a former boyfriend had insisted she keep, even though she had refused his proposal. The box also contained her birth certificate, social security card, her baby picture and the title to her VW Beetle. Most importantly, the box held Cady's true treasures: two of her baby teeth, a sepia wedding photo of 22-year-old Claire Winters (neé Roberts) with Henry "Hank" Winters, a crotchet needle, a bald-headed Monchichi doll, a dried bud rose, the stub of her first *Herald-Star* paycheck and an assortment of objects that held no significance or value to anyone other than Cady. Stuck against the side of the box was a wrinkled, yellowing piece of lined paper. Cady sat back on her heels as she read her own handwriting from 26 years ago:

Today is The Winter Festival.

Clara danced in the Winter Festivl.

Clara fell down to times.

Clara bowed.

Clara gave me her ribben.

A slow smile bloomed on her face as she looked at the large, uneven letters. Like a drunken sailor, a lower case 'h' leaned against an upper case 'T'. The words were separated by one finger-width, just as Cady's first-grade teacher had taught her.

In her hands, Cady held her first story and it was called, surprisingly, "The Winter Festival." The story didn't interest Cady as much as the comments written in ink in the margins.

"This one's all mine." Cady smiled and sighed wistfully.

Two and a half decades fell away as she read the faded ink markings that overlapped her bold, broad pencil strokes. Her father had edited her story while she sat on his lap. She closed her eyes and vividly saw the way the cords and tendons had moved beneath the rich, brown skin of his hands as he'd added an 'a' to her 'Festivl', changed the 'e' in 'ribben' to an 'o', and popped a 'w' between the 't' and the 'o.' As if in a dream, she remembered the sound of his voice as he'd said, "You're a natural-born writer, Scoop," and then explained to her what "Scoop" meant. For the merest instant, she could smell him, and feel the warmth of him. And then the moment was gone.

She tucked the paper back into the box and returned the box to her safe.

"I have my stories." Happy tears sprang to her eyes. "I have my words."

She went to her hall closet and withdrew her leather satchel. She grabbed a fresh reporter's notebook and a micro-point pen and went back into the bedroom. She sat cross-legged on the floor on Keren's side of the bed, the window side, so that she could work by the light of the moon.

A few hours later, when the pale of the moon had faded to the grey light of dawn, Keren opened his eyes to see Cady's bowed head before him. "What are you doing up so early?" His voice was growly with sleep.

She didn't answer.

"Cady?"

Still, she didn't answer. He sat up and finally saw what she was doing.

She was writing.

Cady's kitchen was small but inviting. Her personal touches—homemade curtains with a cheery apple print, ceramic cabinet knobs in the shapes of mangoes, pineapples and bananas, the artwork of her nieces and nephews covering the ancient General Electric fridge—were everywhere. When Keren looked for a large cooking pot for pasta, he wasn't surprised to stumble across an extensive collection of well-seasoned cast iron skillets in the cabinet under the counter. He heaved up a twelve-inch frying pan, appreciating its weight and condition.

The cozy kitchen and Cady's cookware summoned a hazy memory of long-ago Sunday mornings, when he could hear sizzling and sputtering from the black skillets on his mother's stove. He'd been too little to see the contents of the skillets, but he'd been just the right size to devour the eggs, bacon, sausage or ham his mother had prepared in them every morning before she had taken to her bed.

Keren's eating habits had changed considerably since then. He couldn't recall the last time he'd eaten bacon or sausage, and he hadn't eaten ham in years, prior to Claire's repast. But holding Cady's skillet, he had a sudden craving for a big Sunday breakfast, the way his mother used to make it.

"Cady's rubbing off on me," he mumbled as he replaced the skillet and took an aluminum pasta pot from the recesses of the cabinet.

Keren prepared his specialty—cappellini tossed with olive oil and roasted red peppers—and brought it to Cady for lunch. Other than to gather two more blank notebooks, Cady hadn't moved from her place near the bedroom windows. Keren set the dish of pasta on the bed and sat on the floor beside Cady. She finished the sentence she was writing before she looked up at him.

"Good morning." She capped her pen and used it to mark her place before closing her notebook and settling it on top of the two she had already filled. "You look so cute!" She ran her hand along his denim-clad thigh.

"Actually, it's afternoon, and thank you." He handed her the plate of steaming pasta.

Her delight gleamed in her eyes. "You cook?" She inhaled the delicious aroma.

"*You* cook. I boil."

Cady didn't realize how hungry she was until her first bite. While she slurped up the tasty strands of pasta, she listened to Keren talk about a chemotherapy program at Brigham and Women's Hospital that he wanted to check out. "Why don't you go this afternoon?" she suggested.

He almost didn't hear the question. He was too preoccupied with the sight of her using the tip of her tongue to catch the end of a strand of cappellini. "I thought you wanted to see some of my Boston places."

"I'm not up for another cancer ward just yet." She set her empty dish aside and crawled into his lap. She was still in her nightclothes: a vintage CoCo Puffs T-shirt, pink cotton bikinis and snowy white anklet socks.

Keren nuzzled her neck, loving the combination of little girl playfulness and womanly sultriness in his lap. "I'll stay here with you, in that case."

"I won't be much fun." The movement of her backside and hips in his lap belied her words. "I want to keep writing. I have a few more thoughts I need to get down, while it's all fresh."

"I could give you a foot massage while you write," he offered.

"I couldn't concentrate on writing if you were massaging my feet." She laced her fingers together at the back of his neck. "You don't want to leave me alone. Is that it?"

"It's more like I want to be with you."

"I'll be fine, you know. I'm…working on letting go."

"You're writing about Claire?"

She nodded toward her notebooks. "I'm just gathering the pieces. I'll make the quilt later."

He looked at her, a question in his eyes. "I'm not sure what that means, but why don't you use your laptop? It would be faster and more efficient."

"The laptop is for work. Pen and paper are more comfortable for me, more personal." She changed the subject. "You go to Brigham and Women's, and I'll treat you to dinner at Magnolia's tonight. Is it a date?"

She had spent most of the night and all morning writing, but she looked relaxed and refreshed. Whatever she was working on, it was doing her good. He wouldn't take her from it. "Should I meet you there, or come back here first?"

"Meet me there at six," she said. "And wear your jeans."

"Good evening, Dr. Bailey," the pretty hostess greeted the moment Keren stepped into the tiny restaurant. "Welcome to Magnolia's."

"Have we met?" Keren was sure that he hadn't met the woman. He might not have remembered her face but he certainly would have recalled her thick Creole accent.

The hostess led him past the bar and into the dining area. Recessed lighting gave the place an ethereal, romantic glow. It was early, so there weren't many diners. Several children, their homework papers and books spread before them, occupied a table near the bar. The children seemed to fit in with the casual sophistication of the small restaurant.

"Cady called to make a reservation, even though she knows she doesn't ever need one here," the hostess said. "She's one of our special favorites." She brought him to a table in the center of the restaurant and gave him an incisive stare as she asked for his coat. "Cady was right about you."

"I beg your pardon?"

"When I asked Cady how I'd recognize you, she told me to just look for the handsomest man I'd ever see. That you are, Doctor."

The hostess, who introduced herself as Evie before excusing herself to greet a couple at the door, left Keren with a wine list and beverage menu. He sat at the table, noting the restaurant's décor. The place was cozy. The square tables were covered in pale linen and set with polished silver and gleaming crystal. The chairs had high backs and plush cushions, perfect for lounging in after a good meal, and the tables were spaced well—not so close that conversations could be easily overheard, but not so far apart that the room seemed cavernous.

Each table had its own collection of flickering votive candles in cut crystal holders. Keren watched the merrily dancing flames as he thought back on his day and his visit as a whole. He had seen more of Boston in a week with Cady than he had in all his years at Harvard. She'd given him behind-the-scenes, reporter's eye views of the State House, Boston City Hall, the World Trade Center, Fenway Park and Symphony Hall. All he'd had to offer her was the greasy spoon diner in Cambridge that he'd gone to for dinner every weekend for seven years, and tours of Boston's finest oncology departments.

He'd lived in New England through college, medical school and his internship and residency, yet it hadn't felt like home. Not until now. Everywhere they had gone, it seemed that everyone knew Cady. The women who sold T tokens, the staff at Guiglio's Bakery, the merchants at the Haymarket Square farmer's market, even the South Ocean Chinese delivery driver—who spoke no English other than "Hi!" and "Thank you very much!"—greeted Cady and conversed with her as though she were a favorite relative. A trip to the corner store for milk had taken over an hour because the Pakistani shopkeeper, his wife and two children had each spent a turn catching Cady up on the past few months of neighborhood gossip.

Cady had given big, bad Boston a hometown comfort that made it harder for Keren to think about leaving. And the harder he tried not to think about his few remaining days, the easier it was to consider staying.

He struck a thoughtful pose as he sat mesmerized by the candlelight. I could stay, he reasoned. I still have my connections at Harvard, if I wanted to teach, and my visit to Brigham & Women's couldn't have gone better. The chief of oncology offered me a position outright.

"What's to stop me from taking it?" he murmured. "There's nothing keeping me in St. Louis."

Contemplating an exit from Raines-Hartley gave him a sudden rush of fondness and affection for Renyatta and Zweli, but the feelings were feathery and shallow compared to what he felt for Cady. Love, passion, comfort, understanding and home—in Cady he had found everything he had ever longed for. He hid a coy smile behind his fingers as he thought of an inspired way to hold on to the gifts she had given him.

"Evie?" he called, waving her over.

She hurried to his table. "Yes, what can I do for you, Dr. Bailey?"

He patted Claire's rings, which were in the breast pocket of his jacket. He'd kept them close to his heart since he'd received them. "I was hoping you could help me surprise Cady…"

"Exactly what did you do to get service like this?" Cady quivered at the touch of Keren's lips to the side of her neck as he seated her at their new table. "Evie never seats me in the private gallery."

Keren took his own seat, pleased with Cady's reaction. The private gallery, as Cady had called it, was a section of the restaurant separated from the main dining area by a gauzy curtain. In keeping with the restaurant's theme, the curtain was printed with a lush, Impressionist-style rendering of a bayou scene. The gallery was lit in such a way as to allow the couple within it to see out while other diners couldn't see in.

"I asked Miss Evie, very nicely, if we could have some privacy while we dined," Keren explained. His gaze caressed the skin exposed by her off-the-shoulder dress. The winter-white cashmere gave her an angelic, otherworldly look that managed to be achingly alluring. The tight-fitting garment revealed nothing, yet hid none of her shapely assets. "You look beautiful."

She smiled. It was kind of him to say aloud what his expression had said so much better when he'd first seen her enter the gallery. "You've been so patient and understanding about me spending the day writing, I thought you'd like seeing me in something other that a T-shirt and panties."

He took her hands on either side of the votives. "Just for the record, I have no objections whatsoever to your T-shirts and panties."

Cady drew her fingertips along one of his palms. He felt the small gesture all the way down to his toes. "I missed you. How was your day?"

"Very productive. Very interesting."

She wasn't sure what to make of the peculiar smile accompanying his answer.

"Did you finish what you were working on?" he asked.

"Yes, for now." She took a sip of ice water. "I know you don't want to talk about it, but—"

He reached across the table to cup her face. "Is that what you think? That I don't want to listen to you talk about Claire?"

Candlelight danced in the liquid depths of her honey eyes. "No. But you were right. I've been keeping her alive in the wrong way."

Evie politely interrupted to bring in appetizers, compliments of the chef. Cady realized how hungry she was when the aromas of crispy, fried green tomatoes and blackened shrimp assailed her. They thanked Evie before leaping into the dishes.

Cady closed her eyes to better savor the mingled tastes of the tomatoes and their horseradish sauce. "Every time I have these it makes me feel as though I've never truly tasted food before. These are the best in the world, even better than my grandmother's."

"That's high praise," Keren said around a mouthful of the plump, tasty shrimp. "Did Claire agree?"

"I never brought her here."

Keren paused. "Why not?"

Cady shrugged a shoulder. "I've never brought anyone here before tonight."

Oddly flattered, Keren stopped eating. "You are the most perplexing person I have ever met. This place is amazing. Why would you keep it to yourself?"

She cast her eyes downward and played with her cutlery. "I guess I'm a little territorial. I feel like it belongs to me. When I come here, I can write and have a fantastic meal without having to amuse or suffer a date. I like this place too much to spoil the experience with bad company."

"Claire wouldn't have been bad company."

"I know. But it never occurred to me to bring her here. Some women browse through Shreve, Crump & Lowe and dream about the engagement ring they hope to get someday. I used to come here and fantasize about sharing the perfect meal with a man of my dreams."

"That's a very modest desire."

"Modest, yes, but damn near impossible to accomplish. Until now. Until you."

He leaned closer over the table. Cady's heart swelled as she met his expectant gaze over the candlelight. "This visit has meant a lot to me, Cady. I never thought that Boston could feel like home. It's a shame that I have to go back to St. Louis." He stroked the backs of her hands with his thumbs, unsure how to proceed. "I want to talk to you about that."

"Keren, what is it? You're starting to scare me."

"I love you." Those words came so easily. "I never knew how much I liked Boston, until I shared it with you. I guess I'm saying that I want to keep sharing—"

"Excuse me, loves!" Evie crooned as she parted the curtain and entered with a large circular tray balanced on her shoulder, "but dinner is served."

Keren reluctantly retreated to his side of the table. Cady's eyes widened at the assortment of pleasantly steaming dishes on the tray. "You ordered all this?" Cady asked.

"Actually," Keren started, "I—"

"Chef decided what you'd be having tonight," Evie said. "For you, Cady, Chef prepared herbed salmon with sweet potato strings and sautéed winter squash." Evie set a plate before Cady. "And for you, fine sir, Chef prepared his bleu cheese encrusted filet mignon with honey-ginger roasted carrots and parsnips."

"What would you have ordered, Keren?" Cady asked.

He chuckled. "I don't think it matters." To Evie, he said, "Please, give my thanks to your chef."

Cady tasted the salmon. "Give him mine, too. This is…I can't think of a word good enough to describe how good this tastes."

"Chef cooks from his heart," Evie said as she served the rest of the side dishes. "The quality of the meal reveals how happy he is that you've come back to us, Cady. Chef missed you." She poured a fragrant white Beaujolais while Keren and Cady dove into their meal.

Keren tasted his steak. The flavors danced on his tongue and the meat melted in his mouth. "Chef" clearly more than missed Cady. The food tasted like he adored, worshipped and loved her. Chef spoke Cady's language of culinary seduction.

"Exactly how often do you eat here?" Keren asked once Evie had departed.

"At least once a month. Why?"

"I was just wondering why 'Chef' would miss you this much." He indicated the assortment of food with his fork.

"Chef Jean-Pierre is sixty-four years old. He's like a grand-father to me."

"You don't have to explain," Keren said, although he was relieved.

"Apparently I do." She grinned. "You're jealous."

"That's ridiculous."

"I'm flattered. But you don't have to worry about some other man catching my eye or winning me over with great salmon. You're the one I want, Keren."

Her assurance brought him back to where he'd been when Evie brought in the food. He took a sip of his wine to calm the butterflies flitting in his belly. "And you're the one I want. I think we should talk about you and me and Boston. And the future."

"I've done a lot of thinking on that in the past two days myself," she said. "I wasn't quite sure how to bring it up with you."

Sure that she was of the same mind as he was, he relaxed a bit. Knowing that she would accept his proposal would make it easier for him to deliver it.

"I'm not sure what the future holds for me," she said quietly. "I need to take some time to sort a lot of things out. It's not just because of Claire, although that's a big part of it. I need to spend some time alone, to figure out what I want to do with the rest of my life. When I was writing about her today, and thinking about all the things she wanted to do with her life and never did…it just made me think about my own life. Claire devoted her life to me and my sisters. She always made me feel like I could accomplish anything I wanted. I don't feel like I've accomplished very much. I'm doing myself, and her, a disservice, by not living up to my own expectations. I have to change that. I can go on without her, but I still have to make her proud. I owe her that."

Keren's appetite faded. "What do you think you have to do?"

"I'm going to write," she smiled. "I'm going to cast my fate into God's hands and see what comes of it."

"You can write anywhere, can't you?"

"Sure. But I think I'm going to start in Mississippi."

Keren was struck speechless.

"That's where my grandmother's family originally came from, long before the Civil War."

"How long do you plan to do whatever this is that you're planning to do?" He set his napkin on the table.

"Until my savings run out. Until I find a publisher. I don't know. Until I don't feel the urge to do it any more. I finished my friendly hospitals story when I got back to Boston, so it's time I started working to get it published. I'd like you to read it, though, before I submit it."

"Sure," he said, not really paying attention to what he was agreeing to. "So how long do you think it'll take for you to sort out your new career plans?"

"I figure six months is long enough to give myself a fair shot."

Six months! Keren thought of the engagement ring in his pocket, and he was glad that he hadn't taken Evie up on her suggestion to place it atop the key lime sorbet he'd planned to order for dessert.

"Are you upset with me?" Cady asked, noticing his sharp change in posture and demeanor.

"No." He sat up and resumed his meal, although he had lost his taste for it. "I'm not upset. Just surprised."

"This doesn't have to change things between us, Keren. I can still come to St. Louis to visit you and you can come to Boston, or wherever I am, to visit me. You're so busy with your patients and the hospital, the time will pass quickly."

The sound of his own words being used against him made him cringe. He wanted to ask her to reshape her plan so that it included marrying him. The only way he could force himself from bursting out with a proposal was to grit his teeth. She had found a way to let go of Claire as he'd told her to, and he had no right to ask her to change her plans to accommodate him. But he would have kept his counsel to himself if he'd known it would lead to her leaving him.

Six months…he could wait. He'd waited all his life for her, so he could handle another six months.

The question was, would she wait six months for him?

Keren lay back in a nest of pillows, cradling Cady against his chest. He had been quieter and somewhat withdrawn since dinner at Magnolia's. When they returned to her apartment, there had been an urgent intensity to his lovemaking. It had been no less satisfying, but Cady didn't quite know what to make of the change in him. She attributed it to the fact that their time together was running out, and perhaps he felt it more keenly than she had first assumed he would. But now, lying together in the wake of their physical union, he was talkative and open, which put her worries to rest.

"I don't know very much about my ancestry, other than something my father used to tell me," Keren said. "He said that one of our ancestors was a slave, a Muslim whose name was Bul-Ali. It was Americanized to Bailey. I used to wonder if that was true, but I never had anyone else I could ask. My grandparents died before I was born, my parents were only children and Great Aunt Bernadetta cared more about money than history when it came to family. I really admire the way your family has kept track of its ancestry."

Keren spoke from his heart. Cady had thrown him with her announcement during dinner, but the shock and disappointment of it had slowly given way to his respect for her and her decision. It was selfish of him to bemoan what she needed to do to find happiness, even if that quest took her away from him.

"I could help you find your ancestors," she offered cheerfully. "We can start with birth certificates and social security records, and check out the halls of records in the states your people come from. I think it's important to know where and who you're from."

He tipped her face up to his. "You would help me discover my past?"

"I would do anything for you."

Would you stay here in Boston and marry me? he wanted to ask.

His intent must have been plain on his face, because she asked, "What's on your mind?"

"Uh…did you know that Zweli asked Kyla to marry him?"

"She told me. She thought it was a joke."

"It wasn't. He loves her."

"I think she loves him, too. Kyla's always been a little blind when it comes to things like that. I don't know why it is, but she's always had a strange insecurity about herself. About her looks, about her talent…she never thinks she's good enough. I don't know how she can stand being in Hollywood, where you're constantly judged on the very things she's most insecure about."

"Maybe it's a birth order thing," Keren said. "She's had to compete with you and Ciel and Clara all her life. You three are hard acts to follow. You're all smart, beautiful, caring—"

"You make us sound interchangeable."

"I don't mean to. I like your sisters, but none of them can compare to you, Cady." He kissed her forehead. "Did Kyla give you any other reasons as to why she refused Zweli?" His arms involuntarily tightened around Cady.

"She thinks he's too egotistical. I think they would have made a strange couple. A woman who hardly loves herself and a man who loves himself a little too much. They're different in that regard, but alike in so many other ways. I actually think they could have made each other happy."

Keren thought back on Zweli's accusation that he and Cady were too much alike. "What about you and me? Are we a strange couple?"

Cady moved beneath the sheets and covered his bare body with hers. "We're perfect for each other."

"Could we make each other happy?" The question was hard for him to get out with Cady's warm, supple body working its magic on him.

"Is this the proposal you've been starting and stalling on all night?" she asked breathily.

"It's just a question." Suddenly annoyed that she had known his mind all along, he punished her by turning his face when she tried to kiss him. His plan backfired when she settled for his earlobe rather than his lips.

"Yes," she said. "I think we could make each other happy."

"When?" He resisted her touch for as long as he could— exactly three seconds—before taking her head in his hands and kissing her fully, deeply.

"When I come back," she murmured.

He wouldn't argue with her, or try to talk her out of her plan. All he could do was give in to the passions she aroused, and cherish the last few days they had together.

CHAPTER SIXTEEN

Keren started turning heads on his first day back at Raines-Hartley when he stopped in the cafeteria for an orange juice on his way up to fifteen. He checked in on Rosina Ippolito first, and nearly gave her a heart attack just by stepping into the room. Keren was pleased to see that Rosina's bone and brain scans showed no signs of new tumors, and that the original tumor in her stomach had shrunk by forty-two percent since she'd begun radiation therapy.

The shocked and surprised looks continued as Keren traveled down the corridor, visiting each of his patients on his way to his office. Rod Millbrook was so stunned at Keren's appearance he considered asking for another surgeon, convinced that Keren had lost his mind. Three new patients had heard stories about the "Iceberg," but after meeting Keren, each made a point of telling Renyatta that Dr. Bailey was nothing at all like the cold, impersonal robot they'd expected.

Renyatta had rushed to Keren's office, and when she opened the door and saw him standing at his filing cabinets, she almost fainted.

Dr. Keren Bailey was wearing blue jeans.

She would have been less surprised to see a pig in tap shoes and she stood staring at him, her mouth hanging open.

"Hello, Renyatta," he said. "Good to see you. I've scheduled a meeting for two this afternoon, so you and the staff can update me on the charts."

"Uh huh," she said, still not believing her eyes.

"Cady sent some heavenly hash and divinity for you," he added. "I left it at home. I'll get it on my lunch break and bring it to the meeting for you."

Renyatta finally found her voice. "Dr. Bailey, what happened to you in Boston? People are talking. Since you came in this morning, all I've heard is whispering about you."

"What do you mean?"

"Never mind." She decided to leave well enough alone. "I'll be at the station if you need anything."

"Renyatta," he called after her before she left the office. "Could you do one thing for me?"

"Depends on what it is," she said suspiciously.

"Tell everybody that all I changed was my pants. I haven't been brainwashed by aliens, or replaced by my own twin, or smoking crack. I bought some new pants. That's all. If I'd known it would cause such an uproar, I'd have done it years ago."

Renyatta laughed out loud. "I'm so glad you went to Boston. Lord, I am so glad!"

Keren's behavior over the next two weeks belied his declaration that all he'd changed was his pants. Zweli was the first to notice that the changes in Keren ran deeper than the clothes he wore. When Keren failed to show up for lunch as they'd previously arranged, Zweli went looking for him.

He'd gone to Keren's office first, and not finding him there, he'd enlisted Renyatta to aid his search. They checked Keren's usual haunts: the hospital library, the records room and the conference room. They visited the patients' rooms one by one, sure that Keren was somewhere on fifteen.

But none of the patients had seen him. Zweli and Renyatta were passing the utility closet when Renyatta swore that she heard a sound from within it. No stranger to the convenience and privacy of a hospital utility closet, Zweli tiptoed closer to the door and listened.

Renyatta moved in close to Zweli. The two of them pressed their ears to the door, holding their breath to better hear what was happening on the other side of it.

There were voices; a high, female one was louder than the lower, muffled one. "This is wonderful," the female voice gushed. "This is amazing. I can't believe you."

Renyatta, her eyes as wide and round as golf balls, pursed her lips as she looked at Zweli.

"Oh, I like that," the female voice crowed enthusiastically. "I've missed you so much. That feels so nice."

The other voice mumbled something Zweli and Renyatta couldn't make out. Whatever it was, it made the female voice giggle.

"You don't know what a treat this is for me," the female voice said. "I—ouch! No biting!"

Renyatta pounded on the door with her fist, nearly popping Zweli's eardrum. "Get dressed and get your asses outta my closet!" she boomed. "This is a hospital, not a cathouse!"

She flung the door open. What she saw glued her tongue to the roof of her mouth. Keren was in the closet—with one of his new patients, an attractive blonde who was in for a breast lumpectomy. The woman wasn't terminal, but she'd heard that Dr. Keren Bailey was "the best," and wanted him to perform her procedure.

Renyatta wildly looked from Keren to the blonde, finally pinning her death stare on Keren. "You are the last person I'd expect to find foolin' around in a closet!" she thundered. "I'd expect as much from him." She jerked a thumb at Zweli.

"Hey, now," he said indignantly.

"But I thought you had better sense, Dr. Bailey," Renyatta continued. "Cady's been in Mississippi for only two weeks, and already you're messing around with this…this…"

"Hey," the blonde said, insulted.

"*Person*," Renyatta finally said. "I knew something was wrong with you when you showed up here in those blue jeans, lookin' like a rock star instead of a doctor." Renyatta swore an oath. "How could you do this to Cady? I had such hopes for the two of you. And Claire…Claire is probably looking down from heaven right now, asking the Lord to smite you with his slippery sword!

"Hell, I just might smite you myself, you sneaky, two-timin' rascal!"

When Renyatta stopped to catch her breath, Keren was able to get a word in. "Exactly what do you think I was doing in there?"

"Oh, I think we all know what you were doing," Renyatta declared.

"Mrs. Packard here was nervous about her surgery and was missing Bongo," Keren calmly explained. He bent over and picked up the Jack Russell terrier cowering behind a mop bucket. "Renyatta, this is Bongo. Bongo, this is Renyatta. She's our resident watchdog."

Keren lifted Bongo's paw and made the dog wave at Renyatta.

"I have truly seen everything," Zweli muttered under his breath.

"You were in the closet...with Mrs. Packard...and a dog?" Renyatta faltered. "She was talking to the dog? About the 'feels so good'? And the 'no biting'?"

Mrs. Packard took Bongo from Keren, and the dog began wildly licking her face. "I don't mind the licking," she said. "But the biting hurts."

"I think you owe Mrs. Packard an apology," Keren said.

"Sorry," Renyatta said, not looking at Mrs. Packard or sounding the least bit contrite. "What the hell was I supposed to think, with you two hiding in a closet?"

"You were supposed to think that I was trying to make my patient feel more at ease," Keren said.

"Well, that's exactly what I thought. Only I didn't think there was a dog—other than you—involved in it."

"Dogs aren't allowed in the hospital, Renyatta. I thought I could get away with a private reunion in the closet. I was wrong."

"Can't Bongo stay, just a little while longer?" Mrs. Packard pleaded. "Mrs. Ippolito told me that there was a whole horse up here once. Why can't Bongo stay?"

"Because I'm not paid to scoop pooch poop," Renyatta said. "Let's get you back to your room. Bongo can stay for as long as it takes your husband to get here and take him home."

Zweli hung back with Keren while Renyatta took Mrs. Packard and Bongo back to her room.

"I wouldn't have believed what just happened if I hadn't seen it with my own eyes," Zweli said. "Did you really smuggle that dog in just to make her happy?"

Keren grinned as he closed the closet door and started down the corridor with Zweli. "It didn't seem like such a big deal. She's terrified of going under the knife. Nothing I said seemed to make a difference. I told her that the lump was small and that it had been caught very early. The borders are nice and clean, so we'll get the whole thing with minimal tissue loss. She won't even need reconstructive surgery. Her prognosis is very good. But she was stuck in a cycle of panic. I had to do something. She has three children, but she doesn't have any pictures of them in her room. She's got three framed photos of that neurotic dog right on her nightstand. I figured he would be the best way to settle her down. Plus, he weighs two thousand pounds less than a horse. He was easier to smuggle in."

"You're fast ruining your reputation as the Iceberg of Raines-Hartley Hospital," Zweli said. "Minerva said she almost passed out when you smiled at her in the common room this morning."

"Who's Minerva?"

"She's the head housekeeper for our floor. She's the one with that long twisty hair growing out of her right eyebrow."

"Oh. I never knew her name. I never noticed the hair, either."

"I guess you haven't changed completely."

"No," Keren smiled. "But I'm working on it."

"Did you see my story?"

Cady sat on her bed in her hotel room holding a copy of the February 14th *U.S. Daily*, which had run the freelance piece she had started in St. Louis.

"I got the fax this morning," Keren said. "It's a great story, Cady. Your research was tight and you covered all the pros and cons. 'Friendly Hospitals: A Healthy Approach to Sickness,' " he said, reading the title to her. "You didn't take my recommendation to put Claire in it."

"Claire was personal," she said. "The story was business."

"I like the points you brought up about patients being advocates for their own care. That's something too many patients don't do."

"This is my first national piece," she said. "The Lifestyles editor asked me if I had any other story ideas I could pitch to him. I told him that I was working on a genealogical study of my family's ancestry. He thought that might be a good story idea. Since I'm African American and some of our records are harder to find, readers might be interested in knowing the paths I take to discover my heritage."

"I'm interested," Keren said. He carried the cordless phone into his bedroom. "When you've finished tracing your roots, I'd like you to help me weed mine."

"I gave my notice at the *Herald-Star*," she said softly.

"What?"

"It was my Valentine's Day present to myself. I'm leaving the newspaper. I've been there for ten years, since I graduated from college. It's time for a change and I like freelancing. I can set my own schedule, pick and choose my own stories, and I can live wherever I want to. Sean Murphy, my editor, extended my leave, hoping I'd change my mind about resigning, but I know this is the right thing for me to do."

Keren reclined on his bed. "When can I see you?"

"Right now."

He heard the smile in her voice and movement as she settled more comfortably on her bed. "Don't tell me you're calling from right outside my bedroom window."

"No. I wish I were. I'd love to spend Valentine's Day with you. Are you in your bedroom?"

"I'm in my bed."

She moaned, and over the phone, it sounded like a purr. "What are you wearing?"

"I thought I'm supposed to be the dirty pervert and you're supposed to be the naïve sweet thing on the other end of the phone."

"Just tell me what you're wearing," she persisted.

"Black turtleneck, black sports briefs, blue jeans…"

She sucked in a sharp breath.

"What are you wearing?"

"A black T-shirt. No bra. And a teeny, tiny pair of black silk bikini panties."

"Take off the T-shirt," he said.

She giggled, excited by his willingness to play her titil-lating Valentine's Day game. "No. First you take something off."

The sound on his end faded as he set the phone aside to take off his turtleneck. "There," he said, picking the phone up again. "The turtleneck is gone. Now you."

She wriggled out of her T-shirt. Though she was alone in the hotel room, she felt totally decadent, stripping for him by phone. "It's gone. The jeans."

He teased her from hundreds of miles away by letting her hear the sound of his steel buttons popping as he removed his pants.

"I'm going to make you pay for that," she promised as her heart beat faster and harder. "And when I'm finished, I'm going to make you pay some more."

"Cady?"

"Yes?"

"Lie down…"

She did as he commanded, holding the phone to her ear. With choice words and his melodic, sexy voice, he drove her into a writhing frenzy that made her question her decision to run South in search of her past when she could have begun a glorious future in the Midwest with Keren. He tormented her with images of what he could have done to her with his hands and his lips, if only she were there with him. Her skin steamed at the positions he described, and her memory of how his flesh felt against and within her. He showed her a creativity and imagination she had never guessed him capable of, and when he had left her a gasping, quivering mass weak with desire, he had stoked her fires higher with words of love and devotion that had made her want him more than she ever had.

They talked some more, catching up on her writing and her family and his work at Raines-Hartley and Renyatta and Zweli. After they bid one another good night, Cady hung up the phone and stared at it, as though she could see him across the miles. As she drifted off to a contented sleep, the thought of six months away from Keren began to seem like a lifetime.

Cady went straight to the hospital from the airport. It had been three weeks since she'd last seen Keren, and two days since their erotic Valentine's Day phone call. She couldn't stand to be away from him any longer.

Renyatta was waiting in the hospital lobby as Cady's taxi pulled to a stop before the wide, revolving doors. The driver waited patiently while Cady and Renyatta screamed and fell into each other's arms in greeting.

"You didn't tell him I was coming, did you?" Cady asked as she pressed a few bills into the driver's hand and picked up her suitcase from the curb.

"Girl, let me look at you," Renyatta cooed, holding Cady's hand. "You look wonderful! Got some sun down in Miss'sipp, didn't you?" Renyatta laid a hand on Cady's face, which had deepened to a terra cotta bronze.

"All they have down there is sun," Cady remarked, "especially in the dried-up, two-horse town I was working in. I found some good stuff, though. I discovered some property records from 1790 that list an Ismael Winters."

"You go 'head, girl!" Renyatta said triumphantly.

They took the elevator up to fifteen. "Dr. Bailey has made a lot of changes since you were last here," Renyatta told her. "He's changed a bit, too."

"I think he's learned some things about himself," Cady said. "He knows what he wants and now he's willing to do what he needs to, to keep it." She turned to hide a shy smile. The Keren that had thrilled her on Valentine's Day was a different man than the one she had met the day she had stormed into his office with vinegar in her veins.

"What he wants is you, lady," Renyatta said. "Wait until you see fifteen."

Determined to keep her surprise intact, Cady sent Renyatta out of the elevator first, to run interference in case Keren was lurking nearby.

Renyatta was built like Winnie-the-Pooh but she had the stealth of a ninja as she eyed the corridor for Keren before waving Cady out of the elevator car. Cady took one step out of the elevator before she stopped, frozen in place. Her suitcase dropped to the floor with a loud clack.

There before her, mounted on the wall, was a framed blow-up of her friendly hospitals article. Beneath it, on a polished half table, was a giant vase of flowers. Cady went to them, convinced that they were too pretty to be anything other than silk. She used her fingertips to gently lift the heavy blossom of a bright orange tiger lily, and she saw that the flowers were real.

Who died? Cady wanted to ask, but knew the question was distasteful on a floor like fifteen. She forgot about her suitcase as she traveled farther down the corridor, toward the nurses' station.

The station had been remodeled. A waist-high counter of Lucite had replaced the tall, wood-paneled counter that had formed a wall between the nurses and the rest of the floor. A subtly patterned Persian rug in muted gold, burgundy and violet had replaced the drab, decomposition-gray carpeting.

Cady peeked into the patients' rooms as she passed them, and saw fresh flowers and plush armchairs in each one. One patient had a visitor who slept comfortably on a twin-sized day bed, rather than on the squeaky and unyielding cot Cady had suffered while staying with Claire.

As stunned as she'd been by everything else she'd seen, Cady's jaw dropped when she entered the common room. Other than during the luau, she had rarely seen more than two or three people in the room. The room was now busy with patients, visitors, doctors and nurses. Chess, checkers and backgammon games were in progress at low tables designed especially for the respective games. A group of older children played a boisterous game of Monopoly, while near the wall of one-way glass, a group of adults played Trivial Pursuit.

Rod Millbrook, his traveling chemotherapy pack attached to his hip, sat on an oversized, overstuffed chaise, watching a videotape of the Super Bowl on a giant, flat-screen television that looked like the JumboTron at Kiel Auditorium. Next to the television was a sound system complete with wireless headsets and ports for multiple listeners to hear different music at the same time.

Cady clutched her heart when she saw that one corner of the room had been converted to a children's play area. The brightly colored padded climbing toys gave the room the cheerfulness it had lacked. The smaller tables and chairs, and bins and cupboards filled with Legos, building blocks, Lincoln Logs, dolls, trucks and tea sets made it especially inviting.

"This is unbelievable," Cady said, once she found her voice. "All these things came from my story."

"These are just the surface changes," Renyatta said proudly. "In the next few weeks, we're going to have two full-time massage therapists, an aromatherapist, and our own grief counselor, too. And Dr. Bailey is financing all of it with his own money."

Cady whirled on Renyatta. "No…"

Renyatta nodded proudly. "He wrote up a proposal for the hospital the day after he read the draft of your article, but it would have taken them two years to requisition the funds. Even then they only wanted to give him half of what he needed to make this place friendly. He thought it was quicker to just cut the check himself. He can afford it. He's worth millions. He's had people in here every day for almost three weeks working on the renovations."

"I suppose it counts as a business expense," Cady said absently. "I can't believe he did this."

"*You* did this," Renyatta said. "Even before you wrote that article, you showed him how to take care of people. You taught him how to show people that he cares for them, and that he loves them."

"I did a good job," Cady chuckled.

Renyatta looked at her watch. "Honey, we better hurry along now. He'll be coming through on his afternoon rounds soon, and he promised to play gin rummy with Rosina's grandson."

"Rosina's still here?" Cady said as she followed Renyatta back to the nurses' station. "I thought she was released last week. Keren said that she was going home."

"She is at home," Renyatta said. "She's in remission. That grandson of hers latched on to Dr. Bailey. He's kind of like the kid's surrogate big brother." She clapped Cady on the back. "You created a monster, honey."

"I love that monster, and I came here to take care of some unfinished business." Cady trotted to the elevator and retrieved her suitcase. She opened it at the nurses' station and pulled out a foil banner and a bottle of champagne. "Do you have a permanent marker I could borrow?"

Renyatta read the banner as Cady doctored it to suit her purpose. "You said you had something subtle planned."

"This is subtle," Cady said. "Well...for me."

Cady started for the common room. Renyatta grabbed a roll of tape and followed her.

"Do you think he'll be surprised?" Cady asked as she stood on a chair in the archway, taping up one end of her banner.

"Oh, I think a lot of people will be surprised," Renyatta said.

"What are you doing here?"

Cady, who was trying to hide behind a potted palm at the opening of the common room, spun at the sound of her mother's voice. "Me? What are *you* doing here?"

"Renyatta and I have lunch every Saturday here at the hospital," Abby said. She avoided Cady's gaze even as she pulled her in for a long embrace and kiss on the cheek. "I just fell in love with the food here."

"The meatloaf is especially good," chimed Renyatta.

"I didn't tell anyone I was coming home except for you, Renyatta," Cady said. "How did Mama know I'd be here?"

"I guess I might have let it slip," Renyatta grinned. "Is it two o'clock yet?"

"Oh, you're not running off like that," Cady said. "I trusted you, Renyatta, and now my surprise is—"

Renyatta's wristwatch alarm went off, beeping twice. "Two o'clock!" she proclaimed. "I'm on."

Cady scanned the suddenly crowded room with a wary eye. "Something is going on here. What is she up to, Mama?"

Abby took Cady by her shoulders and ushered her to a chair that had been placed in the center of the room, facing the corridor. "You only like surprises when you're the one doing the surprising, Cady. Sit down, be quiet, and enjoy the show."

Flummoxed, Cady allowed Abby to plop her into the chair. As if triggered by Cady's bottom hitting the seat, Zweli's voice filled the common room. "Ladies and gentlemen, welcome to the Raines-Hartley Players' production of *Disco CinderFella*!" He bowed in the center of the entryway, flourishing a baton made of notebook paper.

Cady's eyes bulged from her head. Heat bloomed in her cheeks as she sought her mother's gaze. "Mama, you didn't!"

"Oh, yes, I did," Abby laughed.

"Once upon a time," Zweli began dramatically, reading from the unfurled baton, "there was a princess who lived in a marvelous paradise called Plaza Frontenac."

"Plaza Frontenac is a mall," Renyatta hooted.

"I was twelve," Cady explained above the laughter. "It was paradise to me at the time."

Zweli continued the story. "She had everything a princess could want. Clothes…" He paused as Clara sashayed past the archway bearing giant shopping bags from Cady's favorite stores stuffed with tissue paper. "Food…" Ciel appeared, displaying a huge tray filled with empty fast food cartons set amidst a giant plastic roasted turkey. "And friends," Zweli finished. Kyla, Renyatta, Adele Harrison, Rosina Ippolito and Gloria Williams scooted past, waving and blowing exaggerated kisses at Cady.

"But there was one thing the princess couldn't buy." Zweli swept his arm toward the common room.

"True love!" everyone responded on cue.

"The princess decided to have a party," Zweli read. "She invited all of the kids in Plaza Frontenac to Ricky's Roller World for a skating party. All the handsomest boys came, but only one made the princess's wheels spin. His brown eyes sparkled. His teeth twinkled?" Zweli looked over at Cady. "Twinkling teeth?"

"I was twelve, dammit," Cady growled behind her smile.

"And he had a gorgeous afro," Zweli said.

Keren, dressed in a tight black T-shirt and blue jeans, stepped into view to lean against the frame of the archway.

"What the…?" Cady cried, grabbing the sides of her face. Her mouth fell open as her eyes wandered over Keren, taking in his shiny black afro wig and his roller skates.

Zweli laughed as he continued to read. "And on his feet, the boy wore the most magnificent roller skates the princess had ever seen. They were blue and white Nike sneaker skates with orange, glow-in-the-dark polyurethane wheels with independent truck action that—"

"Was she in love with the skates or the boy?" an anonymous voice asked.

"The skates," Kyla answered with a roll of her eyes. "I'll bet she still has them."

"I was twelve!" Cady insisted.

Keren loudly cleared his throat, prompting Zweli to read more of the story. "The boy wasn't just handsome, he was also the best skater in the rink."

Grinning, Keren straightened. His usual grace and assured movement vanished the instant his front wheels hit the seam dividing the tiled corridor from the carpeted common room. His arms windmilled wildly at his sides, his legs seemed to have separate plans for the direction his body should go, and his wig slid down to cover his eyes. His vision impaired, he rolled backwards and out of Cady's line of sight and crashed into something that sounded quite heavy and breakable.

"I'd better call central supply and order up some crutches," Renyatta whispered in Cady's ear.

Cady stood to go help Keren, but sat again when she saw his hands grip the archway. The rest of his body inched its way into view.

"Just step onto the carpet," she advised, her heart fit to burst with love for him. "It'll slow the wheels down."

Keren, his wig now covering only his eyebrows, stiffly hugged the archway as he struggled into the common room.

Zweli shook his head and sighed deeply. "No one knew the handsome boy's name or where he came from." He flashed a devilish glance at Cady. "Or where he learned to skate."

"It's been 20 years, but I know I didn't write *that*," Cady said. "Quit editorializing."

Cady turned her gaze back to Keren, who steadily worked his way toward her, his arms rigid and straight out for balance, his legs stiff and unsure on the skates.

"Lord, he looks like Frankenstein on wheels," Abby muttered.

The thick carpet caught Keren's wheels and his stiff-legged maneuvering failed him halfway to Cady. Zweli trotted over to him and towed him the rest of the way. Relieved, Keren dropped to one knee before her.

"He's on his knees!" squealed a female voice.

"I don't think he had much choice," Renyatta said under her breath. "He'll break his neck if he stands up in those things again."

Cady curled her arms around Keren's neck and slid off the chair to plaster her body to his. "I can't believe you did this," she said, "all of this. I'm so impressed and…" Her gaze locked with his, and they may as well have been the only two people in the world. "I missed you. Did you miss me?"

He answered her by way of a kiss that left her dizzy and humming all over. "Will you marry me?" he whispered in her ear.

"Funny you should ask me that." She tipped her head toward the forgotten foil banner.

Keren noticed it for the first time. The banner had been printed with colorful letters that spelled out WILL YOU MARRY ME? Cady had crossed out the "WILL," written the word over again between "YOU" and "MARRY," and closed the loop on the question mark to form an exclamation point.

"I had something more subtle planned," she giggled.

"I guess I've rubbed off on you in some ways," he said, kissing her again.

"I'm looking forward to some more of that rubbing," she whispered.

"We came here for a show," Renyatta interrupted. "That was the opening act. We want the headliner."

Everyone clapped. Abby and her daughters moved in closer to witness Keren's proposal. He awkwardly set Cady back in the chair, again facing her on one knee, and took her hands.

It took him a moment to jumpstart his tongue. He couldn't stop looking at her. He wanted to remember every detail of how lovely she was right now, on the verge of joining her life to his.

"Claire told me a long time ago to think of something nice to say to you, and to tell you how I feel about you," he began. "I've wracked my brains trying to come up with a way to say that I love you that really tells you just how much I love you. I keep coming up short. You are the lioness who fiercely guards her own. You are the tigress who tries to stand alone. You are the kitten whose playfulness and charm makes everyone love her. You are the sleek and sexy black pantheress, who hypnotizes with her beauty. And you are the blazing hellcat who fights for what she wants. You are every woman I could ever want, the one true love of my heart. Will you marry me, Zacadia Winters?"

She wanted to respond, but she couldn't move words past the emotion clogging her throat. The crowd advanced to catch her answer.

Keren smiled at the diamond-shine of tears in her eyes. "You know how the fairy tale ends, don't you?" He clasped her hands to his chest.

"Yes, but it doesn't end like this," she blurted on a nervous laugh. "The boy loses a skate when he flees the party to get home before his mean stepfather notices that he's gone. The princess finds it and searches all of Plaza Frontenac, looking for its owner. She finds him and rescues him from a life where no one loves him, but they don't get married. They go to Ted Drewes and they get ice cream."

Keren grinned. "They're twelve. We're not. Our story ends differently, doesn't it?"

Her curls bobbed as she vigorously nodded and bit her lower lip in a futile attempt to stave off a torrent of happy tears. Keren framed her face in his hands. "How does it end, Cady?" He set a soft kiss on the end of her nose. "Tell me what happens next."

With tears of sheer joy trickling down her face, she pitched herself into his arms and said, "I marry the handsomest fella on rollerskates!"

The applause from her family and friends was deafening, and her eyes widened when Keren pulled Claire's engagement ring from his pocket. "I thought Sharonda stole this," she laughed through her tears.

"Claire gave her rings to me." Keren slipped the ring onto the middle finger of her left hand. It was a perfect fit. "She told me to keep them in the family."

"That's not all she wanted to keep in the family."

Keren looked at her sideways, unnerved by the crafty glint in her eyes.

She laced her fingers together at the back of his neck and said, "How do you feel about taking my last name?"

EPILOGUE

Fifteen Months Later

The nurse rushed from the room, her loud sobs echoing as she scurried down the corridor. Keren, in a fresh sterile gown, caught the woman by her shoulders. He didn't know her personally, but she had been at Raines-Hartley for twelve years. Keren had asked for her specifically, based on departmental word of mouth. The woman was supposed to be an excellent, experienced nurse, and Keren had wanted only the best for his team.

"Nurse Kelley, is there a problem?" Keren asked. "Everything was fine when I left a minute ago."

Nurse Kelley clutched a crumpled tissue in her pale, thin hands and pressed it to her nose. "I'm sorry, Dr. Bailey," she wept, "but this is worse than anything I've ever experienced. I'm sorry, but I can't go back in there."

On the edge of a full-out panic, Keren raced into the room Nurse Kelley had just escaped. A single, vicious word pinned him to the spot the second he entered the room.

"*You,*" Cady accused. Her face, her soft and beautiful face, was a twisted mask of sweat-drenched hatred. Her floral gown was almost transparent with perspiration as it hung low on her shoulders and the cords in her neck stood out like telephone cables as she sat forward, assisted by Renyatta and Abby, and rode out the last seconds of a powerful contraction.

"You did this to me!" she grunted between gritted teeth as she gasped for breath. "You and your high-powered, turbo-charged, heat-seeking *SPERM!!*"

"Good heavens," Abby exclaimed.

"That's nothing compared to what she said right before her head started spinning around," Renyatta said.

Keren had been warned about the diabolical turns a laboring wife could take, and he had fully expected Cady to be particularly colorful. What he hadn't expected was her determination to labor naturally, without the help of an epidural. Once it seemed safe, he went to her side and took Renyatta's place. He curled his hand around hers and mopped her forehead with the cool cloth Renyatta handed him.

"Will it be soon, Doctor?" Keren asked Lorna Wilkinson, the obstetrician hunched at Cady's feet.

"She's at eight centimeters and progressing rapidly," Dr. Wilkinson said. She stood and removed her latex gloves, and tossed them into a trash receptacle. A broad smile beamed from Dr. Wilkinson's mahogany face. Keren had asked Dr. Wilkinson, a twenty-year veteran of R-H Obstetrics, to attend Cady's labor, specifically because of her soothing and unflappable demeanor and her competence as an obstetrician. "She's been putting on quite a show for us."

Cady spat a particularly colorful stream of off-color words that she had once overheard in the sports department at the *Herald-Star*.

Keren's eyes widened as he looked at his wife. He could hardly believe that the same mouth that had spoken sacred vows in their wedding ceremony had just let loose with curses that could make a Marine blush.

"Replace each curse word with the name of a flower, and you'd have a poem," Dr. Wilkinson said with a chuckle.

"What happened to Nurse Kelley?" Keren asked quietly while Abby held ice chips to Cady's parched lips. "She's crying in the hallway."

"She told Cady to stop being such a crybaby," Abby answered.

"And Cady asked her to try...*eliminating*...a bowling ball, and see if she didn't feel like crying, too," Dr. Wilkinson said. "Amanda Kelley just isn't accustomed to being spoken to that way."

Keren bent over his wife. She had been in active labor for ten hours, and he knew that she was exhausted physically. "Cady, it's almost over, love. Remember, you have to see these people again once this baby is born and the pain is over."

With the speed and accuracy of a striking cobra, Cady's hand shot out and grabbed Keren's collar. She dragged his face close to hers, so he wouldn't miss any of her hissed words. "Don't talk to me about pain, man. I think I'm a little more qualified than you when it comes to that subject right now." She released him as another contraction built up.

"Use your breathing, baby," Keren said calmly as he helped her curl into a position to better manage the pain.

Cady whimpered as the shattering, pulling pain filled her body. "I can't breathe! I just want to choke you!" She took a few deep, fast breaths. "I never should have had that second daiquiri. I never should have let you buy those jeans!"

The contraction ebbed and Keren kissed the crown of her head. "That's not what you said when the stick turned purple," he reminded her. "You were so happy to be pregnant, you did a cartwheel right there in my office."

"It's not fair," Cady sobbed. Abby wiped her cheeks with a soft cloth. "Everybody else gets to have one baby at a time, but I have to do this twice in a row."

"What?" Keren grunted as another contraction gripped Cady.

Dr. Wilkinson slipped on a pair of gloves and moved to the foot of Cady's bed to check her cervix once more. "I think it's time we told him. And…I think it's time you started pushing, Mrs. Dr. Bailey."

Cady did as requested. Her face turned golden-red, then rose-red as she pushed for all she was worth.

"Cady, what did you mean 'twice in a row?'" Keren asked when she was allowed to rest.

"Take a deep breath and give me one more good push, Cady," Dr. Wilkinson said.

"Cady?" Keren persisted as he and Abby helped her sit up to push.

She rolled an eye at him, unable to speak through her pushing.

"She wanted to surprise you," Abby said, her face close to Keren's over Cady's shoulders. "This was her payback, for the way you surprised her when you proposed."

Keren's head spun. He'd been called to surgery and missed her 10-week ultrasound, but Cady had later shown him a photo.

"That was Clarence's sonograph," Cady said, answering his next question before he could get it out.

"Twins," he said dully. "We're having twins!"

"*I'm* having twins," she groaned as she collapsed against her pillows at the end of a push. And with that push, her first child emerged into the world.

"She's a girl!" Dr. Wilkinson announced as she cut the cord and turned the mewling baby over to a neonatalist, who placed the baby on a blanket atop Cady's chest.

Another strong contraction seized Cady's body, and the neonatalist lifted the baby from Cady and cleaned and weighed her while Cady's second baby entered the world. "He's a boy," Dr. Wilkinson said happily over the baby's cries. "Well done, Cady."

Cady, in a pleasant haze of relief, slumped into her pillows. "Are they okay?"

Keren, torn between comforting his wife and wanting to meet his children, could only nod as he watched the neonatal nurses clean, weigh, diaper and dress his children. They worked quickly, yet still seemed to take forever before they brought the swaddled babies to Keren and Cady.

Dr. Wilkinson took care of Cady as Keren set his new daughter in Cady's arms. He cradled his son close to his heart and squeezed onto the bed beside Cady. A tearful Abby grabbed her camera and took the first photo of the Winters-Bailey family. "I'm going to go and let everyone know that you're okay and that I have two perfect grandbabies!" Abby said.

"You and your high-powered, turbo-charged, heat-seeking sperm," Cady said tenderly as she gazed upon the faces of her children. Her daughter wore a pink knit cap, from beneath which poked sweet, silky curls of gold and copper. Her son's bald head was covered with a blue knit cap.

"There are about a hundred people out there waiting to meet them," Keren whispered. He kissed Cady's forehead, and then kissed her lips. "How do you feel?"

"Like I just won the lottery and the Pulitzer Prize at the same time. I love them so much and I only just met them."

"Twins," he chuckled. "Why didn't you tell me that we were having two?"

"You're a doctor," Cady said. "You should have been able to tell. I was as big as a baby elephant."

"Why didn't *you* tell me?" Keren demanded of Dr. Wilkinson.

"Patient confidentiality, Doctor," she said. "I was sworn to secrecy."

Abby poked her head into the room. "Cady, everyone out here is getting restless. Do you feel like bringing the babies out?"

"Give me a few minutes to get cleaned up," Cady said. "And Mama, could you get me a piece of that cornbread? I smelled it while I was in labor, and I'm starving."

"I didn't bring any food with me, Cady," Abby said. "You were probably just imagining things."

Cady marveled at the tiny, perfect features of her daughter's face as she thought about what her mother had said. I didn't imagine it, she told herself. I smelled Grandma's cornbread as if I were standing in her kitchen while it rose in the oven. A wistful smile came to Cady's face. The Lord worked in mysterious ways. Claire Winters apparently did, too.

"My grandma came to see you," Cady murmured to her children.

The common room on the eighth floor, the Raines-Hartley Obstetrics Department, wasn't big enough to accommodate all the people who had come to welcome Cady's children into the world. Cady held the babies on her lap while Keren stood proudly over her wheelchair. He dipped his head to kiss Claire Elizabeth's ginger-gold curls and Samuel Zachary's serious brow. He kissed his wife, amazed at how motherhood enhanced her beauty.

Keren was high on the love and pride he felt for his family, for all of it. His family, the one he had married into and his extended Raines-Hartley family, filled both the room and his heart.

"Our children have been born into so much love," Keren said softly into Cady's ear.

"I know," Cady smiled. A mischievous twinkle lit up her eyes as she whispered, "We should have sold tickets at the door."

ABOUT THE AUTHOR

Crystal Hubbard is a former Boston Herald sports copy editor. She resides in New England with her husband, with whom she eloped on April Fool's Day, 1996. She has three children and is currently pursuing a full-time writing career. *Suddenly You* is her first contemporary romance novel. Her hobbies include sewing, cake decorating and boxing.

2008 Reprint Mass Market Titles

January

Cautious Heart
Cheris F. Hodges
ISBN-13: 978-1-58571-301-1
ISBN-10: 1-58571-301-5
$6.99

Suddenly You
Crystal Hubbard
ISBN-13: 978-1-58571-302-8
ISBN-10: 1-58571-302-3
$6.99

February

Passion
T. T. Henderson
ISBN-13: 978-1-58571-303-5
ISBN-10: 1-58571-303-1
$6.99

Whispers in the Sand
LaFlorya Gauthier
ISBN-13: 978-1-58571-304-2
ISBN-10: 1-58571-304-x
$6.99

March

Life Is Never As It Seems
J. J. Michael
ISBN-13: 978-1-58571-305-9
ISBN-10: 1-58571-305-8
$6.99

Beyond the Rapture
Beverly Clark
ISBN-13: 978-1-58571-306-6
ISBN-10: 1-58571-306-6
$6.99

April

A Heart's Awakening
Veronica Parker
ISBN-13: 978-1-58571-307-3
ISBN-10: 1-58571-307-4
$6.99

Breeze
Robin Lynette Hampton
ISBN-13: 978-1-58571-308-0
ISBN-10: 1-58571-308-2
$6.99

May

I'll Be Your Shelter
Giselle Carmichael
ISBN-13: 978-1-58571-309-7
ISBN-10: 1-58571-309-0
$6.99

Careless Whispers
Rochelle Alers
ISBN-13: 978-1-58571-310-3
ISBN-10: 1-58571-310-4
$6.99

June

Sin
Crystal Rhodes
ISBN-13: 978-1-58571-311-0
ISBN-10: 1-58571-311-2
$6.99

Dark Storm Rising
Chinelu Moore
ISBN-13: 978-1-58571-312-7
ISBN-10: 1-58571-312-0
$6.99

2008 Reprint Mass Market Titles (continued)

July

Object of His Desire
A.C. Arthur
ISBN-13: 978-1-58571-313-4
ISBN-10: 1-58571-313-9
$6.99

Angel's Paradise
Janice Angelique
ISBN-13: 978-1-58571-314-1
ISBN-10: 1-58571-314-7
$6.99

August

Unbreak My Heart
Dar Tomlinson
ISBN-13: 978-1-58571-315-8
ISBN-10: 1-58571-315-5
$6.99

All I Ask
Barbara Keaton
ISBN-13: 978-1-58571-316-5
ISBN-10: 1-58571-316-3
$6.99

September

Icie
Pamela Leigh Starr
ISBN-13: 978-1-58571-275-5
ISBN-10: 1-58571-275-2
$6.99

At Last
Lisa Riley
ISBN-13: 978-1-58571-276-2
ISBN-10: 1-58571-276-0
$6.99

October

Everlastin' Love
Gay G. Gunn
ISBN-13: 978-1-58571-277-9
ISBN-10: 1-58571-277-9
$6.99

Three Wishes
Seressia Glass
ISBN-13: 978-1-58571-278-6
ISBN-10: 1-58571-278-7
$6.99

November

Yesterday Is Gone
Beverly Clark
ISBN-13: 978-1-58571-279-3
ISBN-10: 1-58571-279-5
$6.99

Again My Love
Kayla Perrin
ISBN-13: 978-1-58571-280-9
ISBN-10: 1-58571-280-9
$6.99

December

Office Policy
A.C. Arthur
ISBN-13: 978-1-58571-281-6
ISBN-10: 1-58571-281-7
$6.99

Rendezvous With Fate
Jeanne Sumerix
ISBN-13: 978-1-58571-283-3
ISBN-10: 1-58571-283-3
$6.99

2008 New Mass Market Titles

January

Where I Want To Be
Maryam Diaab
ISBN-13: 978-1-58571-268-7
ISBN-10: 1-58571-268-X
$6.99

Never Say Never
Michele Cameron
ISBN-13: 978-1-58571-269-4
ISBN-10: 1-58571-269-8
$6.99

February

Stolen Memories
Michele Sudler
ISBN-13: 978-1-58571-270-0
ISBN-10: 1-58571-270-1
$6.99

Dawn's Harbor
Kymberly Hunt
ISBN-13: 978-1-58571-271-7
ISBN-10: 1-58571-271-X
$6.99

March

Undying Love
Renee Alexis
ISBN-13: 978-1-58571-272-4
ISBN-10: 1-58571-272-8
$6.99

Blame It On Paradise
Crystal Hubbard
ISBN-13: 978-1-58571-273-1
ISBN-10: 1-58571-273-6
$6.99

April

When A Man Loves A Woman
La Connie Taylor-Jones
ISBN-13: 978-1-58571-274-8
ISBN-10: 1-58571-274-4
$6.99

Choices
Tammy Williams
ISBN-13: 978-1-58571-300-4
ISBN-10: 1-58571-300-7
$6.99

May

Dream Runner
Gail McFarland
ISBN-13: 978-1-58571-317-2
ISBN-10: 1-58571-317-1
$6.99

Southern Fried Standards
S.R. Maddox
ISBN-13: 978-1-58571-318-9
ISBN-10: 1-58571-318-X
$6.99

June

Looking for Lily
Africa Fine
ISBN-13: 978-1-58571-319-6
ISBN-10: 1-58571-319-8
$6.99

Bliss, Inc.
Chamein Canton
ISBN-13: 978-1-58571-325-7
ISBN-10: 1-58571-325-2
$6.99

2008 New Mass Market Titles (continued)

July

Love's Secrets
Yolanda McVey
ISBN-13: 978-1-58571-321-9
ISBN-10: 1-58571-321-X
$6.99

Things Forbidden
Maryam Diaab
ISBN-13: 978-1-58571-327-1
ISBN-10: 1-58571-327-9
$6.99

August

Storm
Pamela Leigh Starr
ISBN-13: 978-1-58571-323-3
ISBN-10: 1-58571-323-6
$6.99

Passion's Furies
AlTonya Washington
ISBN-13: 978-1-58571-324-0
ISBN-10: 1-58571-324-4
$6.99

September

Mr Fix-It
Crystal Hubbard
ISBN-13: 978-1-58571-326-4
ISBN-10: 1-58571-326-0
6.99

October

November

December

The More Things Change
Chamein Canton
ISBN-13: 978-1-58571-328-8
ISBN-10: 1-58571-328-7
6.99

Other Genesis Press, Inc. Titles

A Dangerous Deception	J.M. Jeffries	$8.95
A Dangerous Love	J.M. Jeffries	$8.95
A Dangerous Obsession	J.M. Jeffries	$8.95
A Drummer's Beat to Mend	Kei Swanson	$9.95
A Happy Life	Charlotte Harris	$9.95
A Heart's Awakening	Veronica Parker	$9.95
A Lark on the Wing	Phyliss Hamilton	$9.95
A Love of Her Own	Cheris F. Hodges	$9.95
A Love to Cherish	Beverly Clark	$8.95
A Risk of Rain	Dar Tomlinson	$8.95
A Taste of Temptation	Reneé Alexis	$9.95
A Twist of Fate	Beverly Clark	$8.95
A Will to Love	Angie Daniels	$9.95
Acquisitions	Kimberley White	$8.95
Across	Carol Payne	$12.95
After the Vows	Leslie Esdaile	$10.95
(Summer Anthology)	T.T. Henderson	
	Jacqueline Thomas	
Again My Love	Kayla Perrin	$10.95
Against the Wind	Gwynne Forster	$8.95
All I Ask	Barbara Keaton	$8.95
Always You	Crystal Hubbard	$6.99
Ambrosia	T.T. Henderson	$8.95
An Unfinished Love Affair	Barbara Keaton	$8.95
And Then Came You	Dorothy Elizabeth Love	$8.95
Angel's Paradise	Janice Angelique	$9.95
At Last	Lisa G. Riley	$8.95
Best of Friends	Natalie Dunbar	$8.95
Beyond the Rapture	Beverly Clark	$9.95

Other Genesis Press, Inc. Titles (continued)

Blaze	Barbara Keaton	$9.95
Blood Lust	J. M. Jeffries	$9.95
Blood Seduction	J.M. Jeffries	$9.95
Bodyguard	Andrea Jackson	$9.95
Boss of Me	Diana Nyad	$8.95
Bound by Love	Beverly Clark	$8.95
Breeze	Robin Hampton Allen	$10.95
Broken	Dar Tomlinson	$24.95
By Design	Barbara Keaton	$8.95
Cajun Heat	Charlene Berry	$8.95
Careless Whispers	Rochelle Alers	$8.95
Cats & Other Tales	Marilyn Wagner	$8.95
Caught in a Trap	Andre Michelle	$8.95
Caught Up In the Rapture	Lisa G. Riley	$9.95
Cautious Heart	Cheris F Hodges	$8.95
Chances	Pamela Leigh Starr	$8.95
Cherish the Flame	Beverly Clark	$8.95
Class Reunion	Irma Jenkins/ John Brown	$12.95
Code Name: Diva	J.M. Jeffries	$9.95
Conquering Dr. Wexler's Heart	Kimberley White	$9.95
Corporate Seduction	A.C. Arthur	$9.95
Crossing Paths, Tempting Memories	Dorothy Elizabeth Love	$9.95
Crush	Crystal Hubbard	$9.95
Cypress Whisperings	Phyllis Hamilton	$8.95
Dark Embrace	Crystal Wilson Harris	$8.95
Dark Storm Rising	Chinelu Moore	$10.95

Other Genesis Press, Inc. Titles (continued)

Other Genesis Press, Inc. Titles (continued)

Hard to Love	Kimberley White	$9.95
Hart & Soul	Angie Daniels	$8.95
Heart of the Phoenix	A.C. Arthur	$9.95
Heartbeat	Stephanie Bedwell-Grime	$8.95
Hearts Remember	M. Loui Quezada	$8.95
Hidden Memories	Robin Allen	$10.95
Higher Ground	Leah Latimer	$19.95
Hitler, the War, and the Pope	Ronald Rychiak	$26.95
How to Write a Romance	Kathryn Falk	$18.95
I Married a Reclining Chair	Lisa M. Fuhs	$8.95
I'll Be Your Shelter	Giselle Carmichael	$8.95
I'll Paint a Sun	A.J. Garrotto	$9.95
Icie	Pamela Leigh Starr	$8.95
Illusions	Pamela Leigh Starr	$8.95
Indigo After Dark Vol. I	Nia Dixon/Angelique	$10.95
Indigo After Dark Vol. II	Dolores Bundy/ Cole Riley	$10.95
Indigo After Dark Vol. III	Montana Blue/ Coco Morena	$10.95
Indigo After Dark Vol. IV	Cassandra Colt/	$14.95
Indigo After Dark Vol. V	Delilah Dawson	$14.95
Indiscretions	Donna Hill	$8.95
Intentional Mistakes	Michele Sudler	$9.95
Interlude	Donna Hill	$8.95
Intimate Intentions	Angie Daniels	$8.95
It's Not Over Yet	J.J. Michael	$9.95
Jolie's Surrender	Edwina Martin-Arnold	$8.95
Kiss or Keep	Debra Phillips	$8.95
Lace	Giselle Carmichael	$9.95

Other Genesis Press, Inc. Titles (continued)

Last Train to Memphis	Elsa Cook	$12.95
Lasting Valor	Ken Olsen	$24.95
Let Us Prey	Hunter Lundy	$25.95
Lies Too Long	Pamela Ridley	$13.95
Life Is Never As It Seems	J.J. Michael	$12.95
Lighter Shade of Brown	Vicki Andrews	$8.95
Love Always	Mildred E. Riley	$10.95
Love Doesn't Come Easy	Charlyne Dickerson	$8.95
Love Unveiled	Gloria Greene	$10.95
Love's Deception	Charlene Berry	$10.95
Love's Destiny	M. Loui Quezada	$8.95
Mae's Promise	Melody Walcott	$8.95
Magnolia Sunset	Giselle Carmichael	$8.95
Many Shades of Gray	Dyanne Davis	$6.99
Matters of Life and Death	Lesego Malepe, Ph.D.	$15.95
Meant to Be	Jeanne Sumerix	$8.95
Midnight Clear	Leslie Esdaile	$10.95
(Anthology)	Gwynne Forster	
	Carmen Green	
	Monica Jackson	
Midnight Magic	Gwynne Forster	$8.95
Midnight Peril	Vicki Andrews	$10.95
Misconceptions	Pamela Leigh Starr	$9.95
Montgomery's Children	Richard Perry	$14.95
My Buffalo Soldier	Barbara B. K. Reeves	$8.95
Naked Soul	Gwynne Forster	$8.95
Next to Last Chance	Louisa Dixon	$24.95
No Apologies	Seressia Glass	$8.95
No Commitment Required	Seressia Glass	$8.95

Other Genesis Press, Inc. Titles (continued)

No Regrets	Mildred E. Riley	$8.95
Not His Type	Chamein Canton	$6.99
Nowhere to Run	Gay G. Gunn	$10.95
O Bed! O Breakfast!	Rob Kuehnle	$14.95
Object of His Desire	A. C. Arthur	$8.95
Office Policy	A. C. Arthur	$9.95
Once in a Blue Moon	Dorianne Cole	$9.95
One Day at a Time	Bella McFarland	$8.95
One in A Million	Barbara Keaton	$6.99
One of These Days	Michele Sudler	$9.95
Outside Chance	Louisa Dixon	$24.95
Passion	T.T. Henderson	$10.95
Passion's Blood	Cherif Fortin	$22.95
Passion's Journey	Wanda Y. Thomas	$8.95
Past Promises	Jahmel West	$8.95
Path of Fire	T.T. Henderson	$8.95
Path of Thorns	Annetta P. Lee	$9.95
Peace Be Still	Colette Haywood	$12.95
Picture Perfect	Reon Carter	$8.95
Playing for Keeps	Stephanie Salinas	$8.95
Pride & Joi	Gay G. Gunn	$15.95
Pride & Joi	Gay G. Gunn	$8.95
Promises to Keep	Alicia Wiggins	$8.95
Quiet Storm	Donna Hill	$10.95
Reckless Surrender	Rochelle Alers	$6.95
Red Polka Dot in a World of Plaid	Varian Johnson	$12.95
Reluctant Captive	Joyce Jackson	$8.95
Rendezvous with Fate	Jeanne Sumerix	$8.95

Other Genesis Press, Inc. Titles (continued)

Other Genesis Press, Inc. Titles (continued)

Other Genesis Press, Inc. Titles (continued)

Unbreak My Heart	Dar Tomlinson	$8.95
Uncommon Prayer	Kenneth Swanson	$9.95
Unconditional Love	Alicia Wiggins	$8.95
Unconditional	A.C. Arthur	$9.95
Until Death Do Us Part	Susan Paul	$8.95
Vows of Passion	Bella McFarland	$9.95
Wedding Gown	Dyanne Davis	$8.95
What's Under Benjamin's Bed	Sandra Schaffer	$8.95
When Dreams Float	Dorothy Elizabeth Love	$8.95
When I'm With You	LaConnie Taylor-Jones	$6.99
Whispers in the Night	Dorothy Elizabeth Love	$8.95
Whispers in the Sand	LaFlorya Gauthier	$10.95
Who's That Lady?	Andrea Jackson	$9.95
Wild Ravens	Altonya Washington	$9.95
Yesterday Is Gone	Beverly Clark	$10.95
Yesterday's Dreams, Tomorrow's Promises	Reon Laudat	$8.95
Your Precious Love	Sinclair LeBeau	$8.95

Order Form

Mail to: Genesis Press, Inc.
P.O. Box 101
Columbus, MS 39703

Name _____
Address _____
City/State _____ Zip _____
Telephone _____

Ship to (if different from above)
Name _____
Address _____
City/State _____ Zip _____
Telephone _____

Credit Card Information
Credit Card # _____ ☐ Visa ☐ Mastercard
Expiration Date (mm/yy) _____ ☐ AmEx ☐ Discover

Qty.	Author	Title	Price	Total

Use this order

form, or call

1-888-INDIGO-1

Total for books _____
Shipping and handling:
  $5 first two books,
  $1 each additional book _____
Total S & H _____
Total amount enclosed _____

Mississippi residents add 7% sales tax